I0615831

# Champagne

## &

# Sour Grapes

*Gary Buslik*

# Early Praise for Champagne and Sour Grapes

"These entertaining, moving, gorgeous stories depict complicated humans and relationships at their best, worst, and funniest. Readers will enjoy unmatched turns-of-phrase, surprise endings, and moments of reverence sandwiched between hilarious observations."

~ JANNA L. GOODWIN, author of *The End of the World Notwithstanding*

"*Champagne and Sour Grapes* is tender and vicious, kind and cruel, spew-your-drink-while-weeping funny. Buslik is Hunter Thompson reborn."

~ JAMES O'REILLY, publisher of Solas House/Travelers' Tales

"*Champagne and Sour Grapes* is a potent mixture of humor, anger, love, and gut-wrenching loss that will stay with you long after you've put the book down."

~ KIMMY BEACH, author of *Nuala: A Fable* (University of Alberta Press)

"Gary Buslik is a master of weaving together quirky, everyday moments into something truly entertaining. His ability to infuse his stories with dry humor and wit makes for an enjoyable and relatable reading experience in his new collection of short stories."

~ LYNDA R. EDWARDS, author of *Redemption Songs* and *Friendship Estate*

"With *Champagne and Sour Grapes*, Gary Buslik delivers the brilliant combination of humor and poignancy that I first discovered years ago in his story 'Killing Sparrows.' This is a superb series of tales. Highly recommended!"

~ T.D. JOHNSTON, author of *Reciprocity* and winner of the International Book Award for Best Short Fiction for *Friday Afternoon and Other Stories*

## Other books by Gary Buslik

*The Missionary's Position*

*A Rotten Person Travels the Caribbean*

*Akhmed and the Atomic Matzo Balls*

This collection is a work of fiction. Names, characters, places, and incidents are either a product of the author's imagination or are used fictitiously. Any resemblance to actual events, locales, or persons, living or dead, is entirely coincidental.

*Champagne and Sour Grapes*

Text copyright © 2025 **Gary Buslik**

Edited by Benjamin White

All rights reserved.

Published in North America and Europe by Running Wild Press. Visit Running Wild Press at www.runningwildpublishing. com. Educators, librarians, book clubs (as well as the eternally curious), go to www.runningwildpublishing.com.

Paperback ISBN: 978-1-963869-89-7

*For Mom, Andrew, and our sweet little Pepe.*
*We love and miss you to the stars and back.*

# Table of Contents

# Killing Sparrows

I come down to breakfast to find Marsha in the library putting the finishing touches on a diagram for a sparrow mass-execution device. She dusts off the last of the eraser shavings and holds the paper up to the light.

"It's a three-quarter-inch plywood floor with fine wires tacked half an inch apart in parallel rows of alternating current," she explains, her fingernail running over her drawing, which she rendered with architectural care in three-dimensional perspective—properly scaled—showing measurements of all elevations. "We run an extension cord back to the kitchen with a switch. I sprinkle it with seed and wait. Their claws should just touch two wires at the same time. When there's a bunch of them, I hit the switch. These are drain holes so water can't accumulate, otherwise we'll just get a short. Frank recommends an in-line circuit breaker, whatever that is. We'll plug it into a surge protector anyhow."

"When did you talk to Frank?"

"The other day."

"Where was I?"

"I don't know. Around. He said to let him know when I'm ready. I'm ready."

I look at the drawing. "I can make this."

"Better let Frank."

I gaze outside at the vast open field and the lake, still mostly frozen, beyond. "It's early for martins," I point out.

"Not for the scouts," Marsha reminds me. Purple martin scouts return in late March to inspect prospective habitats. "I'm cleaning their house today. We can't take a chance on the sparrows."

The sparrows have stayed through the hard winter, eating the seed Marsha puts out for the cardinals and nuthatches and doves. Immigrant squatters, thieving gypsies, the sparrows have survived and prospered, grown fat and arrogant. Viciously territorial—even when the territory is not their own—sparrows are savage, genocidal slaughterers of indigenous birds. Even when they have plenty to eat, they will try to rid the neighborhood of more beautiful species. Marsha calls them the Jeffrey Dahmers of the bird world.

Marsha dons her long underwear and old jeans, her mud shoes, and fleece-lined gloves. In her dark stocking cap and long down overcoat, she resembles a soldier marching off to the front—her steely eyes and downturned lips the only evidence of a human being beneath the layers of insulation.

I come up to my office to do some paperwork but cannot stop watching my wife go about her chore, which is at once nurturing and sadistic. Even cocooned as she is in wool and Gore-Tex, she is beautiful. I love her more now, in fact, than during all of the ten years we have been married. A couple of springs ago, I offered to kill the sparrows myself, but she refused, not wanting me to steal time from my work. Not that this is easier for her. A gentle woman, Marsha would risk her own life to spare an animal from suffering. But if the martins are to come, this sparrow business must be done.

Beautiful, sweet-sounding, loving birds, purple martins are a breed of native American swallow. Every winter they migrate to Brazil and every spring return to the same neighborhoods as in previous years. In the *Purple Martin News*, we read many tales of humans endearing themselves to individual martins. Those that hang around our house line up on our gutters like violet garlands, talking to us as we sip drinks under our deck umbrella. Sometimes they swoop down so close, we think they might land on our shoulders. We have named several. They remember us, and we remember them.

In mid-spring the birds start pairing off to their chosen nesting sites. By May, the flock has dispersed to martin houses throughout the neighborhood, although the group still congregates chattily at dusk—often at our house. Like humans, they enjoy eating together, renewing friendships, maintaining the bonds of their extended family. They flit about frenetically, trilling sweetly, scooping up huge numbers of mosquitoes—which, when they visit us, permits Marsha and me to spend precious extra minutes watching sunsets from our deck or boat. Martins eat an enormous number of insects, so it would be worth the effort of attracting them even if they were not so cordial.

The problem with martins is their fussiness. They are very discerning, and sometimes even when you do everything right to attract nesting couples, they will reject the little house you have prepared for them and break your heart. They look it over and decide. You work hard and you hope.

A scout arrives a few weeks before its flock. If he is last year's vanguard, he greets you with a welcoming trill, a reminder to take the covers off the doors of the house. He pops in to inspect each compartment like a drill sergeant, darting from one hole to the next. Martins are scrupulously clean, refusing to move into a house that is not spotless—let alone a hole that has been sullied by a degenerate sparrow. Wasps also are fond of martin holes, and although an adult martin could pluck his weight of the insects on the wing, martins are disgusted by the idea of the creatures nesting in any apartment in their building.

We have no way of knowing if we pass muster until the main flock appears. Anxiously we wait.

Our first season here, seven years ago, we were lucky. A pair of martins settled into the twelve-hole, green-and-white metal martin house we had installed atop a sturdy fifteen-foot pole set in concrete. They built their neat nest of grass and flower petals, and the female laid her delicate eggs. Each late afternoon we watched from our deck as the male flitted about for mosquitoes, melodically announcing his impending fatherhood, then returned to his mate with a beak full of bugs. When we lowered the house every few days to check on the imminent family's progress, the male would sit unperturbed on the roof, chirping mirthfully as we peeked in to see Mom peeking back at us with half-closed eyes. We were proud of them, and they were proud of themselves. We were part of the family.

Then there was a tragedy.

One early morning in June, Marsha, surveying the prairie from our bedroom window, shook me violently awake. As I sprang to the edge of the bed, she was already bolting downstairs. From the window I watched as, in her robe and slippers, she ran across our deck, clapping to scare away the sparrows attacking our two martins, screaming for me to help.

By the time I joined her, it was too late. There was nothing we could have done anyhow. The male martin must have put up a valiant fight, as they always do, but he was doomed. He lay dead on the ground, both eyes ripped out, his head plucked almost naked. Marsha held him to her cheek and sobbed. I lowered the house to find the female still in her hole, eviscerated, and her three tiny eggs disemboweled.

Sparrows are accomplished hunters. A male and female will gang up on a martin, attacking from all sides. But the martin never gives up, never leaves his mate or babies.

Even after he is blind and in shock, he will block his hole and try to lash back, peck for peck. He never gives up until he is dead. If other martins see what's going on, they will rally to defend their brother, and they will often succeed in chasing away a pair of sparrows. But in all-out gang warfare, the martins never stand a chance. The sparrows kill with impunity. It is almost a sport.

All afternoon of the murder of our martins, the two vanquishing sparrows copulated on the ledge of their newly won hole, taunting Marsha. That evening we took our two martins out on the boat and eased them into the lake, Marsha whispering a prayer, I saying a few words commemorating their short, joyful lives. That's when Marsha decided to fight fire with fire.

And yet spring after spring of Marsha trapping and suffocating sparrows has not enticed the martins to nest again at our house. After that first June's tragedy, nothing. Year after year, nothing. The scouts would come, and everything would be ready. Our flock would return, but the couples always settled somewhere else nearby. At twilight they would visit us, bruising the sky. By midsummer fledglings would join their parents to introduce themselves. They were happily breeding somewhere, but not here.

Despite my reassurances, Marsha couldn't help but think she was doing something wrong. Maybe the martin house was too close to the lake. Maybe too close to our own house. Maybe we should have put down a wood-chip, not gravel, path through the prairie. Maybe they liked bigger houses; maybe smaller. Now she has convinced herself the problem is and has always been the sparrows.

A hundred years ago the first two sparrows were brought to New York's Central Park from England. Every sparrow in America today sprang from those progenitors. That is how easily the sparrow has scythed the territories of our native birds, how quickly it devoured competition for food and shelter—breeding maniacally, plundering rivals' nests, destroying eggs, murdering offspring, mutilating parents.

What the sparrow's hacksaw-like beak does not kill, its filth will. Unlike the fastidious martin, which removes its waste immediately in small membrane sacks like miniature garbage bags, the sparrow fouls its home with malignant abandon. Living amidst its dirty feathers are defecation-feasting mites that, symbiotically, the sparrow uses as a kind of land mine. Should a sparrow covet the nest of a rival species, it has only to drop off a dab of poop and a few of the microscopic marauders. When the legal resident returns, the tiny parasites infect the victim, sucking the joy and eventually the life from its bones. In the case of a martin house, the sparrow merely goes from hole to hole, leaving a dollop of crap in each. Then it watches and waits.

Maybe the sparrows' hatred of purple martins is simple envy. Martins fill the sky with flutes and clarinets, while sparrows sound like drunken fans at a hockey game. The martins build tidy, symmetrical, meticulously woven nests of fresh grass and flower parts, while the sparrows' nests are ramshackle constructions of garbage scraps, decaying leaves, or the feathers of mourning doves just killed by falcons. Also, whereas martins pair for life and will not take other mates if their partners die or are infertile, sparrows' *raison d'etre* is to breed and multiply—to copulate, fornicate, and procreate with as many other sparrows as energy will allow.

From my office, I watch Marsha perform her spring ritual of lowering the martin house, lifting the front panel of each compartment, and scrubbing the interior with a brush and soapy water. With another sponge, she rinses. With a lint-free diaper, she dries. This takes almost an hour. Every few minutes she runs her coat sleeve under her nose. It is only the end of March; we will certainly get more snow. If there is a prolonged cold snap, there will be no bugs, and the martins will starve to death. One more thing to worry about.

Marsha inserts a sparrow trap into a hole. It is a simple, effective device for killing one sparrow at a time: a guillotine-like door snaps shut when a bird enters the compartment; Marsha will then fit a plastic bag over the hole and open the door, releasing the sparrow into the bag, which she will then seal, suffocating the interloper.

Marsha raises the martin house, comes back into the kitchen, watches with her binoculars, and waits. The little trap door is painted Day-Glo orange. Even without binoculars she will see it close on the doomed sparrow.

The binoculars are to keep an eye on prefatory events in case a martin scout or a bluebird or barn swallow should happen to pop into the hole for an inspection. If so, she merely releases the fellow and resets the trap. The problem with a friendly bird getting accidentally caught is that sparrows have keen criminal minds: once they see Marsha release a bird, they are that much more wary of the trap. As it is, a sparrow will approach with caution, hopping suspiciously around the hole fitted with this strange contraption for several minutes before it sticks first its head, then half its body inside, tentatively in and out, before finally popping inside completely, springing the door. Sparrows may be smart, but they just can't help themselves. Their irrepressible urge to screw does them in. What goes around comes around.

Despite the fact that we have a large house—too big for the two of us, really—I can hear Marsha all the way from my office as she urges on a curious sparrow—one of a pair that has decided to inspect the newly opened house. "Get in there. That's it, go in. Look inside. It's nice and clean. You want to make it filthy, don't you, you dirty little bastard? That's it, all the way...."

Not normally one to swear or be impatient, Marsha's personality changes somewhat during these stressful vigils. Hearing her voice scrape through her teeth and echo up the atrium to my second-floor office is almost like listening to a stranger in the house, and is even a little frightening. If I let my imagination go, I can believe she is an intruder who has bypassed our security system and is barking instructions to an accomplice.

"Get the bastard!"

This is a quick catch. It is probably a sparrow which was not here last year, which did not witness its brethren meeting their demise. I hear Marsha psyching herself up as she re-dons her overcoat.

It could be just a false alarm. It's a sparrow, all right—I saw it enter the compartment myself—but it might be a female. Females are a better catch than nothing, and Marsha will kill it anyway. But males are the prize. Caring nothing for the fate of a dead female, a male will quickly call for and attract another mate to his chosen hole. A newly widowed female, on the other hand, will fly off to answer the chirp of another male at some other nearby site—and our martin house will be liberated. And so I can read Marsha's mind as I watch her lower the martin house. *Be a male.*

This time of year our prairie looks its most forlorn, its most barren, and never more so than with my bundled wife standing in the field, fighting the forces of nature. The snow having mostly melted, the earth is pale and apathetic, and I gaze out at our land with a gnawing sense of lost time. This is the seventh March I have watched Marsha lower the martin house for cleaning. The martins might nest here or they might not. Soon there will be goslings and baby mallards and new cygnets paddling past our pier, almost close enough to feel their creamy feathers brush our cheeks. Red-winged blackbirds and finches and chipmunks and groundhogs will return to our feeders in increased numbers. But the martins might shun us yet again. It seems that as the little green-and-white house gets older, its pole more bent from winter winds, it becomes less desirable; that the longer the martins stay away, the less likely they will ever return. Maybe nothing we can do now will make any difference. Perhaps, despite our Herculean efforts, the house simply lacks whatever it is that martins find attractive. Maybe that first year was just a fluke. One thing is certain, though: the martins have not nested with us since the year of the sparrow attack. Marsha is sure the problem is the sparrows.

She scurries down the three deck levels, across the lily pond, down the gravel path. She cranks the windlass on the pole, lowering the enameled house. In her belt is a plastic bag, which she places over a holder in front of the hole. She raises the trap door, takes a step back, and waits. A moment later the sparrow shoots into the bag. Quickly Marsha pinches the bag closed and removes it. She inspects it as she returns up the path.

I meet her on the deck.

"It's a female," she says with disappointment, dangling the bag.

Inside, the little bird is wriggling, gasping for breath. I can hear its tiny, hopeless peeps. Its eyes are already closed, but its beak keeps moving, then moves without sound. And still the mouth sucks in what it can, finding only plastic.

"Let me knock it out on the railing," I offer, reaching for the bag. "Hit its head against the railing," I advise. "Put it out of its misery."

She yanks it away and holds the bag at her side. I can

see the sparrow's beak still faintly moving.

"Let me, then."

"I want it to suffer," she says, holding it up in front of her, knowing I won't take it from her. She is entitled to this.

Still, it is unsettling. The sparrow is, after all, just doing what nature permits. Even the falcons who regularly feast on our mourning doves, Marsha allows without remonstration, must eat. The owls must dine on chipmunks; the hawks must devour mice; the crows must suck out an occasional robin egg. They cannot wander the aisles at the supermarket, tossing Mrs. Paul's fish sticks into their carts. Marsha has nothing against the hierarchy of nature. She holds no philosophic grudges against predators.

But these are sparrows, the birds who keep away our martins. These are the vicious, disease-ridden enemy of our sweet purple songbird. Butchers of joy. To root them out and kill them is not enough; they must be made to suffer.

For an instant I am tempted to grab the prisoner and stomp on it. But I hold back. It simply is not worth the inevitable quarrel and icy silence that would follow, perhaps for days. It is not worth sleeping on opposite sides of the bed or, worse, in separate bedrooms. Marsha has plenty of bedrooms here to choose from, and I'd rather not give her a reason. So the sparrow chokes slowly, agonizingly, silently, to death.

Timidly I return to the house. I do not feel like working in my office anymore. So I go to the basement to see what I can do about making a mass sparrow electric chair. In addition to being more efficient, it seems like the more humane way to go. Frank would build it if we asked him, but he's usually pretty busy. I hate to impose.

Our basement is big and unfinished. We built it extra deep, with extra high ceilings, thinking we would turn it into an apartment for an au pair and a playroom. It has a working fireplace, roughed-in plumbing for two bathrooms and a sauna, and a huge walkout patio facing the lake. But we never did finish it.

At one end I have my workout equipment—some free weights, bench press, sit-up bench, stationary bike, treadmill—and in the middle we neatly store boxes of records, old photo albums, transfer cases of memorabilia, and board games we will probably never play again—all labeled and stacked. I have a sports section: wall hangers laden with mitts, balls, bats, skates, fishing gear, and golf accouterments. Next to this is our boat paraphernalia: cushions, life vests, emergency flares, oars, inflatable raft, pumps, water pistols, and inner tubes. Every item is bagged or covered to keep it dust-free. Marsha calls me "the curator."

At the other end of the basement is my workroom, temporarily separated by a pegboard partition and lined with sturdy wood shelves that Frank built a few months after overseeing construction of the house. Frank, an excellent carpenter, tends to overbuild. If two-by-twos will do, Frank will use two-by-fours. If two-by-fours are the norm, he'll insist on two-by-sixes. He'll always use ten nails where other carpenters use five. Frank's motto is "glue *and* screw." Under Frank's watchful eye, our house was built to withstand any ravage and to last forever.

In appreciation for the generous bonus Marsha and I gave him, Frank built the shelves and my workbench for free. Afterwards he took me to the hardware store, where he helped me pick out the parts and tools to complete a true workroom. It was all new to me and very exciting, as Frank led me through the aisles of wrenches, saws, screwdrivers, hammers, pliers, bolts, screws, washers, and other small parts. He caught me admiring a handsome pair of tin snips but pointed out that they were for southpaws. If there is anything you ever want to know about tools, ask Frank. He will explain why water-filled levels are better than oil-filled; he will patiently teach you how to use a surveyor's transit; he will demonstrate why you should never use a plastic anchor in drywall (use a toggle bolt).

During the building of our house, with hammers droning over the prairie like the call of a strange bird, I became an unabashed contractor groupie. I admired the precision of miter cuts and the raw power of raising a twenty-five-foot window wall. I marveled at the way Frank coordinated the work of his subcontractors—graders and concrete pourers and water proofers and steel fabricators; carpenters and heating-and-air-conditioning experts and well diggers and septic installers; glaziers and insulators and masons and electricians; security system specialists and lightning rod technicians and roofers and plumbers; gutter installers and drywallers and tile layers and painters; cabinetmakers and carpet installers and asphalters and landscapers—to produce this beautiful, complicated network of systems called a home. I found the structured chaos heady.

I knew very well the workmen talked about me and even laughed at me behind my back. "The weekend warrior," they derisively called me: the rich guy who fantasizes about getting blisters. I admit it, I enjoyed watching all the scurrying up and down ladders and thrilled at leaning over the unobstructed second-floor balcony, open to the basement thirty feet below. The buzz of circular saws, the clouds of sawdust, the aroma of freshly cut lumber, and the ear-splitting crack of nail guns made me feel rugged and potent. When drywall taping mud splattered on my glasses, I wouldn't clean them until I got home. I liked getting dirty with the guys, liked asking questions, liked learning how to bend conduit and feather spackle and flash skylights. I delighted in poring over our blueprints, comparing the real with the conceptual, watching the lines leap off the paper and come to three-dimensional life exactly as Marsha and I had visualized, had talked and dreamed about over so many dinners.

I think building our house was the time Marsha and I were the closest. On four different nights we made love in our unwalled home amid the crickets and shooting stars. On one of those nights, Marsha remarked that there are about the same number of neurons in a newborn baby's brain as there are stars in the Milky Way.

Marsha didn't spend much time on the construction site. Her time would come later, when we decorated. When she did show up, it was with doughnuts for me and the boys. She'd stroll around a few minutes, compliment the workmen, compliment Frank, kiss me, and make a quick exit. We were proud of each other. Marsha is a beautiful woman; I looked forward to her showing up, being attentive to the workmen without being overly friendly, looking sexy but not provocative, being generous in her praise yet just aloof enough to suggest inaccessibility. God knows what the workmen said about *her* behind our backs.

Frank was pretty good-natured about the whole thing. He kidded about his men making fun of me, saying it was natural for blue-collar workers to dislike a guy not yet forty who could build such a house. He seemed to take my side. He acknowledged that ours is a culture of envy. His men weren't proud of their blistered hands; they were ashamed. It had nothing to do with being hard or soft. He assured me he would trade his rigorous life any day for a chance to make an honest living with his brain. Those mopes who laughed behind my back would rather sit around drinking beers after work and complain than go home and read a book. But who really built America? Not the guys who pounded the nails, not the guys who drew the blueprints, but the men who created jobs. Men like me. I appreciated Frank's reassurances. He meant well.

One day after his men left, Frank and I climbed up to the newly shingled roof. While we drank a couple of Heinekens, we gazed over the prairie and the lake. The view was magnificent. The goldenrod and baby's breath and Russian sage undulated in the late-September breeze. The shadow of the house frame stretched far in the amber afternoon. It was the first time I got a true perspective of my property—the house being the tallest structure within miles. The cool air and smell of fresh cedar filled my lungs. I wondered if Frank really understood the pride I felt in the house and all it represented. I told him how much I appreciated his good work, and then we fell silent. He too gazed at the unending landscape. Perhaps he did understand. We watched a brown fox scouring the grass.

I whispered, "Marsha and I are going to leave the prairie natural."

Frank agreed there were too many lawns in the world.

"It'll be a good place to raise a family," he replied, as the fox trotted off clutching a mouse. "A kid should have nature. It's good to know what to do." He fell just short of mentioning hunting.

Frank is a hunter. With his men he would sometimes talk about shooting fowl or deer, bow hunting, skinning. But when he'd see me, he'd shut up. I knew he was an expert hunter, though. As we now watched a kestrel falcon sitting motionless in a hickory tree, staring into the weeds, Frank said, "He's looking for something slow. An old or sick bird. He'll wait there all week if he has to, but sooner or later he'll feast."

We climbed down from the roof, and I walked him to his truck, where he gave me a quick lesson in cutting a miter joint. His table saw was still set up on his tailgate. He found a length of two-by-four and showed me how to measure and adjust the angle of the blade. Then, with his knee pinning down one of the studs, he fastened two sections by hammering in a couple of corrugated cleats. "Normally we'd just use nails on rough lumber," he explained, "but this'll give you an idea how to join your cabinets. Of course, you can always call me if you need help. I'll show you the right tools, too. You'll have a great workroom."

And so I do. Well-stocked, organized, and inventoried, my workroom would be the envy of any professional craftsman, let alone a weekend hobbyist like me. Well, what I thought I might be. The truth is, all these wonderful, expensive tools looked a lot more appealing in the hardware store than in my basement. In the beginning, I did build a couple of things—a toy chest, a doll house—from plans I bought at a crafts center. But then I sort of lost interest. It seems a lot easier just to buy what you want when the time comes.

But here I am with Marsha's diagram, determined to build her instrument of mass avian destruction. It seems simple enough—not the kind of project we need a home builder for. I will construct a sparrow fryer that Marsha will be proud of. Not only do I have the tools, but I already have all the materials I need. In the crawl space is a stack of extra lumber Frank left seven years ago. From a four-foot-square piece of three-quarter-inch plywood, I'll cut the execution platform. Some one and one-half-inch plumbing pipe and a flange will do nicely for the pole. I still have a couple half-rolls of electrical wire and plenty of outdoor extension cord.

I prop a six-foot ladder against the foundation wall, lean into the crawl space, grab the plywood, and pull. In the dimness, I do not see the nail.

A large nail sticking out from a length of baseboard

molding first scrapes, then digs viciously into the back of my hand. I recoil, lose my footing, fall off the ladder. But the baseboard, with much scrap wood on top, hardly budges. For a moment I dangle by the nail as it pierces deeper and deeper into my flesh, scraping along my bone. With my other arm, I claw for something to grab as my feet thrash to find a ladder step. But I have kicked the ladder too far, and I can't find the strength to lift myself into the opening. So I scream for Marsha.

The nail burrows deeper and slices through soft meat until it catches on my knuckle. Then, at last, my weight starts to pull the baseboard from beneath the pile of scrap lumber. In a moment all tension is released, and I crash to the concrete, the nail dislodging from my hand, the baseboard flying out of the crawl space and bouncing clangorously off the hot-water heater.

With my other hand, I grip my wound, trying to squeeze in the pain. Blood oozes from between my clenched fingers. Marsha must still be outside. When she doesn't come, I get to my feet and hobble to our middle storage area. I grab the corner of a bedsheet and press its clean underside to my gushing wound. Under the sheet are the toy chest and doll house I made six years ago. I wrap the sheet around my hand and stagger upstairs.

Marsha is outside. I start to go for the door but stop. My hand throbs. I pull away the sheet, which is sticky and thick with blood. Marsha is rigging up her trap again. I want to go to the emergency room. I'll need treatment—an exam and tetanus shot, antibiotics and painkillers. Ointment and a real bandage. Marsha will have to drive.

But I don't call her, and I don't wave to get her attention. Instead, through the French doors, I merely watch her as again she lowers the martin house. The first sparrow is dead. She is after the male. Sensing me watching, she turns and squints toward the house. I hide my hand with the bundled sheet behind my back. She nods, not noticing anything wrong. She returns to her project.

Without a word, I go to the garage, throw the sheet into the back of my car, and wrap my hand in one of the clean diapers we now use for rags. Although the throbbing has reached my head, and my wrist and forearm are already beginning to swell, I decide to drive to the emergency room alone. If I am careful, I can steer with one hand. If I take deep breaths with the windows open, I can keep from passing out. It is better not to let Marsha see me sick.

# Secret Cigars

The day they were leaving St. Martin, Keith decided to sneak back some Cuban cigars.

After breakfast he went to a tobacco store in Phillipsburg and picked out three stout Havanas with colorful bands. He left the shop carrying a flimsy plastic bag that you could almost see through if you were a regular civilian and definitely see through if you were a seasoned CIA operative.

He spent the next two hours packing his contraband so it couldn't be detected at customs. This was probably futile since the old clerk in the tobacco shop had no doubt given his customer's description to his superiors, and Keith's vital statistics were now on a mainframe computer somewhere in the bowels of an ersatz flower shop in Arlington, Virginia.

Keith inserted the first cigar into a sweat sock, knotted the sock, and put that into a black sock and stuffed it into a running shoe so that if it showed up on X-ray it could be mistaken for a shoe horn or perhaps a bone. Cigar number two he slipped into the vomit bag he had pilfered from their arriving airplane. He blew into the bag to give it some fluff, hopefully suggesting to the customs agent that it already contained a bit of regurgitation. The third illicit stogy he suggested putting in Leslie's carry-on, but she told him over her dead body, to please leave her out of his funny business, and if he got caught to make sure to tell them they were legally separated. Keith thought and thought and finally decided to put the cigar in his toiletry case because it seemed unlikely that a customs agent would risk pricking himself on Keith's nose-hair scissors.

Leslie checked her watch and tapped her foot and told him they were going to miss their plane and was it worth three stupid cigars? He told her to just go and check out while he finished packing and to take her suitcase with her if she didn't trust him after fifteen years of community property which, to be honest, was really his. Where did it say that it's always the man who has to check out while the woman makes sure they didn't leave anything in the room?

When she left, Keith unpacked his cigars and tried to think of three different places for them that, at the airport, his so-called life partner's surreptitious eye movements wouldn't reveal.

Okay. One cigar inside the box of guava berry liqueur. Another rolled up in the Spot Marley, Rastadog T-shirt. The third nestled in the hotel room's New Testament with center pages ripped out and for which Keith left twenty bucks on the nightstand.

They got a cab to the airport. The driver stopped on the way to "get change," but Keith suspected he was really getting puffer fish powder with which to turn guilt-ridden tourists into zombies and suck out their souls and make them slaves for the rest of their lives.

Just like having a cat.

They got to the airport with Keith's free will—such as it was—intact, but the plane was late, giving him plenty of time to sit in the lounge to consider the nature of betrayal. A sevenish-year-old kid stared at him the way Black kids stare at White men who bite their nails to the nub. The little bugger was probably in on the zombie thing, too.

At the gate an agent took his ticket, and Keith definitely knew she was in on it because she creased a little triangle on the corner of his boarding pass, which was a secret sign to the flight attendant that this was their guy, and when he dozed off, to put drops in his ear. It was Keith's absolute last chance to change his mind. He still could claim he had to relieve himself and go back to the terminal and flush the cigars down the toilet. (Who could tell the difference?) Leslie knew he had a weak colon because of the many times he had squeezed past rows of patrons at the ballet until they threatened him with their little binoculars, so that now Keith and Leslie Netflixed at home. Just not ballet.

"Why do you look funny?" she asked him on the plane.

"No reason."

"Do you have to go to the bathroom?"

"I'm just thinking."

She gave him that look.

"Why can't wives just assume their husbands are *thinking*," he said.

"Maybe because they can't even figure out which seatbelt goes into what buckle."

"Okay, fine. No, I don't have to go to the bathroom."

"You should have gone before we got on board."

"I'm going to ask you nicely, one time. Give it up."

"Just trying to help."

"You want to help?"

"Yes, I do," she said.

"Then help me find my damn buckle!"

She strapped him in. She wedged his bag under the seat too. He could swear he saw her fingering his case, secretly feeling for his cigars. But he kept his cool. When she glanced up at him, he looked away. When they were at cruising altitude, he tore off small pieces of the flight magazine, rolled them up into his ears, closed his eyes, and pretended to doze. But he watched her from one eye slit.

How well did he know this woman, really? Nothing but what she had told him over the years. Force-fed facts without antecedents; a history that upon reflection was a bit too impeccable; a background so full of dead air that even Facebook might have felt mildly uncomfortable.

She was born in a brick bungalow on the far south side of Chicago on a street with letters instead of names that looked so identical to every other bungalow that when he and Leslie were dating, Keith couldn't find her parents' block let alone their house, and he would often inadvertently enter the home of a family named Zimmermann with two *n*'s from East Germany, so it was obvious that in those bungalows was where they relocated former SS storm troopers, although old Mrs. Zimmermann made a pretty good schnitzel, so Keith would usually stay for dinner and play a little pinochle.

Leslie's "father" worked at U.S. Steel in Hammond, Indiana, and claimed to work in "management," which, if you ever talked to him for more than thirty seconds, you knew was laughable. Here was an implanted foreign agent if there ever was one—trying a little too hard to seem "American"— buying a new Ford or Chevy every two years; refusing to buy any article of clothing or appliance made overseas; pretending that Chinese food gave him diverticulitis.

Keith's so-called mother-in-law was a devout Protestant who looked like the husband in Grant Wood's painting *American Gothic,* and liked to hide eggs at Easter, and then forgot where she hid them for decades, and made most of her Christmas decorations herself, and wound up with emphysema due to years of yarn-particle inhalation. She vacuumed her floors to the joists, and sometimes her hand would cramp-lock onto the handle of her Electrolux, and Leslie's "father" would call the paramedics, and they'd carry her "mother" on a stretcher with her vacuum cleaner still attached to her grip and take her to the hospital where it would be surgically removed.

As a teenager, Leslie didn't use or deal drugs, didn't have any abortions, was not in a carjacking gang, and, in fact (so she claimed), had no criminal record. Her "sister" was not in any bizarre cults, unless you counted East Side Brownie Troop 9. Her "father" did not abuse her, and to the best of her knowledge she did not live a past life as a sixteenth-century Salem witch or a Hebrew princess named Harriet Garber.

A life story just a little *too* perfect, Keith reminded himself as their plane approached the land of the "free," where awaited a dragnet of cigar-sniffing, skull-gnawing DEA German shepherds and FBI agents wearing Menards jackets and blood-stained belts.

But maybe it still wasn't too late. He unsnapped his seatbelt, unwedged his suitcase from under the seat, and started for the bathroom—which they called a "lavatory" in order to confuse passengers born after 1970. But just as he took his first step toward the back, the pilot came on the speaker and announced that they were "making our final descent, so sit back down immediately and do not take any suitcases to the lavatory! Ha! Ha! Ha!"

The attendant, a woman with a square jaw who was the model for those Soviet "Workers Unite!" murals and whom they hired because it was an employee-owned airline, blocked the aisle with her steroidal shoulders. "Going somewhere?"

Keith sat back down.

"You don't look so good," Leslie said.

"I'm hyperventilating."

"Try thinking of something pleasant."

Sure, like dancing the tango with Manuel Noriega.

They "disembarked"—which used to be called "getting off the plane"—and followed signs up and down escalators and through a labyrinth of corridors obviously designed by the same architectural firm that built the hotel in the movie *The Shining*.

Eventually they debouched into a well-lighted open area with television monitors, a white tile floor highly polished to reflect up your shorts for evidence of hidden cigars, and many rows of inspection counters and customs agents dressed like theater ushers with sleeves ten sizes too long—the kind of dorks whose heads you threw popcorn at when you were a kid and who grew up to start Microsoft.

Leslie—or whatever her real name was—refused to stand in line with Keith. She saw how much he was sweating and shifting his weight and working his tongue around the inside of his cheek like a tiny scuba diver stuck under ice, and ostensibly she didn't want to be affiliated with a soon-to-be felon. The real reason, of course, was to blend back into the crowd and "disappear" into other false identities, to romance and remarry more unsuspecting schmendricks, laying her trap again and again, until one day she would come in "out of the cold" and retire to a chateau in Switzerland with her numbered bank account and Elvis.

While Keith was waiting his turn, Leslie nowhere in sight to offer support and comfort, the security TV sets gazing down at him unblinkingly, the fluorescent lights bright and cold and soulless, he thought, *Okay, I can probably survive a long prison sentence—as long as my cell mate is tidy.*

He watched the burly agent who was servicing his line. The guy had bushy eyebrows and a concave forehead. For everyone else (everyone who wasn't Keith), he seemed to be asking a few perfunctory questions and letting the citizens move on. Keith tried reading his lips. As near as he could tell, the agent's questions were: "Which do you like better, McDonald's or Burger King?" and "Is AOC hot, or what?" and "Has the subject's 'wife'—yeah, right—made any surreptitious eye movements to indicate the exact location of the cigars?"

Keith realized where he had made his mistake. By spreading the cigars around he had increased by threefold the chance they would find any one. How dumb can you be? The penalty for three cigars is the same for one, so what could he have been thinking?

There were still three people in front of him. One was a fat dude, who provided excellent cover, proving the point that you can overdo the whole exercise thing. So if Keith was very careful, very adroit, he could maybe move the cigars around in his case without being noticed. He pretended to have the sniffles. He sneezed. He reached for a tissue in one pants pocket after another and loudly mumbled, "Oh my, no tissues. I must have left them in my suitcase." He nonchalantly baggage-probed for a Kleenex.

On vacations, Keith traveled light. Sometimes he would wear a pair of underpants for several days, Leslie frequently warning him that one day his life cycle would regret it. However, having read Joyce's *Ulysses*, he had always believed he knew more about everything than his wife. But now, at the moment his fingertips inched their way past articles of clothing that a couple of days ago seemed perfectly innocuous but now were clearly nocuous, Keith had to grudgingly concede that perhaps great literature was not all it was cracked up to be; that being illiterate may not offer the greatest in retirement security, but it sure beats the hell out of wondering if a vicious, pock-faced former president-for-life of a Central American banana republic is a good dancer.

But having read thick novels by famous British writers had worked Keith's fingers into strong and nimble page-turners, fortuitously adroit at quickly and surreptitiously combining three discrete cigars into a single bundle of larceny.

So as he approached the customs agent, Keith was feeling a tad better—though hardly confident—about his chances. On the one hand, no normal person would dare thrust a fist into Keith's suitcase of lost souls once he unzipped it and all those stinky underpants ghouls were let loose. On the other hand, though, maybe this particular customs agent had just come off his lunch break during which he'd had a lobotomy, so even by U.S. government standards he was still not exactly normal. Current college admissions requirements being what they were, was it possible this civil servant with a forehead shaped like a catcher's mitt might have been hired post-graduation on the basis of his ACT score being higher than three? Might he, in fact, actually *enjoy* swishing his hairy fingers around Keith's rotting fruits of the loom?

There was only one person ahead of him in line now, stuffing the last of a family-size candy bar into his cheeks, fortifying himself. Keith's heart raced. He looked left and right but couldn't see his alleged spouse. He figured she was probably in the chief inspector's office sharing a bottle of Dom P.

Almost his turn now, he reached for his suitcase. But all he found was air. It was gone.

"Mine is heavy," Leslie whispered from behind, "and my arms are tired. Here, we'll trade."

He turned all the way around. "How...how long have you been back there?"

"A while."

33

"I didn't notice you."

"You were too busy thinking."

The customs agent was zipping up the fat guy's luggage.

"But—"

"Next!"

Leslie carried her husband's suitcase to the counter.

"Anything to declare?" the agent asked.

"Only what's on the card," she answered, cool as a snow cone.

The agent peered into her eyes, and she peered back.

"Welcome home," he said.

"Nice to be back."

"Next!"

Keith swung up Leslie's suitcase.

"Open it, please."

He spread her lingerie over the counter.

"These yours?" the agent asked.

"Got a problem with that?"

He raised his bushy eyebrow. "My name's Roy."

"Sorry, Roy, I'm already in a relationship."

"Next!"

Leslie was waiting for her husband in the terminal. It was bright and colorful and filled with gift shops. Keith was glad to be home. They went into a drug store, where he bought a coconut patty, and she bought a *People* magazine. They wandered over to their connecting gate and sat.

"Feel better?" she asked.

"I was doing just fine. I had it all worked out."

"Want a neck massage?"

"Not necessary," he assured her.

"Want a double latte?"

"I can buy my own, thank you."

He stuffed the coconut patty into his chops. "The border's a sieve," he grumbled.

"Not everyone's as tricky as you."

He swallowed the patty. They were silent for a couple of minutes. Then she started rubbing his neck.

"You were pretty brave," he told her.

"A good cigar is worth it."

"Things sometimes work out, don't they?"

"Usually."

"Do you think there's something wrong with me?"

"Yes, I do."

"I can be an ordeal," he said.

"Tell me about it." She took his hand. "I like you anyway."

"I always meant to tell you how much I appreciate your tidiness."

"In prose, what's not said can be more important than what is."

They fell silent.

"You're always there for me, aren't you?" he said after a minute.

"Well, you have sexy lingerie."

"You know what else I always liked about you?"

"What?" she asked.

"Your underwear is always so clean."

"Gee."

"I'll have to try it."

"I guess we can all do a little better," she agreed.

"Want a coconut patty?"

"Sure," she said. She held up the magazine. "Want a crossword puzzle?"

# Hammered Notes

He should have been over the divorce, but he was chained to the past. Even when, a year later, he met Jilly and felt the weight lighten a little, the iron ball was right behind him.

He liked Jilly a lot. She was pretty and effervescent and no, not as brilliant or stunning as Miranda, but good enough. He just didn't love her. When she once asked to see his ex's picture, Dave said he threw them all away—although he still had every one stashed in his storage tubs.

"I'll bet she was gorgeous!" Jilly burbled. She wasn't being sarcastic. She thought everything was gorgeous.

Dave was fascinated by what made her think the world was so stupendous.

After dating just two months, one night she chirped, "I know! For your birthday, let's go on a cruise! My treat!"

Jilly made a decent living, but this was over the top. She knew very well how often Miranda and Dave had traveled the Caribbean. Why would she want to visit the same places they had spent their honeymoon and almost every winter vacation?

Was she testing Dave? If he turned her down, would it reveal his still-broken heart? But accepting her offer might have been revealing, too: *Why sure. I'm so over what's her name. Seeing those places again won't bother me in the least. I don't even care if I see her there with some other guy.*

Which, of course, would have killed him.

It was a sticky situation.

———◆———

The history of Caribbean steelpan music began with a viscous abyss in which, once trapped, few creatures escaped. La Brea Pitch Lake, a one-hundred-acre natural asphalt basin on Trinidad's southwestern coast, has been a source of mystery and fear since its fatal attractions of prehistoric giant sloths and mastodons, whose bones, with an occasional human femur or tibia, still bubble to the surface.

Pre-Columbian Amerindians believed their gods created this gate to hell as punishment. Legend had it that the belching lake once swallowed an entire tribe for eating hummingbirds—thought to be the souls of departed ancestors. So the locals were only too glad to lead European interlopers to the black goo. But that backfired when in 1595 English adventurer Sir Walter Raleigh, seeking El Dorado, found the pitch to be excellent for caulking his ocean-weary ships. When, inevitably, exploratory flotillas morphed into cannoned armadas, the tar helped the colonial powers expand their brutal reach.

With the process of tar refinement came, long after the colonial wars had ended, the discovery of an ancillary element that would render this strange land worthy of even greater human suffering: a prehistoric substance more valuable even than Sir Raleigh's gold.

But before the world was ready to fight and die for oil, there happened to be a far less expensive source of energy.

———◆———

Dave agreed to join Jilly in the Caribbean but insisted on paying his half—birthday or not. He was a red-blooded American dude who paid his own way. Besides, he didn't want to owe her.

Because he and his ex had spent overnight on almost every Caribbean island, and not wanting to relive old memories, Dave suggested to Jilly that they take a short, seven-day, cruise—pointing out that because she had never been to the islands, "it will give you a nice overview." The couple of hours they'd be spending in each port would give her the general idea and spare him too much painful nostalgia.

"You're the expert!" Jilly agreed, planting Dave a smooch. "Perfect!"

OK, so their in-port times would be limited to strolling around dockside souvenir shops or, at most, up and down each touristy Front Street: art galleries, crystal shops, eateries, tchotchke stands. They simply wouldn't have time to visit any of the quaint rainforest plantation inns where Dave and Miranda had spent so many nights. What's more, if any of their favorite islands—say, St. Kitts or Antigua— happened to be on the cruise itinerary, Dave could always claim he had a stomach ache from last night's shrimp cocktail and so ditch going ashore altogether.

Naturally, he told Jilly none of this.

After Dave agreed to go, Jilly bought him a present: a Trinidad All Stars Steel Orchestra CD. They played it in the car on the way to and from the movies and as they snuggled on her couch. But the whole time she was swaying and air-pinging imaginary steelpans, Dave wished he was cuddling Miranda.

In the early 1700s, the French began transporting their African slaves from Martinique and Haiti to work their Trinidad plantations. The Africans brought with them their musical traditions, including drumming and singing—for celebrations, religious ceremonies, to pass time while working, and for communication. The playing of animal-skin drums created the rhythms that brought spiritual ecstasy and oneness with their Orisha gods, helping them remain united with their tribal roots and survive the rigors of toil and oppression.

The French also brought their *Carnivale* (from the Latin *O flesh, farewell*) festival to the island, a masquerade revelry traditionally enjoyed by the European elite. Slaves, who could not take part in this pre-Lent merrymaking, formed their own, parallel celebration called *Canboulay* (from the French *cannes brulées—burned cane*), in which their drum-beating was an integral part.

At first the planters encouraged friendly slave rivalry among the different estates, including stick-fighting competitions, in which chants and drum beats spurred on each team's fighters. But when Trinidad became a British colony in 1797, the Englishmen feared the drums would instigate revolt by transmitting coded messages from one plantation to another (in Haiti, hundreds of Whites had been murdered in slave uprisings). So drums and *Canboulay* were banned, the slaves forbidden to practice their heathen religion.

After emancipation in 1834 and the resurrection of *Canboulay*, hand drums were again taken up but were often used as a call for slum-dwelling youths to come together and "mash up" rival gangs. The once-sportive stick fighting now degenerated into open conflict and, often, bloody free-for-alls.

Hoping to curb the violence, in 1881 the Trinidad government again banned the Blacks' annual celebration, precipitating the *Canboulay* riots, pitting the Afro-Creole revelers against the police. Instead of backing down, in 1884 the authorities outlawed skin drums altogether.

With the drums prohibited, but with percussion rhythm so much a fabric of African culture, in the early 1890s the impoverished descendants of former slaves began forming bands called *tamboo-bamboo* (from the French word for *drum—tambeau*), the beating together and stomping on the ground of bamboo tubes of various diameters, dried and cut to different lengths to produce a crude, reverberating soprano, alto, tenor, and bass "music" they paraded through the slums to the sometimes delight and often annoyance of their neighbors.

Eventually the tamboo-bambooers added the beating of bottles with spoons to their instrument arrays, trying to outdo rivals gangs in musicality and cacophony, each neighborhood's band producing a distinctive rhythmic signature.

Soon enough, the musical rivalries turned ugly.

In those days every district in and around Port of Spain was its own tribal-like territory, the band within its boundaries its army, providing warriors to uphold its sovereignty. Disreputable thugs attached themselves to each group. When bands from different districts met or encroached on one another's territory, gang hostilities exploded into violent clashes, their musical instruments suddenly becoming weapons—bamboo bludgeons, bottle brainers, utensil daggers—and beating rhythm gave way to beating the hell out of *bruddas*.

Meanwhile, tribal enmity was taking place on a much grander scale in Europe, requiring more potent and deadly instruments—and the fuel to power them.

—————◆—————

After joining Jilly at the ship's railing as she waved goodbye and threw kisses to people on the dock she didn't know, Dave returned with her to their cabin to unpack. Because she had never cruised before, she had overestimated the size of the room, its closet, and their bathroom counter space. She seemed to think she'd need to change clothes twenty-nine or thirty times a day.

Dave managed to shoehorn his one pair of jeans into the closet. In the bathroom, Jilly had spread out all her toiletries around the sink, so Dave had barely enough space for his toothbrush.

"They give us soap and shampoo," he pointed out, as he stared at her bottles, bars, and tubes.

She hugged him. "Isn't it great!"

Already she had lined the floor with her slippers, sandals, and shoes. Dave imagined himself getting up to go to the bathroom, tripping over her flip-flops, cracking his skull on the nightstand, and lying in a coma in the infirmary. On the plus side, at least he wouldn't need to get off the boat in St. Kitts or Antigua.

An experienced traveler, Miranda had known to travel light. Her suitcase, like her purse, had always been small and efficient. Although Jilly herself was in good shape, her purse resembled a hippopotamus.

But Dave was dating her, not her rucksack, he reminded himself. And he liked her...he really did. She was lively and perky and always ready to see the beauty in everything. He liked her despite those things.

For instance, the mango.

The first day, the ship still docked at Ft. Lauderdale, for a predinner snack they decided to explore the buffet—Jilly in her coronation gown, Dave in his cutoffs and Bob Marley T-shirt. Things were going pretty well until she spotted, behind the sneeze guard, the half-mangoes, raspberries garnishing their deseeded centers. She went bananas.

"They're like a van Gogh!" she declared. "Look at those colors!"

She brought two halves back to their table, one for each of them. "Pure Caribbean," she purred. One by one she spooned her raspberries out of the mango and eased them onto a dish, in a soft arc, each one touching another so none would get lonely. Then, gently running the edge of her spoon over the mango's orangey pulp, she beamed, "Wouldn't you love to paint a whole room in this color? What complexion! And the texture!" She stroked it as if caressing a baby's cheek. "Almost too gorgeous to eat," she cooed. "And these berries! They look like little rising suns!"

Tenderly she shaved up a spoonful of mango, rotating it to catch the perfect light. "So pure...so innocent." She held it there, admiring it like a surf-washed seashell. She ran the spoon under her nose, closed her eyes in ecstasy as she inhaled the mango's aroma, and, finally, eased the sliver onto her tongue, pausing to absorb its first sighs of flavor. Then she closed her mouth, meeting those tiny sighs with her own.

"I've eaten mangoes before," she said after dabbing its sweetness on the roof of her mouth, then gently swallowing, "but never anything like this. It's like little angels live inside."

Dave scooped his out, shoveled it back, and wolfed it down. He was hungry for food, not poetics. "Yeah, yummy," he agreed, scraping the last of the meat off its rind.

Jilly repeated her mango-tasting experience with the first of her raspberries, whiffing, then nibbling a couple of bumps, admiring their juice, then placing the remainder of the berry onto her tongue and imbibing its essence before she lovingly swallowed. Her gaze scanned the voluptuous buffet. "Look at this place! The colors...the smells.... How clean it is. It's like heaven!"

Before she had finished the mango and berries, Dave had eaten not only the fruits but a slice of cherry pie with a scoop of vanilla ice cream and was working on his second cup of coffee.

———◆———

In 1912, having made the connection between Trinidad's massive tar reservoir and possible nearby petroleum sources, Britain's Trinidad Oil Syndicate began drilling around Pitch Lake. The wells proved prolific, immediately producing almost ten thousand barrels of oil per day.

With global political tensions rising, the British admiralty desperately wanted to secure fuel supplies for the Royal Navy. When home secretary Winston Churchill decided to change all warships from coal- to oil-burning, Trinidad's great petroleum rush began.

Although field conditions were mordantly unhealthy—workers suffered from caustic lung diseases, malaria, and yellow fever; for miles around, wildlife died in droves from the refineries' sulfuric vapors; buildings quickly turned black; plants turned blood red in their dying throes; entire villages were deemed uninhabitable—drilling continued unabated, so that by the time war broke out in 1914, Trinidad's yearly oil production had passed a million barrels.

———◆———

Before dinner that first night, Jilly and Dave stood at the railing watching the stars, the Florida coast fading behind them. The moon was silver and almost full but, like the last of Ft. Lauderdale, on the opposite side of the ship. So here the stars were abundant.

She took his hand. "You think anyone up there is looking down at us right now?" she whispered. She was quick to add, "Other planets, I mean."

"Looking *up* at us," he corrected.

"I hope they're as happy as we are."

"You hungry?" he asked, trying to change the subject.

"I love nighttime," she said, squeezing his hand. She gazed at the stars again. "It's so innocent."

He missed Miranda.

"I wonder what the fish do at night," Jilly said, tilting an ear over the railing. "Do they sleep, like we do? Do you think the momma fishes tuck in their babies?"

Dave asked her if she was more inclined to the main dining room or back to the buffet. She said it didn't matter, as long as they didn't eat fish. "Not tonight," she pleaded. "Just not tonight."

They wound up in the boisterous main dining room. The ship's social director got up on a small dance floor to wish everyone a happy time, then spieled about land-excursion specials, great deals, so be sure to sign up early. As she described some highlights—St. Martin's French side, St. Thomas's shopping wharfs, St. Kitts's mountaintop fort—Jilly's eyes saucered, her smile widened.

Dave hadn't yet told her that while in port he intended to stay close to the ship—or maybe even on it.

She ordered a California rolls appetizer, which the waiter served along with chopsticks. Jilly glowed. "I never figured out how to use these," she said, unsheathing them and pulling them apart. "Should I try?" she asked the table. "Sure, why not?" she answered herself. "May as well! What the heck! Go for it, Jilly!" she piped. The table buddies cheered their approval.

After fumbling and dropping her first two rolls, she wound up stabbing one to get it up to her mouth. The sitting neighbors thought it was a riot, as did Jilly. The waiter, spotting the bedlam, padded over just as Jilly dropped one of the chopsticks to the floor. Without a word, the waiter picked it up and replaced it with a fork.

"He's trying to tell me something!" she guffawed, rice-cheeked.

The guy sitting next to her, a gray-bearded gent in suit and tie, reached around her and slapped Dave on his shoulder. Dave wasn't sure if it was congratulatory or sympathetic. *Don't worry. In a week the agony will be over.*

After dessert, two guitarists and a drummer took their places behind the dance floor and began tuning up. Even before they broke into their first number, Jilly was snapping her fingers and wiggling her eyebrows at Dave.

She already knew he didn't dance but probably figured since they were in the middle of the ocean and no one knew him, and his credit rating probably wouldn't be affected, so—*What the heck! We're on vacation!*—he'd give it a go.

At first Dave made no eye contact with her, and when the band broke into "Matilda," he pretended not to notice her swaying in her seat. When he still didn't budge, to keep in tempo with the musicians, she began tapping her coffee spoon on her half-filled water glass, then her empty rum-punch tumbler, then the salt and pepper shakers, then the flower vase, then any glass container within reach. Their table mates who weren't already dancing also began tapping their utensils on the bowls, plates, glassware, with Jilly their bandleader. Then the rhythmic accompaniment spread to the other tables, and soon the entire room of nondancers was having its own sit-down-jump-up.

Dave was happy, too, because now he didn't have to embarrass himself on the dance floor. But when the band began playing a slow song, he finally gave in and escorted Jilly to the parquet. He still felt self-consciously weird that he was up there with someone not Miranda, but now the floor was flesh-full and the lights low, so he endured.

As she snuggled close, Jilly whispered in his ear, "You're my other hero."

So they hung around for the next slow song, and they danced again.

———◆———

In the early 1930s, with band rivalry and their respective gang clashes becoming increasingly violent, the Trinidad authorities—still British—as they had earlier prohibited skin drums, now banned tamboo-bamboo, too.

But rhythm, music, and noise being an irrepressible element of the African spirit, the young men of the Port of Spain and hillside slums began foraging for whatever metal scraps might be made to pound out a beat. Abandoned and stolen food tins (in the East Port of Spain district, a biscuit factory discarded what would become bass drums), cheese graters, milk cans, garbage can lids, paint buckets, old car parts, chamber pots, and frying pans were pinged and thumped with spoons, open hands, knuckles, and sticks. These groups became known as "iron bands."

One youth, Winston "Spree" Simon, while living in a blighted manufacturing district, fashioned a single-tone kettle drum from a scrapped container, which he then lent to a friend, who returned it dented and misshapen. While pounding it to restore its shape, Simon was delighted to find the dents produced variously pitched sounds.

As word of this innovation spread, all the iron band players began dent-tuning their tins, hammering and partitioning surfaces to create actual notes. Through experimentation, trial and error, and serendipity, the paint cans, carbide containers, and biscuit tins evolved into "ping-pongs," raw instruments struck with wrap-tipped wooden sticks. One player fashioned into a can four distinct notes tuned to the chimes of the clock at Queen's Royal College.

By the mid-1930s, automobile brake hubs had joined the repertoire of these roughhewn pan bands, replacing glass bottles, so that by 1937 the first all-steel bands, the hallmark of underprivileged young Black men, were starting to perform at Carnival, causing quite a stir. Led by Lord Humbugger, "conducting" with a baton while wearing a top hat, gloves, and coat tails, these new performers changed the modern musical course forever.

The streets resonated with revelers chanting to the accompaniment of the melodic, metallic sounds that now ruled the lanes, alleyways, and dry riverbeds on any occasion that locals could justify taking a good jump-up, the pulsating vibrations sending the crowds into frenzy.

But this reaction to "primitive" rhythms once again made the authorities nervous. Even Trinidad's Black middle class felt unsettled by these antics. Because the bands' "instruments" were literal trash, as were, socially, their creators—"bad johns" without land, work, or future, clashing over petty jealousies and women—their so-called music was scorned. That their audience—ghetto dwellers and their criminal elements—loved the steel band performances added to the law-abiding-community's disdain.

Steelpan, then, came to be seen by the general population as the noise of hooligans. Indeed, encounters between rival bands continued to end violently, with turf wars flaring between different districts and between panners and the police. It didn't help their cause that the bands liked to brand themselves names like *Desperadoes, Attila, Invaders, Renegades, Red Army,* and *Hell Yard.*

So the more respectable Blacks decided to end the abomination—and embarrassment—once and for all. The editorial pages of the two daily newspapers filled with bitter diatribes, exhorting the authorities to once again ban this primitive, savage expression of Trinidad's dregs.

Had it not been for the intervention of an even greater threat to civilization than stolen garbage can lids, the pan-band warring factions might have indeed come to not just noise, but slaughter.

———◆———

Dave's plan wasn't working. He had agreed to go on the cruise with Jilly, thinking the ship's few-hours-stopovers would somehow insulate him from the pangs of memories on each island where he and Miranda had spent not just afternoons wandering dockside souvenir shops, but days and weeks living up in rainforest inns and hillside B&Bs.

But he soon realized he had wandered into remorse quicksand.

Jilly's and his first stop was at St. Thomas. On their honeymoon, Miranda and Dave had stayed in an old, converted-mansion, hilltop hotel overlooking the bay. From the dock now, walking with Jilly, he glanced up between palm trees at its imposing tiled roof, as blood-red as a poinsettia. Stupidly, he imagined Miranda up there, gazing out the window at him and his halter-topped girlfriend strolling happily in and out of jewelry stores. He imagined his ex, not himself, feeling regretful and jealous.

"What's wrong?" Jilly asked, as she adjusted Dave's cap's visor to shade his eyes. "You okay?"

He pulled his head away and slid the cap back on backwards so the sun was in his eyes. "Nothing."

In an instant it wasn't Miranda he was angry with, but Jilly.

She apologized. "I won't do it again."

"Stop being sorry all the time," he sniped.

They were quiet for a few minutes, still shuffling around. Finally, she said, "Do you want me to go back to the ship?"

"No," he growled. "Why would you say that?"

"What, then?"

Silence.

They walked some more, his gait quickening, she struggling to keep up. In front of an ice cream shop, he stopped, turned around, and gruffly asked her if she wanted any. She shook her head. She was crying.

He hated himself.

By 1940, Trinidad's refined-oil output had reached almost 300,000 barrels a day. The next big war was now roiling in Europe. With England desperate to protect its vital Caribbean fuel source, the prowling Nazi U-Boats equally bent on either taking it over or destroying it, and, with America determined to protect the region's strategic shipping lanes, in September, under the Destroyers for Bases Agreement, the British government granted the U.S. military occupation rights on British possessions in the region in exchange for fifty American warships.

In June 1941, the new United States naval base was commissioned in Charguaramas, on Trinidad's northwest peninsula. By the time, six months later, America officially entered the war, that base and nearby Waller Army Airfield had become fully operational, storing millions of gallons of battle-ready petroleum.

In fifty-five-gallon steel barrels.

From a nearby park came the sound of steelpans, first pinging, then breaking into melodious song. Dave started walking in that direction, his pace slower now. As he and Jilly approached the music, he contritely reached for her hand, and she took his. They sat on a bench, and for a half-hour they listened. They didn't talk, but every so often he'd move another inch to her, and she'd take the cue and lean toward him, and soon their shoulders were touching.

After the band finished its final, rousing piece, Dave got up to put a ten-dollar bill in their tin, had a word with one of the players, and rejoined Jilly on the bench. A few seconds later the pans burst into the Happy Birthday song.

During the war the government officially suspended the celebration of Carnival, sparing a final, probably brutal confrontation between social classes, as the steel band experiment was continuing at a less public, but rapid pace in the backyards of poor, Black Trinidadians.

Because the players were not able to spend time preparing for or performing the traditional pre-Lent celebration, they could now concentrate on developing better instruments, tuning methods, and musical compositions. When the U.S. naval and air bases began discarding empty fifty-five-gallon oil containers, it was almost inevitable that the pent-up creativity of nearby panners would see possibilities in those steel barrels. Hammering their tops to make shallow cavities of various sizes and depths produced distinct, pure notes, more resonant and durable than their biscuit-tin and paint-can predecessors. By cutting the barrels' sides to various-length "skirts," they were able to achieve sonorous tonal range from the lowest bass to the highest treble.

So it was that around 1943, Spree Simon, having hammered four depressions into the bottom of one of those oil barrels, became the first person to put a musical note on a steel drum. An eight-note ping-pong soon followed, then a tenor pan fashioned from an oil drum sawn about twelve inches from its top and played with a cutoff broom handle.

When on May 7, 1945, Germany surrendered to the Allies, the Trinidadian government let its citizens celebrate in the streets. The next day, the first melody pans, forerunners of the sweet steel bands we know today, officially appeared in public, ringing their happy harmonics through streets and across the hills. The Japanese surrender in August saw another street party with even more steel drums and exuberance.

In the words of the *Trinidad Gazette*, "They waved branches and chanted songs to the accompaniment of music thumped out of old iron."

Carnival resumed in 1946, the joyful oil pans becoming an integral part of the celebration, with now-friendlier competition fostering innovation in tuning and design. By then the instruments carried up to fourteen notes and were played with wooden stick tips wrapped with salvaged inner-tube rubber, making them sound more mellow.

At first, the pans' playing surfaces were sledge-hammered convex—domes rather than dishes. Ellie Mannette, a Port of Spain youth, recognizing that a concave surface would accommodate more notes than a convex and retain their tones longer, was the first to bowl out a pan, giving the drum its mature form and sound.

After precisely marking the shape and location of each note with a nail punch, then reverse-tamping them to raise various-size notes in the bowls, the drums were tempered over fires to harden the steel. After cooling, the pans were fine-tuned with tapping hammers until the correct pitches and timbral qualities were achieved, their artisans fashioning exact combinations of overtones and blendings.

With musical competitions between rival-neighborhood bands having replaced their street fights, the steelpan was finally being recognized as a legitimate musical innovation, with progressive middle-class influencers promoting what they viewed as an indigenous art form having been unjustly maligned by colonial cultural standards.

In 1949, pan leaders formed an association that held (peaceful) contests in which each area's band competed for awards for best popular song and best classical piece. Indeed, with almost thirty notes now forged onto tenor pans, and with "bass," "cello," "double seconds," and "guitar" pans providing rhythm, harmony, and melody, the ensembles were now symphonic arrays.

In 1951, the newly formed Trinidad All Steel Percussion Orchestra sent a delegation of its best players to London's Festival of Britain fair. The crowds didn't know what to expect from those beat-up, rusty bins, but as soon as the first ebullient pings rang out, they fell in love, astonished that such a powerful, wondrous sound could come from a simple piece of junk.

*Where was that music coming from?*

*How could such humble people possess such enormous talent?*

In the wake of the war's death and devastation, the sound lit up the ravished land like a holiday on a sunny beach. Enthralled with this new sensation, the Brits affectionately dubbed it "Black magic."

After their showers, Jilly and Dave went to one of the ship's atrium bars. In a quiet corner they sipped piña coladas.

"I wasn't angry at you," he told her. "Just mad at myself."

"Russ said that if everyone likes you all the time, you're probably too needy. Everyone, including yourself."

He fell silent. Silent and ashamed.

She found both of their voices. "He told me not to die with him."

Dave wanted to say how wise and brave Russell was, but nothing came out.

Boasting more than thirty notes, modern pans chime out the full chromatic range, producing a complex sound that enables them to stand alone or accompany any combination of other instruments, from those of small jazz ensembles to full classical symphonies. Today, steel band orchestras perform not just on vacation beaches and cruise ships, but in concert venues worldwide, performing the works of Bach, Beethoven and Mozart as deftly as "Day-O" and "Jump in the Line."

But why does this mystifyingly joyful sound— whether pealing out Belafonte or Tchaikovsky—make us want to feel so happy? Is it because its jubilance is reminiscent of cherry-garnished coladas, windsurfing, powdery sand, cloud-wisped lapis skies, colorful reefs in translucent waters, Caribbean sunsets, and calypso? Does the tempered steel's particular resonance, a kind of auditory drug, release endorphins in our brains to render us ecstatic? Do its frequencies stir subconscious recollection of the lullabies our mothers sang to us? Or do the sonorous tones speak to our atavistic, limbic brains, a collective tribal memory that reminds us to be grateful for our fragile freedoms and ephemeral pleasures?

Do they, like drill bits into ancient oil deposits, tap our indomitable human spirit? A reminder that the steelpan's history is a that of all mankind—that its merry timbre was born of loss, deprivation, and misery? That oppression not only *steels* the will of the enslaved, but also sends a message across parched hills and dry riverbeds that we might be temporarily suppressed but never stilled?

That optimism still pulses in anguished veins.

A year before she and Dave met, Jilly's only child, her fifteen-year-old son, Russell, died. For many months she had watched his body wither, curl, and dissolve. Dave hadn't known Russ except through Jilly's pictures and anecdotes, but knew he had courage and cheerfulness beyond his unimaginable pain. Despite facing the abyss, he remained upbeat. It was there, in him. The notes were there.

Born of bleakness and despair—tar pit, slavery, poverty, criminality, war—thanks to the skill, determination, and delight of its creators, the steelpan has in its relatively young life achieved not just respectability, but social prosperity while its innovators, practitioners, and their acoustic magic are held in almost divine regard. Having evolved from waste-dump cacophony to exhilarating symphonics, the musical mellifluence of these now racially integrated, intergender ambassadors soars blithely around the world.

The days of rusty pans are gone—we now see only chrome-plated or jauntily painted instruments—but their spirit remains its pure, glorious self.

Jilly and Dave's ship went on to visit St. Maarten, St. Kitts, Antigua, and Barbados. They took day excursions to Montserrat, St. John, and Anguilla. In St. Maarten they rented ATVs and drove along the coast to Marigot on the French side. On Antigua, they took a cab to Nelson's Dockyard, on St. Kitts a "cane train" through the rainforest, and on Montserrat they found a driver willing to take them to view the remains of Plymouth, the former capital now buried under the massive ash deposit of 1995's Soufrière Hills volcano eruption.

After the devastation, Montserrat built a new main town and airstrip on the other side of the island. The smoke still trickling out of the volcano doesn't seem to bother the locals much, and you can still pluck and eat mangos right off the trees.

The rich volcanic earth has made them sweeter and juicier than ever.

# Lanterns of Fear

For our honeymoon, my wife and I took a Caribbean cruise. I don't remember much about it. It was a long time ago. I thought if the day ever came when I'd need to remember, all I'd have to do is pad over to our media room cabinet, pluck out a few slide trays, set up the old projector, and have a look-see. I thought my wife would want to put down her book, pop us some Orville Red., and join me down memory lane. I thought when the projector click-clacked and such-and-such picture dropped into place and blazed in Technicolor onto the dining room wall, she would reach over, clasp my hand, and coo, "Oh, I forgot about that! That was the day you bought me that ruby heart pendant. I forgot all about that!" And she would lean over and kiss me, just as she did that day in the St. Thomas jewelry store. That's what I thought.

———◆———

Undoubtedly, prehistoric showmen cast fire-shadow images on cave walls. But the known history of projectors began with sixteenth-century experiments in optics and lighting, at a time when the mystical and magical power of projected images—the Inquisition had burned Bruno at the stake for his devotion to imagistic magic—was giving way to scientific enlightenment.

The camera obscura, a device that, with mirrors and lenses, captured the images of external objects on a surface inside a dark box, so fascinated Renaissance Europeans that artists like Vermeer and Rembrandt included the wondrous invention in their paintings. From this obsession with capturing and casting reality came, in 1659, the "magic lantern," the first projection device using both an artificial light source and a lens—and therefore the modern slide projector's first direct ancestor.

The popularity of this invention spread around the world, resulting in its becoming, by the nineteenth century, a commercialized source of public and home entertainment—though, in the case of children, not always pleasant. The writer Marcel Proust, for example, recalled his childhood fear of the magic lantern slide shows his great-aunt projected on his bedroom wall: "It substituted for the opaqueness of my walls, an iridescence of many colors. But my sorrows only increased thereby, because this mere change of lighting was enough to destroy the familiar impression I had of my room. Now I no longer recognized it and felt uneasy in it."

In her autobiography, sociologist Harriet Martineau records a similar childhood reaction: "Such was the terror of the white circle on the linen sheet of the dark drawing room, and of the moving slides, that, to speak the plain truth, they sat on my heart and soul the black night through. And sometimes even morning light could not drive them away."

Thus the first slide projectors came to be known as *lanternes de peur*—"lanterns of fear."

I don't look at our honeymoon slides anymore, but I'm pretty sure we took shots of the usual tourist scenes: my wife waving in front of pastel, gingerbread Curaçao harbor facades; my wife navigating a bamboo raft down the Martha Brae River; my wife at a St. Maarten beach bar, mugging with her new ruby necklace; my wife aboard ship, leaning on the railing, backdropped by sea and sky, her eyes wide and young and happy—the loveliest blues I had ever seen. I took a lot of pictures of my new wife—I don't recall having taken any without her in them. But I don't much remember specific shots—except the one with her at the ship's railing. She's standing there in her shorts and halter top, the most beautiful woman I ever knew, affecting a saucy smile, pointing with her seashell-braceleted wrist to a sign stenciled on the gunwale: *DANGER*.

That's the only one I'm really sure about. It was a long time ago.

The history of slides is, essentially, the attempt to make illusion seem more real than reality. In 1833 David Brewster invented the stereoscope, an optical device that, when viewed through lenses, made special photographs seem three-dimensional. By "projecting" an image onto the retina with the appearance of depth and texture, the device caused not only its makers but its enthusiasts to claim it provided the "perfect image of reality." Later, Daguerre's huge paintings, his dioramas, cast on transparent materials and presented in darkened theaters and illuminated from behind, imbued his landscapes with breathtaking realism. Manipulation of the light behind the pictures gave the effect of actual changing light and shade or even of complete transformation from daylight to night, and thus an intense illusion of reality. There is a famous story of a spellbound child observing one of Daguerre's dioramas and declaring it "more beautiful than nature itself."

At the time of our honeymoon, cruises were different than they are today. To eat a meal on board that did not involve foraging for peanuts between your mattress and headboard, you had to don a tie and jacket and enter the ship's dining room at a specific time and sit with people you did not know. They herded you into this immense, frenetic hall that had all the characteristics of the Chicago slaughterhouse in Upton Sinclair's novel *The Jungle*, in which upside-down hogs are conveyed squealing with terror to an aproned guy who slices their throats with a rusty knife. I don't know what women had to wear because, to be honest, I never looked at them. I had eyes only for my new wife.

We sat with a group of six other couples, middle-aged folks from Nebraska who had never seen a body of water in their lives, let alone an actual ocean, and who seemed pretty baffled by the concept. So there my wife and I were, shouting across the table at a bunch of devil-may-cares from the Heartland, trying to figure out how to get our food down without chewing and get back to our room to screw. Apparently, our tablemates were part of a group of TV-set salesmen (and their wives) who had won a sales contest that included all the free liquor they could spill on themselves in a week. They talked with their cheeks as florid and bulbous as Bavarian oom-pah-ers, and, while spitting veal cutlet and routinely knocking over highball glasses with the maniacal gusto of a Spike Jones routine, they barked sage marital advice to me and my new bride that included the phrase, "Never admit anything." They were jolly and pickled, they ate off each other's plates, and their wives showed us pictures of their kids and snorted, "Here's our little shits."

————◆————

In 1870 a Venetian, Carlo Ponti, designed the megalethoscope, a beautifully milled tabletop cabinet—itself a work of art—in which photographs were viewed through a large lens, creating an optical illusion of depth and perspective. Backlit by an internal kerosene lantern, translucent albumen pictures were colored and pierced to create dramatic visual effects, such as stars and streetlamps. Unfortunately, the source of the megalethoscope's power was also its downfall: its oil lantern heart would occasionally burst into flame and destroy the device and, sometimes, its owner's house.

The first patent for a 35mm still camera was issued in England in 1908. The first full-scale production camera was the Homeos, a stereo camera, produced between 1913 and 1920. Then came the big-selling Tourist Multiple, which appeared in 1913, and the Simplex, introduced in the U.S. in 1914. The Minigraph, by Levy-Roth of Berlin, another small camera, sold in Germany in 1915. The patent for the Debrie Sept, a combination 35mm still and movie camera, was issued in 1918, but it was not marketed until 1922. The Furet, made and sold in France in 1923, was the first cheap, small 35mm camera, and looked vaguely like more recent models. But it wasn't until the great industrialist George Eastman came onto the scene that America became, as with so many products, the world's leader.

The moment we finished our entrees, my wife started playfully pinching my thigh to get the hell out of the dining room. She was in a hurry to get away from those Nebraskans and back to our room. She would take her after-dinner drink with her. No argument from me. No need to wait for dessert. We'd make our own.

George Eastman was born in Waterville, New York, in July 1854. His father died when George was twelve, the elder Eastman leaving his family destitute. At fourteen, George dropped out of high school to find a job. As the history of the Eastman Kodak Company attests, he managed to overcome his economic adversity. In 1884 he patented the first roll film; in 1888 he perfected the Kodak camera, the first designed specifically for roll film. In 1892 he established his famous company in Rochester, New York—the first firm to mass-produce standardized photography equipment. His gift for organization and management, his tireless work ethic, and his lively and inventive mind made him a successful entrepreneur by his mid-twenties, enabling him to lead his company to the forefront of American industry.

Before making love, my wife and I made fun of the bulbous TV-salesmen and their blustery fraus, my wife braying, "Cooked snails! Cooked snails!" and me wheezing, "Shut up and fill your purse!" Then, after we made love, feeling close enough to her to take a chance, I said, "In a weird way, I like them."

"That would be weird," she said.

"Maybe that'll be us in thirty years."

"God forbid," she said, coughing up Drambuie.

"You know, giving advice to newlyweds, pictures of kids—"

"Synchronized belching."

I realized I had made a mistake. "Okay, I get it." We were quiet for a minute, and then I rolled onto her. "And now maybe I want to get it again."

But something bothered her. She draped her arm

around me and let me nibble her neck, then sighed and went limp. We had been up early that morning for muster drill. We were both tired, and I felt a little rejected. So I just sighed and also went limp.

In the earliest days, photographers had to load their film into reusable cassettes and, at least for some cameras, cut the film leader. But in 1934 there was a huge breakthrough. Eastman Kodak introduced 35mm-wide, daylight-loading, single-use, *cartridge* film, principally for use in its new "Retina" camera—but, of course, adopted by competitors. In 1935 Kodak launched its 35mm Kodachrome color film. Because of its ease of use and stunning transparencies, this slide film quickly grew in popularity, becoming, by the late 1960s, the most popular photographic format. (Its lexicon remains, even if the film does not: the term *slide show* on our computer photo programs was derived from Kodak's innovation.)

Our first slide camera was a Kodak Automatic 35R4, which I bought for my wife as a wedding present, in honor of our many future trips together. I didn't have much money; this sturdy little slide-taker cost under a hundred bucks. What's more, unlike expensive Leicas and Nikons, our honeymoon Kodak was very simple to use. When it comes to photography, I'm kind of stupid. Stupid, stupid, stupid. I never did understand, nor had the patience to learn, the meaning of f-stops or shutter speed or focal lengths or ISO numbers or aperture settings or the dozen various dials and buttons that were the hallmark of upper-bracket cameras.

I don't recall if on our honeymoon cruise I told my wife how lucky I felt every time we sat on the Lido deck in the moonlight or walked together down one island Front Street or another. I wish I had told her more.

As the years rolled along, we traveled a lot. We took a lot of pictures. We would carefully pack our film in lead-lined travel bags, so it wouldn't be corrupted by airport X-ray scanners, and once home we raced to the camera store to get it developed. Ten days was a long time, but that's how long it took. Ten days seemed long. We had an agreement. If we didn't pick up the slides together, we wouldn't peek at them until they were in the projector, so we could view them at the same time. We would cuddle on the couch with a tub of popcorn and relive our recent experiences. I knew she cheated. It wasn't in her not to sneak a look at the pictures before she got home. Sometimes I would notice a number out of order or a slide upside down coming out of the package, or if she had loaded the tray, a slide would appear on the screen upside down or backwards, and I knew she had broken her promise. But I never said anything about it.

In his final years, George Eastman was plagued by a generative disorder of his spine. He had trouble standing, and his walking became a slow shuffle. In intense pain and frustrated at his inability to maintain an active life, on March 14, 1932, when he was seventy-seven, he shot himself in his heart.

Sometimes I will be sleeping, other times I will be lying awake in the dark, watching imaginary bursts of light, listening to the click-clack of a nonexistent slide projector.

*Click-clack.* Here is a picture I took while kneeling on the deck of a chartered sailboat, my wife, wearing a scarlet two-piece, smiling against a backdrop of billowing sails and lapis sky. She is very happy. The breeze washes wisps of her silky blond hair across her smile. The warm, clear sea is in her azure eyes, a morning beach in her high, smooth cheeks. She is very happy. In the slide's outsize projection, colors are so vibrant—reds bursting, magentas pulsing—the images are almost living, breathing beings—three-dimensional creatures hovering long into the night.

I can't recall now if this was one of our actual pictures or just in my head. I don't remember.

*Clack-click.* The slide projector sounds like a semiautomatic weapon. You load a tray like a clip, insert it into its receiver with a sturdy, satisfying *clack*; you press a button, and, *click,* a "shell" drops into place and explodes onto the screen. The original Kodak projector trays were rectangular and held only forty rounds. But the projector my wife and I owned, we didn't have to reload as often. The trays were circular, similar to that of a World War I machine gun's bullet magazine, and they held 160 pictures.

In the bursts of color and dust-swirling blasts from the projector's muzzle, there is something else about slides different from ordinary pictures. If they, with their bigger-than-life, dazzling images that, as in Proust's childhood bedroom, block out the familiar world and blur the distinction between imaginary and real, they might well render the image *more* real than the original, the actual events inferior to the memory. Slides, then, may create a world where false memory—the illusion of an idealized past—replaces the true experience they represent. A frozen smile, a colonial façade glinting in the sunlight, expensive jewelry, the happy glow of sand-smooth cheeks, become billowing sails of illusion.

*Clack-click.* Here is a picture of my wife, hair and halter top drenched, leaning against the owner of the plantation inn where we often stayed in St. Thomas. They are standing under an eave of the great house, rain bullets slicing behind them. They are holding onto each other, half-mugging, half-in-earnest, as Hurricane Lenny mows down the Eastern Caribbean. In my wife's eyes you can see the strain we all felt, holed up for four days, watching our roofs billow, listening all night to their timbers' ghostly wails, wincing from the far-off surf crashing thunder-like against the town. In the horizontal rain, denuded palm trees bend like jackknifed legs, their nesting birds long dead. A torrent of brown runoff roils down the stairs and mountainside, down, down. For once the Kodachrome is lusterless, soaked gray, as if the developing process had broken down. But the soddenness is not the film. It is in the deluged earth. In the slide's absence of color you can feel the utter wetness, the oxygen-starved, muted red of my wife's bathing suit, the winter brown of her hair, the cistern gray of the owner's shirt and beard. He hugs her shoulder, my wisp of a wife, preventing her from being sucked into the storm. He smiles, she frowns. She wants to go home. We have run out of food. There has been no electricity for three days. The only drinking water is what guests collect from the great-house roof. In front of my wife and the owner sits a large cooking vat, which they had just filled with rainwater, each holding a handle, before I told them to turn and face the camera. I do not like this picture. There is something primordially evil about hurricanes, something that suggests original sin. When we found ourselves trapped on the island, I thought it might be an interesting experience, something to tell our (future)

children. But it did not work out that way. Now I remember something else. When I shouted above the wind for the owner and my wife to put down the vat and turn around, when I snapped that picture, how hard it was to breathe.

———◆———

Because digital photography is the new technology, it is virtually impossible to get 35mm slide film anymore. The truth is, for all of its magic, Kodachrome was doomed. It was a difficult film to manufacture and even more complex to process. There are no remaining photofinishing labs in the world processing Kodachrome.

I never bought a digital camera. And I hardly ever take pictures with my phone, although someday I might. In the meantime, my original Kodak 35R4 sits on my closet shelf, collecting dust. I thought I might one day show it to my kids, just as those Nebraskan partiers must now be showing their grandkids pictures of that long-ago cruise. That's what I thought. But it's just in the closet. It may still have a partially exposed roll of film in it. Maybe someday I'll throw it away.

# Nasdaq 16,000

They didn't get to the hotel until after dark. Everything was pretty much as it had been twenty years ago, except a little threadbare. They certainly could have afforded much better now, but Bajan Guest House had carved out a little place in Katie's heart. Even after all those years, the bartender, Horton, remembered them, making her very happy. He served them welcome punches, two cherries each.

"Here's to our second honeymoon," she whispered, wrapping her drink around Paul's.

He looked around the weary bar, at the sagging fishnet above the cash register, the broken starfish, the dusty bottles of rum. Maybe Bajan House was a buyout candidate. Maybe they could fix up the place, flip it, and make a quick couple hundred thousand. But he kept his mouth shut. He just sipped his punch and returned his wife's kiss.

"What're you looking at?" she demanded.

"Nothing." He sucked his orange slice. "I'm just glad to be back."

"Your phone off?"

"You bet."

"Let's walk on the beach."

"Now?"

"What's wrong with now?" She nodded at the bartender. "He'll let us take the glasses, if we promise to bring them back, won't you, Horton?"

"Of course, Missus."

With Paul puffing an outsized Cohiba cigar, they strolled down narrow Rockley Beach to the jetty, then back up Bay Street, reminiscing, Katie snapping her fingers to the rhythm of a steel-drum band playing at a nearby hotel, Paul thinking about Nasdaq. Yesterday it had closed over 15,000.

His phone rang, muffled in his pocket.

Katie cleaved him a death glare.

"I thought it was off, I swear to God. Here, look, I'm shutting it off right now."

"Get to it."

He shoved his hand in his pocket.

"Well?"

"What if it's an emergency? What if I take this one and then turn it off for the rest of the trip?"

She turned and kept walking. He let her get twenty feet ahead, then answered his phone with a whisper.

"I have to turn it off," he told Warren, his broker. "Leave a message at the desk if we get filled on our LorCom July one-tens. Don't call the room. For God's sake, don't call the room."

He turned off the phone, slipped it back in his pocket, and raced to catch up with his wife.

"Off forever," he promised. "I thought I turned it off at O'Hare." When he put his arm around her, she didn't protest. "I'll put this stinky cigar out, too, okay?"

"It's all right."

"It is?"

"But if I hear that phone again, I'll ask Horton to

frappé your nuts in a blender. That would make a heck of a welcome punch, don't you think?"

"No problem."

As they walked hand in hand, Paul could feel the tension drain out of her.

"Everything's so different," she said, wistfully. "But we're still the same, aren't we, honey? I don't mean money-wise. I don't mean financial-wise. I mean really the same inside."

Before he could answer, from the shadows between Café Sol and Half Moon Apartments squirted a cadaverous beggar, his ribs protruding, his stomach concave.

"Want to buy me magic seed?" said the grungy Rastaman, his bony hand extended. "You plant seed in yard, it grow good luck."

Paul puffed harder on his Cohiba to cover up the stench of the nearly toothless, shoeless, dreadlocked peddler. He walked on, assuming Katie was right behind him. But when he glanced back, he saw that she was actually talking to the shirtless vagabond. She took the seed and held it in her palm while listening to his spiel.

Paul walked back briskly, stepped between them, took a buck from his wallet, handed it to the ragamuffin, and took his wife's arm.

"Wait!" the beggar yelled, striding after them. "Where you going wid me seed?"

Paul kept walking, but Katie pulled free and once again stopped. Paul turned.

"Here's you rass dollar, mon!" the beggar shouted, balling up the money and hurling it at Paul. "I don't want you fuckin dollar! Me want me seed back! Me seed worth ten fuckin dollar!"

The brigand was wiry and hard, with features sharp enough to gut fish. Paul sized him up. He had heard that West Indians fight wildly—poking out eyes, ripping out hair, gnawing off fingers. All Paul knew was good old-fashioned American punching. If the villain did rip out his eyes, he would never again be able to watch a ticker tape scroll on the bottom of Fox Business.

Still, he had to protect his wife.

He turned around, and, just as Katie was opening her purse to give the rascal ten bucks, Paul grabbed the seed from her fist and held it out for the beggar.

The pirate cursed and muttered—Paul not understanding a word—and spat like a snake. But, to his relief, he took back his seed. "Tief!" he bellowed, turning back into the shadows. "Damn tief! Tief me land! Tief me sugar! Tief me beach! Tief me coconut! Tief me rum!"

Katie's hand was halfway out with a ten-dollar bill. Paul nudged it back into her purse. He was proud of himself.

"Tief me pickney! Tief me coral! Tief me gal! Tief me fish!" His mud-crusted arms flailing, the beggar disappeared into the night.

"What are you doing?!" Katie snapped, tearing her hand away from her husband's.

"What do you mean?"

"What do you mean, 'what do I mean?'!" She crunched her purse closed and peered for the ruffian in the darkness. "What the hell is the matter with you?!"

"The matter with *me*?!"

"All he wanted was a few dollars."

"Ten dollars for a seed you can find everywhere?" His glance fell on a brown, boomerang-shaped pod in the gutter. "It was a common tamarind seed."

"Obviously, the seed isn't the point. Anyone but you would see that."

"You were actually going to give him ten dollars for that stupid story about good luck? We already have good luck."

"He wasn't referring to Nasdaq."

"He was taking advantage of us."

"We can afford it. Obviously he needs the money."

"To get more stoned?"

"Not *every* fee has to be negotiated."

"What's wrong with you? No one in his right mind would give him ten bucks."

She started to stride away. "Not everyone's Global Paul," she snorted, referring to his trading account username.

"This is crazy," he reasoned, following her quick pace. "I offered him a buck, for Christ's sake. I didn't even want his stupid seed."

"He could have been a homicidal maniac for all you knew," she mocked. "He could have had a machete or something and whacked off our heads."

"That's why I came back to help."

"Yeah, right," she groaned. "You came back to see if you could get a better *deal*."

"He was wearing shorts. Where was he supposed to hide a machete?"

She swiveled. "Don't try to negotiate your way out of this one!"

"Out of what one?"

"The world according to Global Paul."

"I tried to give him a buck for a seed. He insulted us."

"Not us. *You*."

"He spit on me."

"I don't blame him in the least," she snorted, striding away again. "We come here and throw their own seeds back in their faces."

"This is nuts."

"Global P."

"I *handed* it back to him."

She refused to look at him. "For ten lousy stinking dollars, you humiliated him in his own country."

"You just said he was a homicidal maniac. Now you're worried about embarrassing him?" He tried stepping in front of her but scooted aside when she threatened to mow him down. "Most wives would be grateful their husband came to their rescue."

She chuffed.

Walking backwards, he said, "What the hell do I care about ten bucks? My cigar cost twenty-five."

"Global P."

As she turned a corner, he fell behind, befuddled and wounded, wondering what the hell he did wrong.

He followed her back to Bajan House, and, with her safely in the lobby, kept walking. He was plenty ticked. He relit, finished his cigar, and lit another with long, hard, ticked-off puffs. Fifty bucks worth of cigars, just like *that*.

But by the time, around midnight, he got back to the hotel, his anger had shriveled. The truth was, he had been looking forward all day to making love to Katie in the same room where they had spent their wedding night. Love amid the violin-chorus of tree frogs. Love lighted by the twinkle of cruise ships on the horizon or, if they were luckier still, by a cloudless moon. Love fueled by his unebbing adoration of her and by generous portions of Fire Mountain Heavenly Dark, the local rum they had discovered here twenty years ago.

She was just getting out of the shower, steam billowing out of the half-open bathroom door. He hoped and believed that the hot water had softened her spirits.

But when she came out with her face slick with wrinkle cream, he realized she intended to go right to sleep.

She slipped under the sheet and, towel on pillow, rolled over on her side, her back to him, the coral-colored sheet draped over her perfect, teardrop-shaped body. Her waist was so thin Paul had always been able to wrap both hands around it and almost touch his fingertips. He ached with wanting to make love to her.

"I'm going to turn on the TV," he warned. "I'm not tired."

"That's no concern of mine."

"Won't it bother you?"

"It's none of my business."

"I might read. I'll have to turn the light up."

"Do what you want. Oh, by the way, there was a message for you waiting at the front desk."

He acted surprised. "Really? What did it say?"

"It says, 'Screw yourself.'"

He found the message slip on the dresser and, without even taking a peek, crumpled it up for her benefit. He got into bed and leafed through the room copy of *Welcome Bonjour Willkommen Barbados* magazine, rustling pages. When that didn't rouse her, he turned on the television and found *The Maltese Falcon*. "Good old Sam Spade," he muttered. "Yes, ma'am. Who doesn't love late-night murder?"

Nothing.

He looked up at the mosquito net, bundled above their four-poster like a storm cloud. He couldn't stand it anymore. "Why are you doing this?" he moaned, dropping the TV remote onto the magazine.

"Doing what?"

"You know what."

"Because it's been a long day, and I'm tired."

"I don't mean sleeping. You know what I mean. I mean acting like I'm Adolf Hitler."

"Have a nice second honeymoon, Paul."

"I didn't do anything wrong."

"Just tell me if you're going to jabber all night, so I can put in my earplugs."

"I've been trying to figure out how I could have been a better person there."

"You are what you are."

"Are you mad because we haven't taken a vacation together in three years?"

"Good night."

"I've been working my brains out."

"It shows."

"I offered him a dollar for a lousy tamarind seed!"

"You're repeating yourself."

"All right. If that's the way you want it, I'm going for a walk."

"Be sure to turn off the murder."

"By myself. On our second honeymoon."

"Don't slam the door."

He threw on the same clothes he had worn on the plane—khaki Dockers and a long-sleeve shirt with his stockbroker's logo embroidered on the pocket. He uncrinkled the message—also for her benefit—started to leave, then stopped to turn on his phone, which came to life with a one-octave rendition of "God Bless America."

"Oh, good," he said, crackling the message slip again. "Filled at five and a half."

"Global P," she mumbled.

He didn't slam the door, but he sure as hell didn't turn off the murder.

Downstairs, the lobby was dim and deathly quiet. The night clerk was gone somewhere, the bar was closed, the ceiling fans still. A palm frond floated motionless in the pool. Three terra cotta steps led to the beach. Except for soundless lapping, the sea slept, flat as a mattress.

He stepped onto Bay Street. That, too, was quiet, though glowing ghostily in neon. The silence was broken by laughter. Down the block a young tourist couple walked arm in arm, in synchronized footsteps, the young man's arm around his girl's shoulder, hers around his waist.

From between Sugar Reef Bar and Bajan Jewels, the tamarind-seed beggar leapt out of the alleyway in front of the lovers, holding out his hand.

The young man, wearing a white T-shirt and cutoffs, dismissed him with a wave and kept walking, never missing a step. His girlfriend—something told Paul they were not yet married—clung closer to him, but her footsteps never lost the rhythm of his. The beggar walked backwards with them, down a curb, up another, yammering away about his good-luck tree. Finally, in front of a parked car, he stepped out of their way, followed for a few more futile steps, lagged, gave up. The lovers moved on, leaving him standing in the middle of the empty street, holding out his hand.

The beggar did not insult them, as he had Paul, did not accuse them of rape, pillage, or plunder. But when he spotted Paul, still standing in front of the hotel, he grinned, his three front teeth glowing green and orange in the neon. His eyes bulged like a tree frog's. He stretched out his hand, presumably with the tamarind seed in it. "Tief," he called, sucking his gums. "You want to buy me seed now? Twenty dollars now, Massa Tief."

Paul wanted to throttle him. He wanted Katie to hear the man screaming, to step onto their balcony and see her husband thrashing him to a pulp. But when, instinctively, he looked up, their balcony was empty.

"Tief! Bad luck not to buy me seed! Bad, bad, Massa Tief! You tief me island, you pay de price!"

Saying nothing, Paul went back into the hotel lobby. His tormentor stood outside the front door, his face pressed to the glass, his hand cupped, taunting Paul. The woman clerk had returned, yawning, blinking sleep from her eyes. "Don't pay no attention to him," she said. "He's harmless. Sometimes he run around naked, but he don't hurt no one yet."

Paul walked past the bar and the pool, down the steps to the beach—dark but for the hazy glow of a half-moon. It was just light enough to see the message written on an old fishing skiff, drawn well up onto the sand and now used for advertising: *EAT AT SHORTY'S.*

Didn't Katie remember how poor they were the first time around? Didn't she care how much money Paul had made in the market? What was wrong with a little appreciation? A simple thank you. A nice second-honeymoon lay.

He decided his wife was the most ungrateful woman he had ever known. The most ungrateful on earth. He glanced at the gibbous moon. *In the whole cosmos.*

From the shadows he watched the tourist couple sitting on the edge of the jetty playing kissy-face. Even with the moon half-full, the sky smoldered with stars.

Most women would kill to trade places with Katie, he thought. They sure as hell wouldn't come down to Barbados on their twentieth anniversary just to slime their stupid face, roll over, and fall asleep. They'd be *thrilled* to be married to Global Paul.

*To hell with her.*

As he walked back down the beach from the jetty, the moon retreated behind a nugget of cloud. But it was still light enough to see his own solitary footsteps in the sand, already half-dissolved by the incoming tide.

———◆———

"You want to come with me?" he asked her the next morning.

"I think I'll hang around the beach and read," she said, not letting up. "That's what honeymoons are for."

"I thought honeymoons are for having sex with your wife."

"I'd think you'd need to conserve your energy for puts and calls."

He took a taxi clockwise up the coast. Halfway up the island, at Sandy Point, the driver turned inland toward St. Thomas Parish, climbing the bib of what might have been the remains of an ancient volcano, now carpeted with pink, feathery sugar cane, rearing stallion-like in the wind. In the center of the island, on a lush brow, loomed the vaneless ruins of an eighteenth-century sugar mill, casting a ragged shadow. Beyond that nestled a complex of four pale-yellow, wood-plank buildings and two smaller, red-tile-roofed stone buildings. Paul took in the scene with a keen entrepreneurial eye, wondering what opportunities in this undeveloped swatch of fecundity might await a stock-picking genius such as himself.

He considered the marketing potential of this hidden distillery: humble folks, descendants of slaves, applying skills passed down through generations, toiling with pride in virtual obscurity. He liked its romantic quaintness—like those "We'll leave the light on for you" motel commercials or the Secret Valley salad dressings.

As the taxi coiled down the slope, Paul envisioned an advertising concept for Fire Mountain Estates rum. Like most successful campaigns, it would be profoundly simple. One word popped into his brain: *Still*. *Still*, with all its connotations. He rubbed his hands, gleeful at its understated brilliance. *Still*. He sat on the edge of the seat, his head out the window, breathing the redolent breeze. For a moment, he even forgot about Katie.

"It's beautiful," he told the driver.

"Yes, sah."

"You like Fire Mountain rum?"

"Oh, yes, sah. Yes."

"If you wait for me, I'll buy you a bottle."

The driver's eyes lit up in the mirror. "Fine, sah. Fine, fine. I'll wait as long as you want."

Global P.

———◆———

"No one knows for certain the origin of the word *rum*," said Ms. Lilah Pett, the perky docent, "but it may come from the Latin word for sugar cane: *saccharum officinarum*."

She was small but sturdy, with a smooth, almond-shaded complexion. Her short reddish-brown hair, swept back on the sides, covered her ears except for the lobes, from which hung pearl teardrop earrings. She wore a sleek blue dress patterned with white and yellow hibiscuses, a pearl necklace, and fashionable canvas sandals. Her toes were polished clear. She was pretty, with thin Caucasian features. In the corporate scheme of things, Paul saw her more as a media-relations person than a garden-variety tour guide.

For taking people around on factory visits, he pictured a darker, thicker-skinned woman dressed in traditional bright billowing dress and native head wrap. Barefoot, maybe. Mammy type, huggable—like those plush, roving characters in Disney World.

"Lovable mouse," he said under his breath.

"Mouse?" squeaked Ms. Pett.

The visitors' glances darted around the ground.

"No, no," Paul stammered, embarrassed. "I was just thinking aloud."

Ms. Pett cleared her throat. "Or the name could come from the fact that plantation owners gave rum to their slaves to cure their head colds—the French word for cold being *rhume*."

Paul was among a group of six visitors taking the eleven o'clock tour—this, their first stop, being a replication of a colonial distillery.

"In 1687," said Ms. Lilah Pett, "the British Royal Navy officially adopted a pint of rum as their sailors' daily ration—a reward for good behavior."

"Good behavior," Paul muttered, suddenly remembering Katie.

"In the old days of wind-powered mills, slaves

would cut plump cane with machetes, bring it to the mill in ox carts, and feed the stalks twice through the grinding wheel to extract its juice."

Lilah Pett's voice was as juicy and sweet as...well... sugar, and it oozed out her sunny white teeth. Paul imagined her naked, delivering a lecture on the history of the colonial wench, her arms flailing like windmill vanes while she described the process of her perky rump rearing up in the wind. He decided that should he indeed divert some of his Nasdaq riches into this fertile and deserving enterprise, Ms. Lilah Pett would move up fast in his organization.

"From the crushing wheel," she continued, gesturing to three large caldrons, "the fresh juice ran down a sluice to the boiling house, where it was ladled into cast-iron pots and cooked over an open fire of dried cane stalks and wood. As the liquid thickened, lime was added to precipitate unwanted impurities and aid fermentation."

Ms. Pett was very groomed, very professional. Even in the still-steamy late-morning air, not one of her hairs was wilted or out of place, not a single thread of her dress was wrinkled. Her only concession to the heat was a patina of sweat across the bridge of her nose, and even that had a come-hither quality. Paul was surprised. Somehow the image of fat fruit merchants balancing stalks of bananas on their heads had lodged in the back of his mind. But Ms. Pett was a modern, articulate businesswoman—dressed more for a board meeting than a trip through cane fields—and he found it a pleasant surprise, indeed.

He had the impression that Lilah Pett was eminently rational. A clear, logical thinker, unfettered by emotional yolk—unlike another woman he happened to know. He imagined that an idea would enter into Ms. Pett's brain, evaporate to its essence, and, through a process of precise heating and cooling, distill down to an unclouded conclusion.

He was certain she would see the illogic of sympathizing with a beggar, and in the very same sentence, accusing him of being a machete murderer. He believed Ms. Pett would stare agog at Paul's stock-market statement. Perhaps she would even faint. He believed Ms. Pett was herself wondering why Fire Mountain Estates had allowed itself to remain obscure and was longing for a man of Paul's superior business skills to rescue the tiny firm from oblivion. He believed that Ms. Pett was, in two words, sexually frustrated.

"After most of the liquid has been boiled out," she explained, "the result is molasses."

When Paul pictured molasses—thick, gunky, undrinkable—he could not prevent his wife from coming to mind. Eighty-five percent dissolved solids. Impossible to swallow. No kick, no buzz, no reason, no logic.

He had never cheated on Katie, but sometimes she made it a tough day's work. Sometimes it was like cutting cane for fourteen hours in the predatory sun, hitching himself to an ox cart, hauling load after load back to the mill, only to get his schmuck caught under a grinding stone.

"Next we'll go to our working distillery, to show you how fermentation and distillation is accomplished today, here at Fire Mountain Estates."

They followed Ms. Pett through a yard, into a hangar-like building, and up a flight of creaky stairs, where they lined up on a quavering catwalk, overlooking six stainless-steel tanks—an armada glinting under a fluorescent sky.

"Over fifty percent of the molasses is fermentable sugar," she continued, her hip pressed into the railing, beads of sweat glimmering in the cup of her throat. "Here, we add our proprietary yeast formula to the finest grades of molasses. The resulting mixture is known as *wash*. The yeast consumes the sugar in the wash to produce alcohol and carbon dioxide and heat. In approximately three days, the wash is fermented into what we call *wine*—but not the kind you drink. The wine is pumped to the distillation building, which we will go to next."

They went downstairs and, passing through a gangway, entered another building, where gleaming pipes webbed together two-story distillation towers.

"Other small distilleries use one or two columns to purify their rum," said Ms. Pett, "but we at Fire Mountain Estates incorporate *three* copper-clad columns to assure you of the finest premium spirits available throughout the West Indies. A truly unique taste sensation."

Paul wondered what kind of sensation it would be to dribble a few drops of Fire Mountain Heavenly Dark rum onto Ms. Pett's heavenly dark thighs as she bubbled spiritedly under his sensational column. Fiery Ms. Pett. Hot, sweaty, premium, but hopefully not yeasty Ms. Lilah Pett. Gazing hornily at her, that was what he was thinking. Blame Katie.

"In the still, heat under pressure is applied to the fermented wine. The alcohol vapors are cooled in a condensing vat, pumped into the next column, and so on. By the time the distilled rum leaves the third still, it is 94.5 percent alcohol by volume."

Fiery, tangy, *pressurized* Ms. Pett.

"Finally, water is added to this overproofed spirit to reduce its strength. Usually, the alcohol content winds up to be forty-five to fifty-five percent. Any questions?"

"What are the taps used for at the bottom of the columns?" a fellow with bushy white eyebrows asked.

Ms. Pett glanced around the group. "Does anyone know the answer?" Getting everyone involved. Paul liked that.

"To remove non-productive impurities," Paul ventured. Again, Katie came to mind.

Lilah Pett took a long, curious look at him. He felt the other tourists' admiring stares.

"That's exactly right," said Ms. Pett, she of the copper-clad, finest-tasting, most premium gams available throughout the West Indies. "Are you in the same business?"

"Nope. Just read a lot."

"You like rum?"

"I like yours. I like yours a lot."

"We have a saying here: the more informed you are, the better Fire Mountain tastes." Ms. Pett rose up on her toes.

She led the visitors to the far end of the building. They let Paul walk in front, right behind their lovely docent. "The stills yield about one gallon of rum for every fifteen gallons of fermented wash," she explained. "Distilling the first part of a batch produces the strongest spirits, or *high wines*, and the last part the weakest, or *low wines*. We separate and remove these *heads* and *tails* and collect the in-betweens, called *seconds*, which we then age and blend. Before moving on to the aging warehouse, are there any questions?"

"What are those glass pipes for?" the wife of the bushy-eyebrowed man asked, pointing to long vertical tubes at the base of each distillation column. "They look like big coffee urns."

Ms. Pett glanced Paul's way.

"Sight glasses," he offered. "If I'm right, they have beads in them that float or sink depending on the alcohol content of the rum."

"Quite right, indeed. Right again. Three beads each." Ms. Pett's eyelashes danced a silent samba. "Let's move along, shall we?" she told the group, without taking her eyes off her star pupil.

They walked down a gravel path, through a weedy lot, to a stone warehouse. Ms. Pett motioned them aside, to get out of the way of a forklift truck that came rumbling out of accordion doors. Diesel exhaust rose and burled. The wife of the bushy-eyebrowed man coughed a raspy hack.

They went inside. Barrels were stacked to twenty-foot-high ceilings. Row after row of racks, barrel upon barrel. When the diesel smell dissipated, the aroma of tannin and aging rum hung thick in Paul's sinuses.

"We store almost two thousand casks in these old moss-covered walls," said Ms. Pett. "A quarter-million liters of the finest rum in the world."

He licked his lips.

"The rum is aged from between six months to four years. We import oak barrels from distilleries in the U.S. and Canada that have been used to store whiskey, bourbon and cognac. We then singe the inside of the barrels for charcoal flavoring and, after filling, mark them with the date of the batch, lot number, and percentage of alcohol. The bungs, or stoppers, are made of local poplar, due to its superior sealing ability."

Paul imagined himself bunging Ms. Pett so hard and fast that he singed the inside of her barrel, imparting a smoky, savory flavor.

"The casks are stored on their sides, as you see, and rotated weekly to maximize the rum's contact with the oak."

He would certainly rotate Ms. Pett.

She moved through the rum cathedral. "Right this way, please," she said, Paul staying close behind, feeling the warmth of her flesh, inhaling her lilac cologne.

They made a brief stop at the blending building, then returned to the visitors' center, where the tour had begun.

"And now for the best part," said Lilah Pett, standing before a varnished mahogany bar, reflected light glinting off her lips. She gestured to a dozen gleaming brandy snifters, lined up on the counter. "Here you can sample our light, medium, and Heavenly Dark rums." She nodded at the bartender. "And if you dare, try our rare, fifteen-year-old overproofed Extra Dark. But be prepared for a jolt, because it's seventy-percent alcohol!

The bartender dosed the bottom of a snifter with two-year-old, medium-gold rum. Ms. Pett lifted it to the sunlight. "To thoroughly enjoy the experience of tasting fine rum, first hold it up to judge its clearness and color." She swirled it gently. "This creates aroma in the glass. Then, take a deep breath, exhale, hold the snifter to your nose." She demonstrated. "Slowly inhale the delightful vapors. Assess its delicate and subtle aroma." She ended with a tiny sip and saucy half-smile. She side-glanced Paul. "Eating beforehand always improves the experience. Ice water afterwards cools the palate."

He needed his palate cooled—big time. A drop of rum had escaped the corner of Ms. Pett's lips and threatened to dribble down her chin. Without taking her eyes off her number-one student, she licked it, then wiped the crease of her mouth with a shimmering fingertip.

Global P's boiler was about to blow.

The bartender poured him three samples, and Paul gulped them down in single swallows without glancing at them—never mind holding them up to the light, swirling, and sniffing. Then he asked for a shot of the overproofed Extra Dark. He held that on his tongue for a moment, feeling the burn, then, clacking the snifter onto the mahogany, swallowed hard, held his breath, and braced. A second later the percussion came, the fumes rose up his throat, through his palate and brain, and out the top of his bald pate.

He held the snifter out for an encore, and another after that.

With the rum blending in his gut—eight shots in all—and their vapors swirling delightfully in his skull, Paul got up the courage to approach Ms. Pett, who was shaking the last of her visitors' hands. She was only fifteen feet away, but it seemed a long way to go. It was like he was at a singles bar, walking across the parquet to ask the sexiest girl in the place to dance. If it worked, he'd be a hero to his poker buddies, but if she said no, his life as he knew it was over.

He staggered slightly, found his balance, stopped to assess the situation, wondering if his head was too shiny, wondering, idiotically, if his breath smelled like liquor. He silently rehearsed what he was going to say. Finally, he pulled up short, reminding himself that he wasn't just some ordinary tourist schlemiel off a cruise ship. He wasn't a shirtless beggar with a phony ten-dollar tamarind seed. Hell, no. What he was, was...*Global P*.

Here were the salient points of the deal Paul silently and somewhat tipsily negotiated with his future offshore corporation. If perky Ms. Pett showed the kind of interest in him that he hoped she would, he would recommend to his board of directors to promote her to vice president in charge of something or other. If, on the other hand, the docent had worked him into a froth to no avail, he would aggressively pursue the purchase of this small distillery until the day he died for the sheer pleasure of seeing Ms. Pett dressed in native head wrap, shoelessly leading dumb-question-asking tourists around the distillery *while balancing bundles of bananas on her head.*

Blame Katie.

Blame Katie for the fact that the fate of tailored, highly professional, modern, logical, luscious, and thoroughly delectable Ms. Lilah Pett now rested solely, completely, utterly, and absolutely in the hands of her perky-rumped response.

She held out her hand to him as he approached. His palms were sweating like evaporation coils. She could have just said thank you and have a good day, and let it go at that, but she did not. What she said was, "You're the smartest, most virile-looking man I have ever met. The top of your head is so handsomely slick!"

Paul rattled his skull and stared at her dumbly.

She repeated herself: "Thank you for coming. Do you have any other questions, sir?"

All right, maybe the rum was stronger than he thought.

"Do you like me?" he stammered.

"Sir?"

He cleared his throat. The room began to swirl, just as the rum had swirled against the sides of the snifters.

"Do I like you?" she repeated.

"I do." Paul waited. The visitor center was listing about forty-five degrees, a sloop in a Category 5 hurricane.

"Sir, are you all right?"

He raised a finger. "Why can't I find Fire Mountain rum in the States?" He glanced around for a porthole to open for fresh air.

"Oh, our visitors ask that all the time. It's all about quality, you see," she answered. "The best rum takes time to mellow and mature. Our facilities are tiny compared to some of the mega-brands. If we suddenly started selling in huge quantities, we would have to release barrels before their proper aging period. I'm not saying it would be bad rum, it would just be different. We happen to be fond of what we have. We don't really want anything different."

"Don't I what?" he asked after a beat.

She grabbed his shoulder to steady him. "Do you want to sit down, sir?"

He looked around, wondering which of the Lilah Petts was talking.

"Better come to the bench with me, sir."

"I'm all right."

"Are you sure? That's strong rum. I saw you drink all those samples."

"You saw me? You like me?"

"I like you fine, sir. Won't you sit down, though?"

"Okay," he finally agreed.

Then he vomited all over her.

"You should see how stupid you look," Katie said as she fed her husband a spoonful of Pepto Bismol. Paul lay propped up under the hotel sheet, his head cold and clammy, his shoulders heavy as a donkey pack.

"Do you love me?" he wanted to know.

"Do you think I could live with this head and not love it?"

"I love you, too."

"Why don't you get some sun on it? Fresh air and daylight might do it some good."

"I made a real mess."

"Nothing that can't be fixed. Everything can be fixed."

"I ruined her dress. I don't remember much after hitting the floor."

"I gave them your credit card number and told them to be fair. Notice I didn't say *our* credit card number."

"Will you sleep with me tonight?"

She kissed the top of his skull. "Of course, sweet man. I'm sorry about last night and this morning."

"What happened?"

"It's just that Fire Mountain rum is about *us*. You and me—not Global Paul. Barbados is *ours*, not your stockbroker's."

"We were so poor. Don't you remember?"

"Of course I remember. Those days were awful. But they were nice, too. It's what we had. Them and each other."

"Remember the Windjammer?"

"The cold-water shower? The flying food? The green faces?"

"I guess that was ours, too."

She squeezed his nose. "Now you're getting it, moron boy."

"I made a jerk of myself at Fire Mountain."

"That's because you are a jerk."

"I love Barbados."

"Me too."

Paul clutched her hand to his sternum. She kissed his knuckles.

"I'm done with rum forever."

"A little's not bad. Next time, try it in a punch. A punch would be good for you."

"Okay, I get it."

"You do? You finally get it?"

"You know what I've been thinking?"

She tilted her head.

"I was thinking maybe I'll sell our stocks and take our profits."

"All of them?"

He shrugged.

"Didn't Warren say at this rate Nasdaq will be sixteen thousand by July?"

"It's okay. I think we made enough."

She squeezed his hand. "I think you're making the right decision."

"As soon as we get home."

"Why wait?" She handed Paul his phone. "If it's one call he'll answer, it's Global P's."

At midnight—after Paul had called his broker, taken a nice snooze, and he and Katie enjoyed a lobster dinner across the street, then returned to the hotel to make love—they decided to skinny dip in the ocean.

"Just like our honeymoon," he said.

"Just like."

They padded downstairs wearing nothing but towels. The night clerk smiled at them sleepily and returned to her magazine. The pool shimmered, reflecting onto a thicket of hibiscus bushes. Tree frogs were in full chorus. A white-and-gray cat meatloafed on a stack of beach chairs, its eyes miniature moons. Palm fronds rustled under a wisp of easterly breeze. Heat lightning pulsed on the invisible horizon, illuminating nothing but itself.

They draped their towels over Shorty's beached advertising skiff and went into the water, Paul sprinting rambunctiously and Katie easing herself in. Neck deep, they hugged. He scooped up his wife and kissed her breast.

"You're a wild man."

"You look the same as when we got married. *Better*."

"You have a lot less hair."

"But you love me."

"I sure do."

He heard something. Katie heard it too, and it startled her. "What's that?" She turned to follow his gaze.

He thought he saw something moving in Shorty's skiff. He squinted into the darkness, holding Katie tighter. She clutched his neck. "Something in the boat there," he whispered.

"A dog, probably."

But it was the ragged beggar who rose from inside the boat, like a vampire from a coffin. "You wake me up!" he scolded, shaking his fist.

"Oh no," Paul groaned.

"Bad luck, bad luck to wake de Rastaman!" shouted the ragamuffin, climbing out. "You pay price for waking de Rastaman!" blasted the rascal, grabbing their towels. "You trow property in man's house, you lose property! Squatter's rights!"

"He's stealing our towels," she gasped. "And our

room key with them."

The beggar ran away and disappeared down the beach, their towels contrailing over bony shoulders.

"Now what do we do?" she asked.

"I suppose it's too late to buy one of his seeds."

She squeezed Paul. "My business genius."

"Well, I suppose we can either worry about it or keep swimming."

She shrugged. "Maybe the towels will show up later."

"Maybe they will," he said, kissing her other breast, "and maybe they won't."

"I bet you miss your cell phone now, don't you?"

"Not really."

"You still love me," his wife wanted to know, "even though we sold all our stock?"

He jackknifed his legs, and they dropped under the water. He got his head between her thighs, and when he stood again, she was riding his shoulders, a sea beast rising from the phosphorescent tide. She screamed with fake fright, then glee.

"Nothing to hold onto anymore," she said, groping his noggin.

He plowed upshore until the water reached his knees.

She grabbed his eyebrows. "*Whee!*"

He started running, making huge splashes.

The beggar reappeared from between two shacks. When he saw them galloping through the surf, he ran alongside, on the beach, their towels vortexing behind him. "Bad luck to wake de Rastaman!" he screamed ecstatically.

"Ride 'em, cowboy!" Katie shouted, holding onto

Paul's eyebrow with one hand, thwacking his head with the other.

"Buy me seed! Buy me seed!" yelled the beggar.

"She still loves me!" Paul exclaimed.

"I still do!" she bellowed, slapping his scalp.

"Me too! Me too!" shrieked the vagabond, dropping his shorts and, with Paul and his wife, stampeding naked under the moon.

# Prostate Fluid
# On a Hot Summer Day

One night while watching *The Bachelor*, Lilly, eating shoestring potatoes as Ted rubbed her feet, nonchalantly said, "For my birthday, let's drive to Memphis to see Graceland."

"And for Christmas," he replied, "let's scuba dive in Minnesota."

"It's not the same thing. In the first place, Elvis is not analogous with ice. In the second place, our whole married life has been your idiotic metaphors. No normal human being thinks freezing water is the same as a fun weekend in Memphis."

"Don't judge my corn by your bushel."

"Stop it!"

"I'm a runaway freight train."

"I love Elvis."

For a second Ted wondered if maybe he had rubbed her bunion a little too hard, and she had suffered a stroke.

"Always have," she insisted, her glance darting between her foot and her husband's thumb.

This was news to Ted. In all the time they had known each other, she had never once mentioned Elvis, let alone loving him. Not being a lawyer, Ted wasn't sure if that would spare him most of his life savings, but he didn't have to be under oath to assure himself that this was the first time the name *Elvis* had ever come up between him and Lilly, verbally, spiritually, artistically, or Memphis-Tennessee-ally.

So, yes, his thumb momentarily stopped working.

She withdrew her foot. "Our whole married life has been your lack of musical appreciation."

Well, OK, it was true that Ted didn't dance and when driving preferred listening to cassette-tape short stories than, say, satellite radio's Grand Ole Opry at fifteen bucks a month, even if his twenty-eight-year-old-car radio could fetch that service, which it could not. But, in all fairness, he did like the Supremes.

Lilly got up and thudded to the fridge for a tub of Häagen Dazs and a ladle. When she came back, her face covered with fudge ripple, she snarled, "Why are you so selfish?"

"Because Memphis is a nine-hour drive each way, and I hate Elvis."

"You never told me that before we were married!" She stomped her foot, evidently forgetting that his then-functioning opposable digit had tenderized it. *"Ow!"* Hobbling to the ottoman while balancing the ice cream and scooper, she hissed, "Why are you so selfish?"

It was beginning to occur to him that something more than Presley's hound dog was at work here.

"One lousy weekend drive with your wife *on her birthday*," she pressed, fudge rippling. "I don't know what I was thinking."

*Welcome aboard.* "Make you a deal," he said. "We'll have a nice, expensive dinner here in Illinois...say at Applebee's...after which we'll watch a Sandra Bullock movie."

"I can't believe you're so self-centered as not to take a lousy weekend drive with your wife *on her birthday*. Don't dare talk to me about devotion."

Ted's nose twitched.

"What's wrong with your face?" she demanded.

More and more, his olfactories were smelling a rat. Not a dead one, unfortunately.

"I don't know why I let you talk me into marrying you." She ran the ladle across her tongue. "No man ever treated me like this. I can't imagine any other man not instantly, without even having to think about it, doing whatever I wanted."

*Aha!*

By "no man," she meant Albert, the love of her life, man of her dreams. Albert, the smooth dance-floor trotter; the tall, dark, handsome banking executive—mature, wise, sensitive Albert. Her former soulmate, confidant, best friend, high-stepping drinking buddy—morally, sexually, romantically, athletically, financially, and religiously superior Albert. Albert, the man who had loved her *totally*. The man she had loved *totally*. The man who would have done *anything* for her. Except leave his wife, of course. Or maybe rub his wife's bunions.

Bobsled tears were streaking down fudge-ripple slopes. Reading Ted's mind, Lilly whimpered, "The *only* reason he didn't leave her for me is he happens to be a good Catholic. You wouldn't understand that, of course. You have no rhythm."

He got up and tried shaking the circulation back into his thumb.

"Don't you dare lay a hand on me!" she shouted. "I'll call Albert!"

He went to the kitchen, and she followed. He picked up the phone.

"What are you doing?! Who are you calling?!"

"Guess."

"Put that down!"

He dialed.

She put her hand over his. "*Please* put down the phone."

But the line was already ringing in Elmwood Park.

"Hey!" chirped Don Giovanni, no doubt seeing their last name on his caller ID and assuming it was Lilly.

"Hey," Ted replied.

"Oh."

"You sober?"

"Sort of." He hiccupped. "What's it to you?"

"You like Elvis?"

"What's this all about? You need another loan or something?"

"You like long drives, don't you?"

"Don't listen to him!" Lilly yelled into the phone. "He's deranged!"

"Put her on," Albert demanded.

"I'm wondering if you'd do her a favor," Ted said. "I'm sure I don't have to tell you her birthday is coming up. I know you remember those special days for all your honeys. We were wondering if you would drive her to Tennessee. She said you'd do anything she wanted. She said you wouldn't even have to think about it."

Silence.

Lilly grabbed the phone. "Don't break his knees, Al,

I'm begging you. He's still my husband. He's demented, but has a pension...sort of."

Striding away, trying to make it seem as if she wanted to put distance between Ted and the cordless receiver while listening to her old *innamorato* but not wanting to get so far from her husband that he couldn't hear her kittenish chortles or see the grin that suddenly sprang across her kisser, she purred into the phone, "Yes, all right. Yes. Yes." She licked her lips. "That'll work. That's more than generous. I can't tell you how embarrassed I am about this. We have absolutely no right to disrupt your privacy. Wonderful. I look forward to it. Want to say goodbye to what's-his-name? Didn't think so. Well, goodnight and thanks again."

She threw Albert a smooch, hung up, and shot Ted a .38-caliber gaze.

"Had to hang up before his wife gets home from beautician's school?"

"He told me you better pray I don't die before you do," she reported.

"I could smell his breath over the phone."

"It so happens, he's giving me a ride to Memphis."

"Not unless he wants me to invite his wife to go scuba diving. We'd have some pretty interesting fish-fry conversation, don't you think?"

"You wouldn't dare. You're too big a coward. He'll have you buried alive in an Indiana cornfield."

"Fine, as long as I don't have to drive."

The next day the doorbell rang in the middle of the afternoon. Lilly was out hosing the patio, so Ted answered the door. A short, squat guy in his early seventies, with a gray crewcut and a pool-table-wide face stood holding a dozen white roses. Ted peered over his shoulder, looking for an FTD van, but finding only a dented black '80-ish Lincoln with one rear spring broken and a rocker panel missing.

"What can I do for you?"

"I'm supposta deliver these to the missus."

"They from Albert?"

"How'd you know?"

"They smell like gin."

"You the husband guy?"

"Glad to meet you."

"Albert says I'm supposta scare the crap out of you."

"You do."

His weathered face poked out from between the roses. "I'll get rough if I have to."

"You want a lemonade or something?"

"Okey-dokey."

"Come on in."

Ted led him into the kitchen and gestured for him to sit. Nodding at the flowers, the husband guy said, "Can I take those from you?"

"Albert said I got to deliver them in person with an explanation."

Ted poured him a lemonade. "Want something in it?"

"Nah. My rummy kid drinks enough for the both of us."

Ted sat across from him. "You're Albert's dad?"

"Albert One," he said, holding up a hairy finger. "My pals call me One."

"I don't see much resemblance."

"That's because we don't look alike." He nodded to the back yard, where Lilly was filling the birdbath. "That her?"

"The one and only."

"Nice looker. I can see what the fuss is about."

"What explanation?" Ted asked.

"Albert can't make it. He said I got to drive her to Tennessee."

"In your limo?"

"Got almost two hundred thousand miles on it. She likes Elvis, huh?"

"Apparently."

"You don't like Elvis?"

Ted poured himself a lemonade. "I'll tell you a story, One."

"Like Little Red what's her face?"

"Similar."

"I like them kind of stories."

"A few years ago I had a bad urinary tract infection."

The old guy puckered, confused.

"You know...pee-pee?"

He unpuckered.

"Very stubborn," Ted went on. "The doctor tried three or four different antibiotics..." He paused, but when Albert One seemed to know what *antibiotics* meant, he continued: "Nothing worked. Finally, he referred me to a urologist... um, pee-pee specialist...who decided to take a prostate fluid sample. Ever have that done?"

While he was trying to recall, Ted went on: "Doesn't

sound so bad, does it?" He held up his glass of lemonade. "Prostate fluid on a hot summer day."

"Refreshing."

"So the doc leans me over his examination table, sticks a tong way, way, *way* up my behind, finds my prostate gland, and"—Ted pressed his thumb and finger together and twisted—"squeezes."

Albert's dad winced. "You don't mean–"

"I mean *squeeezes*. Like a freaking lemon. Squeezed and squeezed and *squeeezed*."

"Ho boy."

"I was crying."

"Cheez." One shook his head. "A grown man."

"I almost punched the son of a bitch."

"I'da."

"Just so he could get a teeny tiny drop of prostate fluid on a slide."

The old guy wiped his forehead with his bare arm. "This is makin' me uncomfortable."

"You? I couldn't stand up straight for a month."

"You want me to rough the guy up for ya?"

"Where the hell were you when I needed you?"

One gazed at the floor. "I don't remember."

"It was the second most painful experience in my whole life," Ted said.

"The second? What the hell was the first?"

"When I first heard Elvis's 'A Big Hunk O' Love.'"

"Can I be honest with you?" One asked.

"If not you, who?"

"For my money, give me Albert Francis Sinatra."

"Same first name."

"We named Albert Two after him."

"I thought you named him after you."

"Nah. I can't sing worth spit."

"You can't beat Ol' Blue Eyes," Ted agreed. "Some people think his best work was in the forties and fifties, but give me the sixties."

One's eyes got as big as cue balls. "I agree with you fully."

"A guy knows what he likes. Does Albert Two dig Sinatra?"

The old man shook his head ruefully. "It's hard to believe he's my kid, sometimes. Most of the time. All the time. He don't like to paint, neither."

"You paint?"

"You betcha. I paint, my father painted, my grandfather painted, my great-grandfather painted, my great-great—.

"I get it."

"All the Palermo Alberts were painters."

"Portraits?"

"Houses. You can't stand anywhere in Palermo and not see a house that wasn't painted by an Albert. Sometimes we do saints on front doors, though. I guess you could call them portraits."

"I thought you're Albert One."

"We go to five and start over."

"So, Two doesn't paint."

"I got him into the union when he was twelve, but

they caught him goofing off too many times and kicked him out."

"Goofing off how?"

"Smelling the paint fumes, mainly, but a couple a times they caught him beating off into cans. Unions can only do so much."

"So he makes you do his dirty work."

"I can't paint no more with this damn arthur-itis. So I do some odd jobs here and there. It ain't so bad. Although, I got to tell you, driving all that way just to see Presley's house ain't my idea of a day at the beach. I'd sure as hell rather be giving it a fresh coat, but—" He held up his gnarled hands.

"You couldn't rough me up if you wanted to," Ted ventured sympathetically.

A tear came to One's eye. "We all get old. Even Sinatra. Even my kid's going to get old someday. You can't chase skirts forever."

"The world will be poorer for it."

"I like you," said One. "You're a good guy. My kid's an asshole."

Ted refilled the old guy's lemonade. "Say, I've got an idea," he said, glancing out the back door at Lilly. "What if I could pretty much guarantee you won't have to drive my wife to Memphis?"

It didn't seem to register.

"Or Tennessee," Ted added.

"You could do that? We'd be pals if you could do that. *Grandi compagni.*"

"How much is Albert paying you for this gig?"

"Two hundred bucks, plus reasonable expenses. I think he runs it through the bank's petty cash. He just can't help himself."

"Okay, I'll match it."

"No lie?" He turned, suddenly suspicious. "What do I have to do?" He too gazed out at Lilly. "I don't hit broads." He clarified: "Nice looking ones."

"Nothing like that," Ted assured him. "How would you like a simple painting project. Might take a couple of hours."

He held up his twisted hands again. "I ain't as accurate as I used to be."

"I'll take the risk."

"Two hundred bucks for a couple hours? Plus, I get to paint? Plus I don't have to drive to *whatchamacallit*? What's the angle?"

"It's my wife's birthday, so I'd really like to do something extra nice for her...since I'm not driving her to Graceland and all. Um, Tennessee."

*"Compagni."*

"She wants me to repaint the front door, but I'm not much around the house with tools. She's got her family coming over next month to celebrate Martin Luther's Ninety-Five Theses, and she thinks our door is a disgrace. She wants to have it reformed."

Albert One peered out again at the birdbath. "She don't look colored."

Ted was tempted to explain the difference between Martin Luthers, but decided not to crowd the old fellow's brain.

"That's it?" One lowed. "That's all you want me to do for two hundred bucks? Paint that door?"

"I thought a nice portrait of Elvis would make her

extra happy. I can download and print a picture for you from before he got fat."

"No problem," he said, nodding at the foyer. "It's a double door."

"Fair enough," Ted agreed. "Can you do him real big to cover both doors? You can give him a halo if you want, just like in church."

His eyes glistened. "It's a big responsibility."

"I have faith."

"I can give his behind its own halo." He grabbed Ted's hand with both of his. "If only *you'da* been my son. When do you want me to start? I got no backlog."

"Tell you what. Her b'day is this Thursday. I'm sure I can get her out for a nice romantic dinner. You can do it while we're out."

"My arthur-itis is starting to feel better already."

"Want me to pay you now?"

"Absolutely not," One said, waving jaggedly. "The Palermo Alberts never take money in advance. Never!"

"Could I just mail you the money when the job is done? That way, she'll think I did the painting."

"Ooh, I get it. Now I get it."

"So it's got to be a really good job."

"Don't you worry." The old man pucker-kissed his fingertips. "I'll fix you up good." His eyes narrowed. "Just don't be late with the payment."

"Why don't you leave the flowers," Ted suggested, "and I'll pass along Albert's apologies to my wife."

One got up. "I'll leave that part to you." He rubbed his hands. "It ain't just paint, you know. You got to scrape away the bad stuff, and who knows what you find under?

You probably got lots of rot. Some guys use cheap wood putty, but not us. Nothing but real Bondo for the Palermo Alberts. It's part of the Sicilian painters' code."

"Here she comes," Ted whispered. "Better get going. Remember, if anyone asks if *you* did the work, deny, deny, deny."

One handed him the bouquet. "Don't you worry. The Palermo Alberts know how to paint, and we know how to plead the Fifth."

———◆———

"When did these come?" Lilly asked when Ted handed her the flowers.

"I love you."

"If you loved me, you'd drive me to Graceland. I don't want your crummy roses. They're not even red."

"Come on, honey. You know I need to use the bathroom a lot. It would take us two weeks to get there. Besides, that's what you have Albert for. You're not having second thoughts about going with him, are you?"

"Are you?"

"I trust you completely. You and Albert were then, and what's now is now." He put his arm around her. "You guys will have a good time. You'll drink cocktails and be best friends and confidants again. *Grandi compagni.* And just because you'll dance like you're having sex doesn't mean you're encouraging him. All I ask is that you keep him away from open flames."

"You really are a bastard."

"Give me a kiss."

She walked away...heading for the freezer.

The day after next, unsure if Lilly had fully gotten over Two's most recent rejection, Ted decided to go all out for her birthday and took her to the restaurant where they'd had their first date, Bub's Pub and Grub, and then drove by the motel where they had spent that night. "Want to check in?" Ted asked, as he had that magical evening years before.

"May as well," she answered—now, as then.

As luck would have it, their old room was available. It was a little seedier—the furniture hadn't changed, the TV still black and white, the shower dripped faster and rustier—but it brought back fond memories. The only bump in the road was when, in the throes of passion, Lilly called him Albert—now, as then.

This time, they did not stop afterward at Pizza Hut.

"You mad at me?" she asked on their way home.

"Not at all."

"I was trying to remember the words to 'The Name Game' song, and I couldn't think of any other name with an *A*. It just slipped out."

"No problem."

"Seriously? I'm really sorry."

"I'm not upset."

They pulled up their driveway.

"What's that?" she asked, squinting.

"What?"

"There seems to be a dead person on our porch."

Sure enough, Albert One lay sprawled on their front stoop, a limp paintbrush in one hand, the other clutching his chest.

Ted jumped out of the car and ran to his fallen godfather. The old man's eyelids fluttered, his paintbrush quivered, his foot twitched.

"You alive?"

His eyes rolled back.

"Better call an ambulance," Ted shouted to Lilly. He turned to the fallen Post-Impressionist, placed his mouth to his ear and said, "You want some lemonade?" Then he noticed that One had finished painting only half the double door—the one with Elvis's haloed butt.

Albert Two blamed Ted for almost killing his dad. Obviously, he did not understand the physiology of heart attacks, thinking, apparently, it had something to do with masking tape. In the waiting room outside the cardiac ICU that first night, he told Ted, accusatorially, "He shouldn'ta been doing that."

"It's what he loves."

"You better hope he don't croak, pal. We can call in your loan. Read your contract."

Alas, it was so. Three years earlier, in a moment of weakness, but mostly greed, Ted had let Albert talk him into refinancing their mortgage at the bank where Two worked—for a crummy half-point difference. Half a stinking point.

Lilly was just coming out of the ICU. The whole time at the hospital, she had not spoken to either her husband or her old boyfriend.

"So call in your stupid loan," Ted told Two, loud enough for her to hear.

"Interest rates are up now," the banker smirked, snorting vodka fumes onto Ted's face. "If you have to refinance, you're up shit's creek."

"So repossess our house. Try selling it with Elvis's ass on the front door."

Two had to think about that—mentally reviewing his loan-procedures manual, no doubt. Flustered, he blurted out, "We'll hire someone to paint over it."

"Better check with your dad on that one, juniper-berry boy."

The banker looked confused. He had always suspected Lilly's husband of trying to put one over on him. No matter how innocuous anything Ted said was, Two assumed it was designed to make him look dumb.

Ted helped him out. "The Palermo Alberts don't take money in advance, and they don't let anyone paint over their work. Sicilian painters' code."

"What? Huh? Huh?"

Ted motioned for him to remove his finger from his ear. "Sicilian code," he repeated.

"My father told you that?"

"If you dare let someone cover Elvis, it's the kiss of death."

"He never told *me* that."

"Because I understand Sicilian tradition!"

"You're a Yid."

"Your father knows that in here"—Ted poked his chest—"I'm more of a Palermo Albert than you, his own flesh and blood!"

The old boyfriend turned pale.

The husband guy raised his finger to the heavens. "I understand pigments!"

Albert Two turned plaintively to Lilly, who was leaning against the wall. "He told him about the painters' code?" His voice cracked.

She shrugged. "I wasn't there."

"They...they were alone...together?" he asked, his carotid quavering. He turned back to Ted. "I don't believe you."

"Go ask him."

Two gazed toward the ICU door. "He's out of it. I can't ask him until he comes to."

Knowing Lilly was taking it all in, Ted stepped right up into Two's face. Feet firmly planted, chest puffed, dauntless, he grunted, "Then you better hope he don't croak, pal."

She rolled her eyes.

The nurse called them into the ICU. "He's awake now."

Albert One's eyes fluttered open. Kneeling on the side of the bed, his son was weeping into the sheet. On the other side, Ted held the old guy's arm. He was connected to more hoses than a fish hatchery.

"I see a bright red light," he moaned.

"It's God bringing you back to me," blubbered Albert Two.

"It's not God," his father clarified. "It's the lamp reflecting off your nose."

"Papa...you're alive, you're alive."

"Of course I'm alive. I didn't finish the job."

Two cleared his throat. "That reminds me. I have to ask you something." He glared at Ted, but still spoke to One. "God brought you back so I could ask you." He swallowed hard. "Did you tell him"—he tilted his head at Ted—"about a Sicilian painters' code?"

"What of it?"

"Him—a total stranger? Why? *Why?* You never told me, your very own son."

"You've been like a stranger to me, that's why. You never cared about paint. You treated me like just another loan application. You wouldn't even waive your closing fee for me."

"But Papa, I reduced it from nine-fifty to seven hundred bucks. You didn't complain at the time."

Grimacing, the old man turned to Ted. "I can't stand him," he moaned, the tube in his nose popping out. "Get him outta my sight."

Albert Two stood up and bent over the bed, hands clasped. "Papa...you gotta let me make it up to you! I beg you! Let me refund your already highly discounted checking account service charges!"

One grabbed his son by his Armani lapel. "You want to make your dying papa content?"

"*Si, si, mia padre.*"

"Then finish painting my friend's front door." He nodded at Ted. "In fact, paint his whole house."

"The *whole* house?!"

"And if you take a nickel, I'll hex you with the Sicilian painters' curse."

Two buried his face in his hands.

"Make me proud of you at last."

"I'll make you proud of me, Papa," he sobbed, tears squirting from between his manicured, nicotined fingers. "I'll do anything. *Anything.*"

"Will you quit all your boozing and whoring around?"

Two stopped. He stood up straight. He wiped his tears with the heel of his palm and cleared his throat. "Jeez, Dad."

The old man looked at Ted again, silently mouthing the word *curse*.

"Papa!"

"Better to wait until after he paints the house," Ted advised the old man. "Everyone loves a reformed sinner."

———◇———

Next Sunday afternoon, Albert-the-Younger teetered on his father's extension ladder while trying to paint Ted and Lilly's house. It was pleasant outside, upper seventies and dry, but the ground under the ladder was glistening with Two's perspiration.

"You afraid of heights or something?" Ted called up to him as he dodged drops.

"I need a drink."

"Papa said no booze until you're finished."

"My hands are shaking. I can't paint straight."

Ted thought about that. The window trim was a different color from the siding, requiring steady nerves. "Okay," he agreed. "A short one, just to get you to the next can."

Two raced down the ladder, missing the bottom rung.

"Come in the kitchen. What'll you have?"

"What d'you got?" he asked, limping.

They sat at the table where Ted and One had sat a few days before. Ted made his new guest a vodka-lemonade.

Lilly came in. She was all dressed up. She wore a tight, low-cut, Pepto-Bismol-pink evening dress, a pearl necklace with matching earrings, and uncomfortable-looking, but sexy, open-toed high heels. Her hair was combed and lustrous, her lipstick glistening and sumptuous, her eyes mascaraed, contact-lensed, big and green. Her nail polish matched her cocktail-cherry lipstick.

She had been walking around like that all day. From time to time, she would go to a window, gaze at her old boyfriend's paint-spattered silk shirt, his mineral-spirits greaseball coif, the razor crease of his latex-smeared, three-hundred-dollar slacks, and she'd smile daffily. Albert, in return, would inhale a cigarette and blow a perfect smoke ring against the glass, haloing her face. Then, with a sigh, she would retreat to her paper towels and disinfectant.

Ostensibly she was cleaning the house for her upcoming family get-together. The question was, why was she flitting around all day dressed like a *Glamour* magazine cover girl?

The answer, of course, was now sitting at the kitchen table, opposite her husband, with a pitcher of lemonade at his right hand, a bottle of Stolichnaya at his left, and, with a matchbook tucked into its cellophane wrapper, his half-crumpled pack of coffin nails in the middle, closest to his heart. Since there were no ashtrays in the house, Two was using his palm, more or less, to catch ashes.

"What's that horrible smell?" Lilly asked as she "accidentally" happened into the kitchen. "Oh, hello," she cooed to Albert. Then, whiffing, she curled her nose, and looked at her hubby accusatorially.

Ted side-glanced Two. "Sweat doesn't work with silk," he explained. "I offered him my barbecue apron, but he said it makes him look queer. His word, not mine."

She gazed at the bottle of vodka, gazed at Albert, curled over his pack of smokes, gazed at his ashes and sweat dripping onto her kitchen table, gazed at the smoke burling out of his nose. She said nothing, just stared at him, her left cheek pulsating.

"We're taking an eighty-proof break," Ted explained.

She turned to her short, balding, terrible-dancing but nondrinking, nonsmoking, only occasionally bad-smelling, and sometimes too-clever-for-his-own-good husband. He was wearing a tattered T-shirt, threadbare cutoff Levi's, and blue Topsider loafers with a split seam in the right one, bunion peeking through. He was eating a candy bar.

Alternately glancing between her current hubby and her old beau, her goofy smile fizzled. She seemed to be experiencing one of those moments when you suddenly realize you have wasted your entire life, and you pretty much want to press your face into an electric fan.

"Something we can do for you?" her husband asked.

She hesitated.

"Hey," Two said, noticing her for the first time.

"Could you bring the fan up from the basement?" she asked Ted.

"Sure. Meanwhile, why don't you and Albert dance?"

"Dance?" she said. "What the heck for?"

"You look so nice," he pointed out, "it would be a shame to waste it."

"Okay," Albert said, lighting a fresh cigarette from the butt of his old one. "Let's boogie. Just like the old days."

Lilly glowered at Ted. "I don't have time for this. I have to get the house cleaned."

"I'll help," Albert said.

"You stink!"

He looked hurt.

"Not at dancing. I mean, literally, you smell like a dead skunk! You sweated on my table! We eat on that table! Go outside with that cigarette! Do you see an ashtray anywhere in this kitchen?" She tapped her head. "What does that suggest to you?"

He gazed at Ted pathetically.

Hubby shrugged. "Break's over, I guess."

Two slunk out the back door. Ted started to follow.

"Just a second, you!" Lilly screeched. "You!"

"I have to give him moral support. He's afraid of heights."

"You're not going anywhere until you bring up that fan."

"Honey, think it over. Things aren't that bad. At least you live in a freshly painted house. How many women can say that?"

"Basement! Now!"

He went downstairs to find their old floor fan. When, ten minutes later, he came back upstairs, Lilly was reclining on the sofa, dressed in baggy jeans and threadbare *Oh, no! I Forgot to Have Children!* T-shirt. Her pearls were nowhere in sight. Her hair was mussed and her bare feet were propped up on a pillow, orange-tipped toes wiggling like newborn butterflies.

"What happened to Miss Runway Model?" he asked.

"Just do what I tell you and don't ask questions. You've done enough damage for two lifetimes. Plug in the fan and aim it at my feet."

Wincing at the thought of her mulching herself from the bottom up, he said, *"No problemo."*

When the fan was blowing, she barked, "Sit down there and start rubbing."

He sat on the edge of the couch, put her feet on his lap, and kneaded. "You knew he sent the old man to rough me up, didn't you?"

"That's the spot!" she yowled, flinging her head back, seeming not to hear his question, apparently too orgasmic to see Albert Two peeping in the window—wondering, probably, what all the moaning was about. He pressed his Day-Glo nose to the glass and waved. But Lilly didn't seem to notice him, and because Ted was rubbing her foot with both hands, he couldn't wave back, either. He heaved to with all his might, getting up on one knee and leaning into it. This time Lilly didn't seem to be trying to remember the words to "The Name Game" song.

"Yes...oh...oh...yes!" she groaned.

So it wasn't as if Lilly and Ted didn't have their romantic moments. It's just that he couldn't be sure if her "Yes...oh...oh...yes!" was a groan of ecstasy, or if she was, in fact, answering his question about having him knuckle-sandwiched.

Like the Palermo Alberts, she was terrific at pleading the Fifth.

# Kap'n Cy

Trying to reignite the old flame, I bribed my wife with a trip to Europe. Because her family, grim-faced Aryans with the collective personality of measles, believed they were descended from a super-race of Germanic geniuses, including Wagner, Goethe, and the guy who invented beer, and further believing that the high points of human achievement were Heinz ketchup and Christmas ornaments made out of dried *schupfnudels* and *jägerschnitzels*, I thought it might excite my wife's passion to visit Amsterdam, the city that represented, in effect, the Teutonic tiki bar, where those wacky fascist partygoers almost made it under the genocidal limbo pole.

I use the phrase *reignite the old flame* generously, the "flame" having been one of those chemical glow sticks you have to crack and shake to generate a cold, eerie light. In fact, my wife had not spoken to me for the prior six months because, as near as I could figure it, I had forgotten to rinse out my coffee mug before putting it in the sink. Germans fucked up the twentieth century, but they do tend to be tidy. My own people are too busy controlling the world's banking system to worry about Formica stains.

In any event, it being clear that I had something to grovel for, I offered to take her to Europe, and she said, "What about my mother?"

Fortunately, old Affenpinscher Face died a few weeks before trip date, and, just as with the Nuremberg trials, in which Hermann Goering swallowed a cyanide capsule the night before he was to be executed, saving the Allies the cost of a post-hanging reception and union musicians, I was able to secure a complete refund on my mom-in-law's airfare and hotel, said refund, as you shall see, providing me the extra cash to purchase a colossal vibrating dildo.

Our first night in Amsterdam found us, minus croaked Bavarian Mountain Hound, wandering the Old Center's picturesque cobblestone streets and quaint canals. It was the first week of December, and the gingerbread houses and ancient footbridges were twinkling with holiday lights, reflected celestially in the romantic, swan-dotted waterways. We stopped at a cozy restaurant (de Oesterbar, Leidseplein 10—pricey, but pleasant) overlooking an ice rink etched by a dozen Hans Brinkers and warmed ourselves over steaming bowls of sherry-pooled lobster bisque, during which I kept thinking, *If this doesn't finally get me laid, Hitler's dream of world conquest was a total waste.*

After dinner we walked around some more, and I knew the sherry was working because when I reached for the blonde's hand she didn't scrunch her face as if she had accidentally swallowed Passover wine. Her elbow twitched, she took a half-step toward me—the wind whistled in the narrowed space between us—and cupped her mitten, but she quickly thought better of it and picked up her pace, and I fell on a patch of ice trying to catch up.

We turned a corner, and there was a sign for the Anne Frank house (Prinsengracht 267). The Dutch, keen merchants, have turned the building into a memorial museum, the second most visited site in Amsterdam, right after the Prostitution Information Center, a fifteen minute stroll east (Enge Kerksteeg 3, across from the old St. Nicholas church and the Princess Juliana Basic School for children aged 4 to 12).

This was not serendipitous. That afternoon, on our ride from the airport to the hotel, when our cab driver pointed out the Anne Frank House, I happened to notice, right around the corner, the neon-pulsating De Maximus Boutique, and I had a hunch it was a sex shop because its sign featured an erect penis wearing a Roman emperor's laurel wreath and wielding a four-foot-long gladiator sword. It's simple math: if a penis's sword is four feet long, the penis itself has to be, what? Of course this is the kind of dimension you absolutely would want to pulsate in neon, even in daylight. So when, tonight, we got to the Anne Frank Museum ticket seller, I was about to ask for two admissions, when I suddenly grabbed my butt and said, "Uh oh."

"What?" the blonde asked, glowering.

"I have to make."

"Trust me, Germans taught these people how to install indoor plumbing."

I grimaced. "This is the real deal. I need to go back to our room for an Imodium AD. Must have been the lobster bisque. You go ahead, I'll run there and be right back."

"How come you never think ahead? Lutherans always think ahead."

*Except regarding Stalingrad*, I thought. But I kept my mouth shut. Instead, to prove my intentions, I bought two tickets, gave her one, held up the other. "No way I'm going to blow six bucks." I was including the cost of the Imodium, and that seemed to satisfy her. Germans may know exactly when they're going to get diarrhea, but Jews never waste brand-name drugs. (My uncle Irv once got his arm caught in a curb sewer while trying to retrieve a Flomax.)

In fact, I had thought ahead. I figured my wife would shuffle through the Frank museum solemnly shaking her head, frowning ruefully, pretending to be as ticked off at her progenitors as were other visitors, but secretly negating this little blip of ancestral mischief by virtue of Handel having written terrific water music, Eva Braun having gotten a whole line of small kitchen appliances named after her, and Bismarck scoring a jelly roll.

So when our guidebook (Frommer's—I recommend it) mentioned that a typical visit to the Anne Frank House lasts about an hour, I knew my beloved towhead would take every minute of it, because, for one thing, when most visitors' mouths get so exhausted with frowning they need to rush into fresh air to oxygenate their facial muscles, my wife's mouth had never known any other expression but frowning and was therefore incapable of becoming exhausted and needing to rush out.

In the meantime, while she would be milling about Otto Frank's attic, fake-sniffling contrition, I would be meandering De Maximus's aisles of kink, shopping for just the right potion, lotion, toy, or joy to assure long-overdue bedroom bliss. By my calculations—again, thinking a*head*— my life partner, having just spent an hour admiring the evil genius of her forebears, would be in a giddily horny frame of mind. So, the moment she disappeared behind the bookcase, off I scrammed to the giant penis in the sky.

Don't let Holland's principal export being the Dutch date fool you. These folks know how to run a sex shop. However much you might be pissed off at them for having to dig up your tulip bulbs every fall and replant them in the spring, once you set foot in one of these cathedrals of lubricity, all is forgiven. I don't want to go into glorious specifics because there would follow such a run on Amsterdam that the entire country would sink into the Zuiderzee, causing a tidal wave that would inundate Jamaica, an island country I happen to like very much—which I promise to explain at the end, but don't turn to it yet.

De Maximus was not some sleazy, dusty, dark, sticky, rat-hole sex shop like you find in, say, Wisconsin. No sirree.

It was as well-lighted, organized, and—dare I say it?—spankingly clean as a Walgreens laxative aisle. It practically screamed, "We are not tight-ass Puritan Americans! We celebrate our B and D! We don't just drink bubbly on New Year's Eve—we stick it up our *achterwerks*!"

As my contact lenses defogged, I wandered the rows, pushing *Try Me!* buttons, feeling *Lifelike!* fleshy objects, and whiffing open tubes of gelatinous substances that smelled like room-service breakfast. And then I turned a corner and—*whoa!*—my eyeballs zeroed in on the most magnificent machine ever invented since the front loader. I approached it with terror and awe. It was a gigantic, multi-dialed, toggled and gauged, two-foot-long, 220-volt (with step-down transformer for the U.S.), lights-blinking, needles-pulsating, many-and-gloriously-attachmented, Frankenstein's monster of a female orgasm machine, named, with just enough machismo to underscore its lumbering good looks, Kapitein Cyclops. (The Dutch naval hero Maarten van Zoot Jansse Tromp—no relation to The Donald—was affectionately nicknamed "Kapitein Cyclops" after his 1587 victory over Spanish forces, in which van Tromp lost an eye during his decisive maneuver of wrapping his ship's bowsprit with an explosive charge and ramming it up the stern of Admiral Diego de Bobadilla's flagship, *São Filipe*, blowing the Catholic galleon's aftcastles to kingdom come.)

I don't like using a lot of hyperbole in my writing, but in this case I don't know any other way of describing this monument to futtocks-penetrating brilliance. It's an injustice to call it a mere vibrator. It may as well have been sculpted from a single block of marble, a *La Pietà* of cumdom, the G-spot of the Sistine Chapel. Or, since we were, after all, in Amsterdam, a *Night Watch* of vaginal bliss. I don't know if "vaginal bliss" and *"Night Watch"* have ever been used analogously before, and I don't care. *Night Watch* was

Rembrandt's greatest painting, and it has its own room in the Rijksmuseum (Stadhouderskade 42—leave yourself a whole day), and it takes up an entire wall, and it is a picture of a bunch of seriously randy guys trying to force their way into an Amsterdam sex shop.

When De Maximus's clerk gave me the price in guilders, I didn't even bother to calculate. I just handed her my wallet. She said, "It also comes in a diesel model. No problems with electric conversion, *ja*?" Kapitein Cyclops was an entire goddamn power plant. If you ran out of fuel, all you had to do was press him to your lawn, and in fifteen minutes heavy crude would be gushing.

"Optional carrying case with wheels," she pointed out. "Easy on your back, *ja*?"

"I'll take it." I checked my watch. "Hurry."

She hefted it into the case, swiped my credit card—I crossed my fingers—and when it was accepted thanked me for my wise vibratory purchase.

"No," I assured her. "Thank *you*."

And off we rolled, the Kapitein and I, pressing against the North Sea wind, back to the Anne Frank Museum, where you-know-who was just exiting. "Where the hell were you?" she demanded. She looked down at my new suitcase. "What's up with that?"

"I have a tremendous surprise for you," I said. "Something to cheer you up after your depressing ordeal involving the sadism of the Reich."

Her arm stiffened and twitched.

"A *really, really, really big* surprise," I assured her. "A *huge, enormous* surprise. A surprise that will have you shouting my name."

"On what historical basis?"

"You won't be sorry."

"If it doesn't involve vodka, I'm already sorry."

Fortunately our hotel (Schiller Hotel, Rembrandtsplein 26-36—expensive but a Green Key winner for its environmental awareness and sustainable practices, if you give a damn, which I don't) sported a lobby bar (Café Schiller—popular and noisy), and we stopped for what I hoped would be a quick picker-upper, but turned out to be an excruciatingly slow one, but nevertheless with me smirking the whole time and trying not to look at the rolling suitcase.

The blonde's eyes narrowed. "What's the matter with you?"

"I love you."

"Are you drunk?"

"Intoxicated with love."

"Forget it. I'm exhausted."

*"No problemo."*

"Since when?"

Our typical pillow talk. This time, though, I had her. Lutherans may think ahead, but that's only presuming they've never laid peepers on Kap'n Cy. Once I had wifey in the room and lugged that sixty-eight pounder out of its broadside, all her thinking ahead would be as useless as the *Graf Spee* against Allied torpedo bombers.

And so upstairs we went, my sweet Frau Grendel— suspiciously, if I wasn't mistaken—insisting I walk ahead of her. I unlocked the door and waved her in.

"You go first," she said. "And no funny business."

Inside, I asked her if she wanted to slip into something comfortable—for example, the bed.

"What's wrong with you?"

"I just thought, you know—snowy night in a romantic city…"

"I already told you, I'm tired. After a certain point, it's harassment."

So I unzipped the spinner and unveiled Kapitein C.

She made a wounded-hamster sound. "What the… hell…is that?"

"Say *Hoe maakt u het* to our new best friend." (Dutch for "How do you do.")

She reached for the phone. "I'll show you my new best friend."

"Calling for champagne?" I asked.

*"Neun-ein-ein."* (Nine-one-one.)

Which is why we came home early without speaking to each other in any language, and why when we got back to Illinois she told me she never wanted to see my stupid face again and do myself a favor and get help. And also why, a couple of weeks later, I got a letter from her attorney, Müller.

Soon, I only had half the money I'd worked for my whole life and hated my ex very much. I never started out wanting to despise the Nazi bitch, but I see how these things work. Sometimes I would dream that she was flying back to Amsterdam for a jolly night out at the Anne Frank house, and at thirty thousand feet the plane blew up, and she fell into a bubbling volcanic crater. As a veteran travel writer, I know there really are no volcanoes between Illinois and Holland, but this is how psychotic dreams work, so don't write to my publisher.

The first time I had that dream, I woke up in a cold sweat, realizing what I had just done to the two hundred other, presumably innocent, airplane passengers. I got out of bed, made myself some crackers and spit (I could no longer afford cheese), and decided that those other passengers were probably all newly divorced blondes who also deserved to die choking on sulfuric fumaroles. So I went back to bed and self-hypnotized myself to sleep by imagining my ex waking up in a *Twilight Zone* episode in which every women's purse store sells at only wholesale prices, so she goes insane and jumps off the Louis Vuitton roof, but instead of splatting on Michigan Avenue, lands in Gaza wearing the gold Star of David I had bought her for her birthday and that she returned to me the next day with the note, "What the hell are you sprinkling on your matzo?"

The main point here being, not all European vacations are ideal. Sometimes they start out sherry-pooled bisque but end up flesh-dissolving magma. As an eternal optimist, though, I tend to think things usually work out for the best. For example, my cat seriously *loving* crackers with spit.

As another example: In the divorce, I lost my house, car, IRA, dental floss, caffeine-free Diet Coke, furniture, sheets, pillows, blankets, books, wristwatch, other cat, dishes, silverware, and all my tools. I felt the way Czechoslovakia must have felt in 1938. I moved into a neighborhood that features drive-up crack houses, Meetup.com pimp movie nights, all-night slamming doors, and hallway-roaming pit bulls. And sure enough, every morning I woke up and smelled the shit. On the plus side, though, I got to keep Kapitein Cyclops, so, really, I consider it a fair tradeoff. Here's why.

One day I was watching Nancy Pelosi being interviewed while eating Pringles. I, not Nancy, was eating Pringles. What she, Pelosi, was doing was talking without moving her face, like Jeff Dunham's Achmed the Dead Terrorist. So I was already frightened when my phone rang, causing me to jump and launch the Pringles onto my cat, which she happens to like almost as much as you know what.

At first, I didn't want to answer because I figured it was a collection agency, but on the outside chance it was my father calling to tell me my siblings had all suddenly died, and I was now his sole heir, I picked it up.

"Is this you?" came the cheerful woman's voice.

"Never heard of him."

"You sound like him! I bet you're him!"

"I told your boss I'm doing the best I can," I lied. "We worked out a payment plan," I lied some more.

"This is Lois from O'Hare customs! Remember me?! Last December?!"

"Customs? Lois?"

"You were returning from Amsterdam?" She lowered her pitch. "Mr. Grumpy Face."

I tried to think back on what laws I might have broken.

"I'm the short redhead with big ears."

"Lois!"

"You!"

"Lois!"

"I got your number off the entry doc. I hope you don't mind. I think you, um, might know why?"

Indeed I did. Yes, sirree. If she was the short redhead with big ears I was recalling correctly, she had made quite a fuss over one particular item I was bringing back to the good ol' U.S. of A. The short, big-eared customs agent who took one gander at Kap'n Cy and, bulge-eyed, exclaimed, "Wow! He's a beaut!!"

"*That* Lois," she reminded me. "I hope I'm not calling at a bad time."

I turned off Pelosi. "Matter of fact, you couldn't have timed it better. I remember you well."

"And I remember your contents!"

"Short redhead, knows how to work a zipper!"

"Cute guy with stubble beard!"

"Hate shaving!"

"Your Facebook says you're divorced. I figure men lie all the time, but why would they lie on the internet?"

"Very insightful."

"You wouldn't lie, right?"

"Never," I lied.

"I'm wondering if that still might be the case? Unmarried, I mean."

"The Kapitein is at the helm."

"Awesome!"

"You looked great in your uniform," I said. "Very customsish."

"You should see me without! Amazing!"

"Double awesome!"

"Quadruple amazing!"

"You like movies?" I asked.

"Love them!"

"Me too!" I lied.

"Who wouldn't!"

"Want to go sometime?!"

"OMG!"

"Amazing!"

"I'm off Thursdays!"

"I'll check my schedule!"

"I'll give you my cell number!"

"I'll write it down!"

And so I did, and so Lowie and I went to a movie that very Thursday and sat in the back and shared a frosty malt, stopping occasionally to sword fight with our spoons. And that weekend I reintroduced her to the captain, both of us standing at attention and saluting the heroic commander. I turned on a nightlight, plugged in the ol' skipper, and hoisted my mizzenmast.

The problem being, for all its sex-shop brilliance, Amsterdam never reckoned with Lois's own Force 12 *uitbarsting*. So that in the middle of the Kapitein azimuth-thrusting up her *achterwerks*, and her pupils tacking toward the aftcastle of her skull, the nightlight went dark, my refrigerator went silent, and the Kap'n himself stalled in a dead calm.

"Uh oh," Lowie muttered.

"Hm."

"What happened?"

"Don't know."

"Sail him back."

I shook, slapped, cajoled, and pleaded with Kap'n C., but it was not to be. He had abandoned ship. Alas, despite each man paying his own, Dutch genius had let me down.

All was eerily quiet. I got up, slipped on my robe, padded to the window and saw—"Holy crap!"

"What's the matter?" Lois exclaimed, bolting up.

"The whole neighborhood! Power out!"

She stood next to me, tilting the blinds. The crack houses had all gone *pffftt*. Even the traffic lights that hadn't already been stolen were lifeless retinas. "Must have been an overloaded transformer," I guessed.

"*We* did it," she gasped. "Uh oh."

Apartment doors opened and closed. Voices in the hallway. Firearms cocking. Dogs growling.

"What do we do now?" she whispered.

"Maybe we should donate the captain to Goodwill."

She chewed her lip.

"Don't get me wrong," I said. "I love seeing you happy. In fact, I haven't been this happy myself for a long time, maybe never. It's just that right now a gesture of charity might be what's called for. Before the crackheads find out the truth and torture and kill us."

She gave me a hug and a snuggle. "Never this happy? Really, honest?"

I kissed her forehead. "Never, ever."

"Do you think they'll take it? Goodwill?"

"They'll take anything. And you know the best part? They give you a blank tax-deduction letter. You fill in your own amount!"

Under my front door I could see flashlight beams sweeping along the hallway floor. More voices and cocking pistols. A light froze on my peephole.

"Where are you going?" Lois whispered, tugging my sleeve as I slipped on my sandals.

"They're already suspicious of an English literature Ph.D. with a specialty in Shakespeare. No sense stoking the fire." So I headed to the hallway to let my good neighbors know I really was a fellow capitalist. "Stay in the bathroom," I told Lowie, so when I opened the door, the pimps and whores wouldn't spot her undressed and think that I don't respect women.

I stepped out, and a dozen flashlights and semiautomatics took the measure of my sandals, robe, and stubbled mug. And then what do you think? A second later, all the hallway lights came back on. *Woop! Power restored! Grimy bulbs aglow!* And there I was, yours truly, in robe, sandals, and hockey beard, resembling the son of God, gazing divinely up and down the corridor, lovingly, forgivingly, and as the flashlights clicked off and the muzzles lowered, I became the most heavenly neighbor that rathole had ever known. Nazareth on the alley.

They fell to their knees, the shitheads, hookers, and pit bulls, one by one, Rico and LaShawnDa and Jondro and Chlamydia, and with a gentle flick of my hand, I blessed them all, my good friends, canines, and gangbangers, and wordlessly returned to my crib.

"What happened?" Lowie asked, as I ditched my sandals and robe.

"A miracle. They woke up and smelled the shit." Whereupon we returned whence we came, sans Kapitein Cyclops, and I presented the little customs lady with, I trust I'm not seeming immodest here, the holiest Judeo-Christian *shtupping* of her life, if she was to be believed, which I absolutely did. There is something about your neighbors believing you are omnipotent that peps a fellow up. And it's a hell of a lot cheaper than Viagra.

I hope I perked my neighbors up a bit, too. Not sexually or medicinally, but existentially—that believing they lived next door to the Messiah made them feel special in a way other than, say, solitary confinement; that this, yours truly, Almighty was more *Guardian* than *guard*, more *All-merciful* than *all-over-my-muthafuckin'-ass*. I like to think that at least one or two of them changed their self-destructive ways, went back to live with their parents, re-enrolled in junior high, maybe even went on to pharmacy school and became good Republicans.

Sure enough, despite my Shakespeare Ph.D., my community standing picked up. From then on, I never had to fetch my mail—it would be propped up against my newly scrubbed door, along with plates of tinfoil-covered cookies. I now woke up not to the smell of shit, but of Pine-Sol and chocolate chips. The missing stairway bulbs were back, the blood stains washed off the walls, and someone had thoughtfully hammered down the protruding tack heads from the stolen hallway carpet. One afternoon I came home from work to sparkling clean windows with a note taped to one—"Whoever loved that loved not at first sight!" (Phebe in *As You Like It*, III, 82. These muthafuckas had boned up on their Bard.)—and an unbitten corned-beef-on-rye and kosher pickle in my fridge.

Oh, yeah. My ex-wife soon married a fellow Lutheran, Ray—the Drywalling While You Wait guy whose motto was *I May Be Plastered, But I Don't Drip*. On their Las Vegas honeymoon, Ray got tangled in his flip-flops and took a header, impaling his eyeball on a margarita straw. With only one eye, and that one usually checking his toe fungus, Ray subsequently had a hard time judging the top step of his ladder (the one that says *Caution, Do Not Step Here*) and while practicing his line dancing on said top step fell head first into his Spackle bucket. So he retired on government disability, which suited my ex because it gave them lots of travel time. One day they returned from a Caribbean vacation and, at O'Hare customs, happened to stand in you-know-who's line. Lois held up her finger for them to wait while she tooted me on her cell phone. When I confirmed their identity, she politely asked the lovebirds to follow her to two private rooms, where ex-linebacker agents proceeded to search their cavities. Not dental cavities. And, sure enough, between Ray's buttocks they found a beer can he had cleverly fashioned into a mini-safe crammed with—you guessed it—de aromatic weed. Ja love. Real Jamaican gold, mon—de kinda shit, whiff gonna wake you up.

(Not for sprinkling on his matzo, I assume.)

# Sonny and Phyllis

Ma had been dead for only three months when Phyllis ("Filly") moved in, with her Venus fly traps, hundred pairs of flip-flops, eleven different kinds of shampoo, and jars of face cream that took up so much bathroom drawer and counter space, Sonny's razor and toothbrush had to escape for dear life. And, oh yeah, her boa constrictor.

The snake, Toots, and her humongous fish tank went into Ma's bedroom because it faced south (sunlight), and before another month was out, Filly was in Ma's room, too. Of course, she expected Sonny to sleep there when she wasn't pissed at him, but not to actually move his shit from his own bedroom, since she needed her "space," and she was frequently pissed at him.

"This dump ain't bigger than a two-wheel trailer," she complained, and before another month was out, her crappola had crowded out Sonny's bedroom, too. A few dozen pairs of Walmart blue jeans and sweaters with the tags still on them sprawled over his floor, where one day she would get to them. In the meantime, every article of clothing Ma had owned, every can of soup and frozen entree Ma liked, every sheet and pillowcase Ma slept on, Filly had left out at the curb—"spring cleaning."

But it was okay because, in return, she let Sonny marry her.

Once she had wormed her name onto the house's title, she began to redecorate and insisted that Ma's cat Chloe live strictly in the basement.

"Maybe we should talk," Sonny told her one night as he was pulling up the carpet in the living room.

"So talk."

"Well, I was just thinking—"

"Shush! Wait until the next commercial. The bachelor is just about to hand out the roses."

"But you said—"

"Will you please shut your trap?!" In one hand she squeezed a cigarette, in the other a red laser-light pointer— Ma had used it for Chloe to chase—that she was pointing into the eyes of the bachelorettes she least liked. Once in a while Filly also gave the bachelor's eyes a shot, just to let him know what would happen if he picked the wrong bitch.

Sonny shut his trap and went back to the carpet. When the *Tucker Carlson* program was over, Filly nuked herself a tub of popcorn and headed to the bedroom. Sonny brushed his teeth, got into bed next to her, where she was leafing through her celebrity magazine, munching.

"You stink," she said, exhaling gray contrails.

So he took a shower. When he came back, he waited until she reached the staples in the magazine, then said, "Can I say something?"

"This isn't about your mommy's album, is it?"

"No, not about the album. What about the album?"

"Because any shrink will tell you that the sooner you cut the cord, the better."

"What happened to the album?"

She licked a finger and continued flipping the magazine. Without looking up, she snorted, "I thought you said it's not about the album?"

"It's not."

"What, then, for Christ's sake?"

She got him all confused again. He had to think for a second. But when Chloe mewled in the basement, he remembered. "Chloe's not a cord," he said.

"What the hell are you talking about?"

"Chloe. She's not like an album. She's a living thing."

She stopped flipping and stared at him. "Okay, what's on that goofy little brain of yours?"

He swallowed. "I happen to love Chloe, that's all. She's used to sleeping with my ma. Right here in this room."

"Your mother croaked. Get it through your head."

"And now she's all alone down there, and I think she's miserable."

"You love Chloe?"

"She's a sweet cat."

So Phyllis put aside her tub of popcorn, slid out of bed, emptied Sonny's drawers into three shopping bags, and threw them down the basement stairs. "You love her so much, sleep with *her*."

"I never said I love her more than I love you," he pleaded.

"We certainly don't want Chloe to be miserable."

"But how—"

But before he could get out the last syllable, she slammed and locked her bedroom door.

So Sonny and the cat slept together on the damp concrete floor—although *slept* might be the wrong word. All night he lay awake wondering what he did wrong, how he could make it up to Filly. Would he go upstairs in the morning and find her gone, never to return? Would she have overnight moved to another state with a new identity? Ma, of course, was gone forever. He could do nothing about that, could he? Filly was right about that. Ma was dead.

Chloe slept all right, though. For the first time in a while, she seemed content. Curled up in the crook of Sonny's knees, she fell into a deep, purring slumber. Even in Sonny's fear of losing Filly, he tried not to move too much and wake Ma's cat. But even next to his fidgeting, Chloe was too exhausted to open her eyes.

She was a good, loving cat, and when Sonny's mom died and she suddenly no longer had human warmth to sleep with, Chloe, cold, bewildered, and now relegated to the basement, became sullen and depressed. But now, between Sonny's jeans, his fidgeting and occasional farts, Chloe's separation anxiety at last left her like a sweet sigh. In her dreams, she climbed her old tree, scratched Ma's couch to happy shreds, wrestled with her catnip-stuffed toys, zoomied around the house at two in the morning for no apparent reason.

Although he wasn't aware of having drifted off, Sonny awoke after daybreak to the hacking cough of his neighbor Carl's lawnmower. Chloe was still asleep, so Sonny unfolded himself and sat up slowly, trying to creak back into human shape with as little bother to her as possible.

Even in her sleep, though, Chloe was alert to being rejected. When Sonny sat up, she was up, too, and on his lap. He tried easing himself to his feet, but she didn't budge, just kept head-butting his belly, wordlessly begging him not to go.

The problem being, his terror that Phyllis would ditch him. "I'll be right back," he cooed, kissing Chloe's noggin and moving her gently to the floor. "You hold the fort." He quickly stood up, but when she gazed at him wide-eyed, he lifted her again, gave her another smooch, put her back down, and promised to be right back.

His waking nightmare of finding Filly gone had not lessened with the dusty daylight trickling through the window well. His throat was sticky, and his gut floated as he climbed the stairs, Chloe following close behind. At the top, he opened the door a sliver before, holding Chloe back with his foot, he opened it far enough to slip out. "Be right back," he promised again.

He jiggled the bedroom door, but it was still locked—a good sign. Because he didn't want to irritate her by waking her up, he went outside and around to the bedroom window. With the back of the house on an incline, he had to stand on his tiptoes to peek in, through slats in the blinds. When he spotted Filly still curled up in bed, the tub of popcorn at her side next to her ashtray, a godly relief came over him. In his bliss, he considered crawling through the window and lying down next to her, but instantly reconsidered. His glance darted to the aquarium, which he'd have to climb over to get past the dresser. He imagined Toots wrapped around his throat, choking the bliss out of him.

But the main thing was, Filly had not left him. That's all that mattered. For the first time that morning he smelled Carl's freshly cut grass instead of the basement sump-pump fumes, and he felt the warmth of rising sunlight and a wisp of summer breeze.

He decided to leave Filly be and, instead, go back to the basement to feed Chloe. He thought about running over to the mini-mart to buy some kitty treats, but when the terror of Filly not being there when he came back slithered in his gut again, he decided to offer Chloe her usual, bland breakfast.

"Here you go, girl," he said, as he filled up her bowl from the sack of dry kibbles Phyllis had shoved under his workbench. But instead of diving into the food, Chloe clung to his heel like Velcro.

"It's okay, kiddo," he assured her. "I'm right here." Then he washed out her water bowl in the slop sink and filled it again with nice fresh tap. But only when he sat down next to her dishes did she eat, constantly glancing over her shoulder.

"I'll figure out some way to get you back upstairs," he told her. "I'm working on it." But, first, he was wondering how to get himself back into Filly's good graces. "She's not a bad person," he muttered, more to himself than to Chloe, "just a little..." He tried to come up with an undangerous word (Phyllis had eerily good hearing) but couldn't think of any, so he let it go.

In the middle of scarfing the kibs, Chloe's ears perked, and she cast a stare at a stack of boxes in the corner opposite the sump pump. She leaped behind the stack and returned carrying a dead mouse. As a love token, she dropped the rodent on Sonny's shoe. Deep into his thoughts, unable to come up with a Phyllis strategy, at first he didn't notice Chloe's gift, but eventually the Avon lady of mouse scent rang the doorbell of his brain, and he looked down.

"Oh, aren't you a good girl!" He bent down to give Chloe a vigorous cheek scratch. She fell rapturously onto her back, her eyes glazed with joy as he rubbed her belly and chest, exclaiming, "What a brilliant hunter we have! Sweet and brilliant, too!"

He realized his prayer had been answered. Chloe had blessed him not just with a mouse but a miracle. At once Sonny saw the solution to his problem.

"Are you my guardian angel in there?" he asked, scratching. "Angel, angel?"

Chloe purred long and deep. She was a small cat, and usually Sonny had to listen closely, but now, in the quiet of the basement, with only the soft hiss of the water heater in the background, he could hear her little happy engine like it was Carl's lawnmower—purring not just for the scratch but because she believed in her sweet, brilliant, feline soul that she was once more in the household's good graces, that Sonny still loved her, that she would be sleeping again in her bedroom, and that maybe even Ma would come back. She would inhale the delicious aroma of Ma's mattress, feel the warmth of her blanket, her loving, flabby arms, the sound of her voice. She purred because she had no way of knowing that Phyllis had already replaced Ma's mattress with one of those Swedish foam jobs with a billion memory cells that you could put a glass of red wine on in one corner and jump on the opposite corner and the glass wouldn't fall—even though Phyllis drank beer, not wine.

So Chloe was unpleasantly surprised when Sonny picked up the dead mouse, and, as she followed him jauntily up the stairs, he once again slipped out the door, unceremoniously shutting it in her feline face.

———◆———

Sonny prepared breakfast, which he would serve to Filly in bed. He nuked instant oatmeal, dripped coffee, and toasted white bread. When from behind the basement door, he heard Chloe's heartbroken mewls, he silently told her that if all went well, she, too, would soon again be part of the family.

Even though Filly's favorite breakfast was Egg McMuffin, fries, and a quarter-pounder with cheese, Sonny dared not leave the house now, not now. So he made sure to fix her a deluxe second-best morning meal. Like Toots, she was a heavy sleeper and not likely to hear the nuker nuking, toaster popping, or coffee maker clearing its throat. Just to be sure, he closed the fridge door gently.

He buttered the toast and covered the slices with cheese, having lovingly scraped off some green mold. Then he cut the toast diagonally, just the way Filly liked it. On a separate plate, he fanned out crackers into a semicircle, and in the center of the plate placed her aerosol can of whipped cream. Under the counter, he found the same tray on which he had served Ma in her last days, and on the tray he arranged the plates with artistic precision, two plates on each end, resembling a monster truck if you didn't look at them too hard.

In the center he placed a can of her favorite brewsky. Only one thing was missing—besides the Micky Ds—and that was a flower. So he ran outside and snatched a yellow thingy from Carl's yard when Carl was hacking the other way with his lawnmower. It might have been a dandelion or a tulip, Sonny wasn't sure. The main thing was, Filly liked yellow.

He ran back inside and, remembering that Fill had smashed Ma's only vase, put the flower in an empty beer can, which was a nice personal touch and, as fate would have it, artistically balanced the tray even better, even though it was starting to get crowded. For the moment, he put aside the fact that Ma's vase got smashed on account of Filly hurling it at him.

Finally, snugly wrapped in toilet paper, he tucked the dead mouse into his shirt pocket.

Although Chloe had stopped crying, she had not completely returned to the dank concrete abyss. Still harboring a kibble of hope, she squatted dejectedly on the upper basement stair, occasionally sticking her paw under the door.

"Soon," Sonny whispered. "Soon."

Setting the tray on the floor, he poked his belt buckle prong into the doorknob to unlock it, wincing when it cracked open. Balancing Filly's breakfast, he tiptoed in. The instant he took his first step inside, Toots, waking, lifted her head, fixed her inky eyes on Sonny, and flicked her tongue at, first, the tray and then his shirt pocket. As if the snake's stirring tripped a wire in Filly's subconscious, she too stirred, lifting her head from her pillow and testing the breakfasted air with her mucousy tongue.

"Good morning, sunshine," Sonny chirped in as good a British accent as he could muster, trying for all the world to sound like a butler. Standing next to the bed with the tray, he added, "And a lovely morning it is."

She blinked and with a fingernail shoveled gook from her eye. "What the fuck is that?"

"Breakfast in bed, my queen!"

She sat up, toppling the popcorn tub. She scowled. "Where's the Egg McMuffin?"

"I'm certainly glad to run out for one if you find this inadequate," he answered, placing the tray on her thighs and sweeping the popcorn into a little pile.

She went right for the beer.

While she was busy guzzling, he secreted the mouse behind the dresser lamp and pulled open the blinds.

"What the hell are you doing? Shut that!"

"It's a splendid day out," he said, still affecting Jeeves, although sounding more like a cockney preschooler.

"Why are you talking like that? You stoned or something?"

"High on love, my…uh…love. Shall I open a window

142

for madam?"

"You're creeping me out. What's behind the lamp?" She wiped her chin with the sheet.

He jiggled the blinds, but only pretended to close them—better light for her to see his special gift.

"Hey, didn't I throw your ass out last night?"

"I wouldn't put it quite like that, my dear, but that was yesterday, and today is an entirely new beginning, as it were...was."

"What's the matter with you?"

"Eat, drink, and be merry. For I have brought m'lady a surprise."

She sucked a kernel from between molars, took another gulp of brewsky and a bite of toast. She sucked her fingertip, and, her eyebrow raised suspiciously, said, "Where's the cat?" She eyed Toots, flicking the aquarium glass. "What's behind the lamp?"

"Where would you like the cat to be?" The instant it came out, he was sorry. "I mean, in the basement, of course. Where else?"

"Then what's the surprise?"

"Two surprises, actually," he said, pronouncing it *ack...twoo...lee*. "Today is madam's lucky day. I'll bet if you read your horoscope it will say that today is definitely your—"

"Sonny?"

"Yes, Your Majesty?"

"Do you have any idea what it feels like to have your throat ripped open with a spoon?" She pointed to the front of her neck. "Right here, where your apple would be if you had one."

"Um, no?"

"Well come on over here, my lordy. I'll give you *my* special surprise."

"Well, maybe I'll just cut to the chase."

"Splendid. Just drop the voice bullshit."

"Surprise *numbero uno—*"

She aimed the oatmeal spoon at his throat.

"Okay, no problem." He cleared his throat. "You know how when I get a hole in one of my white socks, I like throwing out the other one, even though it doesn't have a hole in it, 'cause I don't want to break up a pair, even though they're both white?"

"You mean like your mommy taught you?"

"So I decided, what the heck, sooner or later I'll put a hole in another sock, and then what?"

"Let me think."

"Then the lonely, unholey sock will have a new partner, see? They'll be a couple again, get it?"

She belched.

"I mean, the main thing is, they're both white, right?"

Again she eyed the snake flicking its tongue. "If you don't show me what's behind the lamp, I'm going to feed your face to Toots. Fair enough?"

Certain that her sense of suspense had been adequately aroused, he began to bow, reconsidered, and said, "Surprise number deuce..." He reached smoothly behind the lamp and grasped the TP-wrapped mouse. "Courtesy of our sweet, brilliant cat, the brilliant, sweet Miss Chloe. Don't thank me, thank her." He placed it onto the bed and undid the toilet paper. *"Ta-da!!"*

Sonny, however, having failed high school physical science class and therefore not fully grasping Newton's Law of Motion, did not reckon that Filly's breakfast tray, powered by her leaping up from under the blanket, would propel said breakfast—oatmeal, toast, cheese, coffee, beer, crackers, dandelion, and whipped cream—onto dead mouse like Jap bombs over the *USS Arizona.*

———◆———

Phyllis leapt, her breakfast flew, the mouse flew, the dandelion flew, the cigarette butts flew, the beer drained onto her new Swedish foam mattress, its billion memory cells sucking up liquor like payday, a cracker sailed with Frisbee grace, and the aerosol can arced like a grenade—which in a way it was, since it missiled directly into Sonny's eyeball, at which time he retinally witnessed Hiroshima and Nagasaki paying the price for Pearl Harbor.

Filly stood on the bed, bunions spread gun range-like, her boobs flopping, her butt undulating, her teeth locked and loaded. She screeched, "What the fuck?!" at which time the mouse bounced off the mattress into her flapping cleavage. Sonny, clutching his whipped cream-canned eye, bounced off the dresser, forehead-first onto the end table, then shoulder blades onto the floor—which, unfortunately, he had not yet finished carpeting.

Outside, Carl, pushing his mower and blissfully unaware that one of his prized weeds had just careened around Sonny's bedroom like a carjacker on crack, spotted Phyllis standing naked on the bed and waved hello.

"Are you fucking nuts?!" she yelled at Sonny, trampolining off the bed, towering over him, and pumping her fists. Naked, mind you, so that the best view he would have had of her since they had started dating was completely wasted on his blurry vision. For all he could tell, he might just as well have been working under his pickup, her crotch a leaky transmission.

She frantically searched for the spoon to eviscerate his gullet. But he knew she wouldn't find it because, at the moment, it was impaling his rectum. So she lurched instead for the beer can—now empty—and began crushing it on his skull.

*"Ow!"*

"I'll *Ow!* you, you dumb bastard!" she hollered, knee-straddling him and working the aluminum into his forehead like a death-mask mold. "This your idea of a joke, huh? So, it was the cat's idea, was it! My brand new mattress!"

He covered up as best he could, like they teach you in self-defense courses, but it evidently worked better in the classroom. "It's for Toots! *Ow!* Toots! *Ow!* I brought her— *Ow!*—breakfast in bed! *OW!*"

"Where's that fucking spoon?!"

Only when at last her flailing was as drained of pep as the can was of drink—and it was too dense to crush anymore, anyhow—did she tumble over onto her back next to Sonny. For an instant, he wondered if the can thing had been foreplay.

She let out a long, deep, cigarettey exhalation. "Well, that felt good." She caught her breath. "For Toots, huh?"

"Chloe hunted it for her. It's like a gift from God."

"God, huh?" she panted.

"A gift."

He reached behind him, yanked the spoon out of his butt, and whispered, "I love you." He turned his head, shut his bad eye, blinked at her nipple.

"You better not be thinking what I think you're thinking," she warned, "because don't."

146

"You want me to feed it to Toots? I will if you want me to. I know I said I never want to feed her, but I think I can do it if I close my eyes...eye."

"Forget it, numbnuts. She only eats living things, and a lot bigger than that. Try a rat or a squirrel next time. If you paid attention, you'd know." Gazing at the ceiling, she chuffed, "I think we'll repaint. Your mother had shitty taste."

"I can do that."

"I'll tell you what you're going to do. You're going to buy me another foam mattress."

"Okey-dokey."

"And a high-def, sixty-two-inch TV."

"Sounds reasonable."

"Then you're going to paint the ceiling teal."

"Teal's good." Whatever that was.

They were silent for a moment, and he, again, took that for a good sign, romance-wise. "Can I move back in?" he asked. "Upstairs?"

"We'll see."

"Really?" He got up on his elbow to kiss her, but she was too busy eating a piece of toast. "I'd haul your ass to the store, if I was you," she mumbled between bites.

He scraped the butter off his nose. "I'm on my way." He craned himself up and headed for the door. "I'll clean up when I get back."

"Honeymoon suite tonight." She was referring to *The Bachelor*, but he took it to mean him and Filly. "And don't forget this," she called, tossing him the mouse. Which he also took as a good sign.

So, only momentarily remembering Chloe as he passed the basement door, he lifted himself into his truck, fishtailed out of the driveway, barely missing Carl, and sped one-eyed to the mall.

Chloe, meanwhile, still curled hopefully on the top basement stair.

———◆———

At first Sonny drove pretty fast, his pickup lurching up Rt. 45 as he worked the pedal in sync with Jimmy Buffett. He was happy. But then, as he swung onto Rt. 60, the main road to the mall, something happened.

Up ahead was Nelly's Family Style Pancake House, Ma's favorite restaurant, where, before she got really sick, he and Ma went almost every Sunday after church. To him it wasn't what most people would call "oat cuisine"—it was a typical Greek restaurant, and Ma knew they didn't go to the same kind of churches, but she didn't care. It had amber chandeliers, and a pastry display case when you came in, and chipped Formica tables like everyone in America used to have before that granite shit, and separate toilets for ladies and gents, and paper towels instead of those stupid blowers you had to rub your hands under for an hour, so you just wound up wiping them on your pants. The owner's daughter cleaned the tables, and their laminated menu had a brazillion items, and a tuna melt you'd kill for, and pretty decent coffee, even if you could see the bottom of the cup, but if you loaded it with cream and sugar, you were set. Their curly fries had a nice tang to them, and they always served the yellow smiley face cookies so they were happy, not sad.

So now, in such a hurry that he wasn't thinking straight, instead of avoiding Rt. 60, like he always did since Ma died, Sonny let the truck go the fastest way, and here was Nelly's coming up, and there was no longer any place to turn off, and he couldn't make a U-turn here on account of the cops always hanging around the doughnut joint, and the kid on her phone behind him honked, so he had to keep going, and whether he liked it or not, Nelly's was right there in front of him.

It was like he had no control over what happened, like it wasn't him holding the steering wheel but some ghost or something—Ma's ghost?—and the pickup made a hard right into Nelly's parking lot, like the wheels did it out of habit. Sonny had no control over it. And like a miracle, their favorite parking spot was empty, right next to the cripple spot, so Ma wouldn't have to walk far. Even after she got sick and was legally entitled to use the crip slot, Ma still liked this one better 'cause she didn't want to take a slightly closer space from someone who was in worse shape than her, and, besides, this was their favorite spot, hers and Sonny's, so who cared about walking a crummy extra few feet?

So the pickup zipped in like Ma was still in the front seat and waited like a loyal pooch for Sonny to turn off its engine. But he couldn't. His hands froze solid on the wheel. All he could do was look inside at the families enjoying Sunday brunch, kids hanging over the backs of booths, no one paying attention to some jerk in a pickup truck.

And then the owner's daughter—Helen?—happened to glance out and seemed to recognize him. She squinted to be sure, then waved. Sonny looked around the lot, but there was nobody else waving back at her, so she must have been waving at him. He jutted his chin over the steering wheel and looked harder through the restaurant's window, and, sure enough, she seemed to be waving at him. So he waved back, sort of, and she smiled like a cookie and waved.

So he had to go in. At that point, he had no choice.

He killed the engine, grabbed his phone, and headed in. His stomach was wriggly, and his toes bit hard into the bottom of his sneakers. In all the years he and Ma had come to Nelly's he never realized that Helen knew who he was, but now she seemed to recognize him. Now, even during Nelly's morning rush, she came over to talk to him.

He introduced himself.

"I know who you are," she laughed. "Where you been? We miss you. You don't like our tuna melt no more? Come on in. I'm glad to see you." She juggled a deck of menus. "No charge for dessert today, my friend." She glanced out at the lot. "Where's your momma?"

He looked down.

"Your ma okay?"

He shook his head.

"Four," called a woman who queued up with her kids.

Helen answered with her palm. "Hang on!" She turned back to Sonny.

"She died," he said, swallowing a sob.

She came around from behind the cash register and hugged him.

He wiped his eyes with the back of his wrist.

"Now I understand," she said, reaching into a basket of napkins and handing him a few. "Come on, you want a nice tuna melt? No charge for you today."

He shook his head. He couldn't do it.

"Okay," she said. "I understand. Next time, huh?"

He nodded.

"Okay, next time. We miss you."

Filly was waiting.

But, as when he couldn't take his hands off his steering wheel to turn off the engine, now that he was inside, he couldn't seem to get his feet to move to the door. "Could I..." He hesitated. He nodded at her deck of menus. "Could I..."

She handed him a menu. He set his phone on the counter, stepped out of line, into a corner next to the newspaper rack, and, with his stomach swirly and his throat narrow and his sinuses burning, he opened it and forced his eyes to find Ma's favorite choice, the French dip. How she loved the French dip, always ordering it with extra juice. He pictured her glowing cheeks, her twinkling eyes, when they brought her meal, her French dip with side of potato salad and fruit side dish and bowl of juice. He could almost see her now, her little crinkled face, her skinny fingertip tucking the beef into the roll, her happy hands squeezing the roll around the meat, picking up the sandwich and dipping it into the bowl. How could anyone have the heart to tell her you were supposed to pour it right onto the beef?

His tears dripped onto the menu, right on the French dip. He handed it back to Helen and thanked her with a nod.

"Come back when you feel like it," she said, patting his hand.

He sat in the pickup for a minute, head bowed, wiping his eyes with the free napkins, before starting the engine. Then he looked up through Nelly's window, gazed at the pastry display as if for the last time, backed out, and drove as steadily as he could to the mall. He didn't turn the radio back on.

When he got home, Sonny unpacked and hooked up their new TV.

"Now go buy me a new mattress," she said. "And stop at the pet store for a rat. A *live* rat. The biggest one they have. Don't forget. She's starting to get hungry." The snake was awake, her head raised, her tongue searching. "Better yet, a rabbit. Just don't tell them what for. And stop at the hardware store and bring back some paint color chips.

Teals."

He glanced at the ceiling and sighed.

"What?"

"Nothing."

"Then why are you still here? Toots is hungry."

"I was just thinking."

"Well, quit it."

He sighed again and got up. As he was halfway out the door, she said, "Oh, and Sonny Boy?"

He turned around hopefully. She called him that when she was in a good mood.

"I thought when you come back you might clean up, and we could go out for a nice dinner."

"Go out? Tonight? Together? Really?"

"I can see you're trying hard. So, what do you think?"

"Oh, I'd like that."

"And then maybe—"

He raised up on his toes. "Maybe—?"

"We'll see, we'll see."

He turned again to go, as light as helium.

She said, "I thought we'd go to Nelly's."

He stopped.

"You know, Nelly's? That nice family-style place on Sixty?"

He rubbed his chin, pretending to try to picture it.

"We've never been to Nelly's, you and me. You know the one, that pancake house, right near Weaber Road?"

"Oh, yeah, yeah. I think I know the one, now that you

mention it. That one right there on Sixty?"

"I thought you might remember it, even though we've never been there, you and me." She paused.

He didn't like the feel of it. The helium had left the balloon.

"You know why I thought you might remember that particular hotspot?"

It had all the earmarks of a deer hunt, with him as Bambi.

"No...I can't honestly say."

"I thought you might remember it because you're so fucking stupid you just happened to leave your phone there a couple of hours ago."

Reflexively, his hand slapped his back pocket, and, sure enough, no phone.

"You left it on the counter, lamebrain."

In his mind he heard the crack of a Remington Model 700.

Filly picked up the new remote and started flicking channels. Pretending to be more interested in the stations than in Sonny, she said with eerie calm, "So what do you think?" *Flick.* "Some whore calls and says she found our phone number right on your memory, and she called to say you left it."

"Oh."

*Flick.* "And, guess what else she told me?" *Flick.* "She told me you came in just to look at the booth where you and your mommy used to eat all the time." *Flick.* "Said she loved French dip." *Flick.* "What a coincidence, because that's exactly what I've had a taste for all day." *Flick.* "French fucking dip."

He swallowed. "It's…not what you think."

She had her back to him. "How would you possibly know what I'm thinking?" *Hard flick.* "That, what, you never took me to Nelly's because it's Mammy's favorite restaurant, and I'm not Mammy?"

"No, that's not—"

*Harder flick.* "That Ma was so special that Nelly's is off limits to your *wife*?"

"No—"

*Really hard knuckle flick.* "That Nelly's is some sort of shrine that you wouldn't want to contaminate with my presence?"

"No, no. I *love* you. I mean, I love *you*. If you want to go—"

She swung around with napalm glare. Her face was…well…teal, her teeth glinting and deadly. "*Now?!* Now that you got caught with your diaper down?!" She took a menacing step toward him, backing him to the wall. "You think I'd go to that shithole *now?!*" She hurled the remote at him and missed. "I'll French dip you, you motherfucker! I use the term literally!"

He ducked and ran, and she ran after him, stopping to pick up an ashtray and pitching it at him as he dived into the pickup and locked the doors. "You better get out!" she screamed as he peeled down the driveway. "And don't come back!"

Filly had some issues, no doubt about it. She was sort of excitable. But she had her good points, too. As he drove back to Nelly's to fetch his phone, he tried to think of a few. *Well, let's see.*

One: She handled the bookkeeping. He hated writing checks, but she didn't mind at all. He was useless on the computer, but she direct-deposited and automatically withdrew and debited this and credited that like a semi on the highway to hell. She knew all about big-time financial matters like life insurance and beneficiaries, and was so credit card-statement savvy, it made him stand back in awe. A bill collector would call, and he'd hand the phone right over to Filly. With her on the job, he didn't even have to sign over his paycheck. Somehow or other, it was all programmed in.

Two: She knew directions like an *effin* GPS. They'd be driving into Wisconsin to buy a Mega-Lotto ticket, and Sonny wouldn't have the faintest idea where they were even if it was perfectly nice weather without fog, and the roads didn't have names or even numbers but letters, like County Road F and County Road D, with nothing but cornfields as far as the eye could see and cows. One time, before she knew better, Filly had made the mistake of sending him by himself across the state line, and he wound up calling her to say he wouldn't be home for dinner and maybe breakfast because somehow he was in Iowa. She told him she didn't care if he was on planet Pluto as long as he came home with a lotto ticket, but by the time he figured out how to get back to Wisconsin, let alone Illinois, the numbers had been drawn, and Filly always blamed him for not winning.

It was right after that that Chloe had to live in the basement. So now Filly always went with Sonny to buy a ticket, and they never got lost. They'd be riding along on a ribbon of road with nothing on either side but silos, and only tractors coming or going, and the stalks so tall he sometimes couldn't see livestock, and she'd say, "Turn here," and he'd say, "Where?" and not see anyplace to turn, and she'd say, "Right here, moron. Hard left," and he wouldn't believe her, but he'd turn anyhow, and there, right in front of them, appeared a gas station and minimart, like it was Oz—not the doctor; the other one.

Three: She showered almost every day.

Four: She knew how to program the TV. Record programs, fast-forward through commercials, rewind like a gold-medalist.

Five: She hated dancing, pointing out that Americans never danced until they met Indians. She was smart that way, history-wise.

Six: She hated karaoke. When the old owner of the Chalmer Road House croaked and his kids sold it and the new owner put on tablecloths and brought in a karaoke machine and a few of his yuppie pals from downtown Chicago, Filly "accidentally" spilled her beer onto the back of the amplifier and burned the place down, and her name was in the paper, which Sonny cut out and taped to his dashboard.

Seven: She was fleshy. Not fat, thank Jesus, but definitely not skin and bones, especially in the upper-chest department. She was cushy. Sometimes—well, rarely—at night she let him start out sleeping with his face buried between her "cushions"—the same ones the dead mouse beelined for—and it was as good or better than any foam memory cells. Nice and warm and comfy, and her skin smelled like the inside of his lunchbox when he was a kid and Ma packed him his lunches because she had to work and couldn't be home for him like the other kids' moms. Filly's skin smelled exactly like a baloney sandwich.

Eight:—

Well, there would have been an eight, if Sonny hadn't gotten to Nelly's. The pickup's favorite spot was taken, but it didn't matter because he was just going to run in and grab his phone. Helen saw him coming and smiled and handed it to him. "You got a nice wife," she said—iffily.

When he got back into the truck he glanced at the phone and saw he had missed Filly's call from about fifteen minutes ago. So, with the baloney-sandwich lunchbox memory still inside his brain nostrils, he called her back.

"It's me," he chirped.

"And it's me," she chirped back.

"You called?"

"Just to let you know I threw out your fucking cat."

———◆———

Chloe had never been an outdoor cat. Ma adopted her as a kitten from a rescue shelter, so Chloe's entire knowledge of the outside world she acquired from looking out the window, watching the finches queuing up at the feeder, the squirrels warming themselves on the driveway, the occasional chipmunk darting across the front stoop. Mice she only knew from inside the house, and they were like toys, not food. Her real food, wet and dry, was always waiting for her in the kitchen, and, if on rare occasions her dishes happened to be empty, she never made a fuss because she knew the little nuggets and meat would soon appear. Some cats, especially brought-in strays—cats who understand that opportunities are precious—will scarf down everything you put in front of them, but not Chloe. She nibbled her nutrition like a runway model, which was why she had always been a furry wisp.

And when she wasn't studying the outside world from the safety of the window ledge, she was learning about it from TV reruns, curled up on Ma's or Sonny's lap. As far as Chloe knew, she lived on Gilligan's Island, Starship Enterprise, in Mayberry, or in Beaver Cleaver's bedroom. She didn't know about cars that ran over you, or teenagers that set your tail on fire, or raccoons that mauled you, or certain kinds of worms that ate your guts, or coyotes that ripped you apart to death. She didn't understand danger. She didn't understand fear.

So Sonny rushed home. He didn't even take the time to pull the truck into the garage. He left it in the driveway and bolted through the front door and right down to the basement. He searched behind boxes, under old furniture, up and down shelving, under the stairs. He looked and double-looked, calling her. But she wasn't there. Phyllis was in the kitchen eating shoestrings. He ran upstairs, searched under the beds, in cabinets and closets, calling her, calling her.

But she wasn't anywhere in the house. Filly had told the truth.

"She can't live out there," he pleaded. "She can't."

"I'm allergic to her. It's not like I didn't try."

"She don't know how to live outside."

"So what're you saying? Better I suffer?"

He shuffled back to the truck, slunk down across the front seat, turned the radio on so Phyllis wouldn't hear him, pulled his sweatshirt over his face, and sobbed. He missed Ma a lot, he missed going to Nelly's, and now Chloe was gone. She was all alone out there, wondering where her bowl of food was, wondering why she couldn't watch TV anymore from Sonny's lap. He had broken her heart.

Phyllis knocked on the glass. He looked up. She tried opening the door, but it was locked. She motioned for him to roll down the window. He rolled it down just enough so she couldn't reach in.

"I don't suppose you remembered Toots's rat, did you?" Her forehead furled menacingly. He half-expected her to try to reach in anyway to take a swipe, but she didn't. She just walked back into the house. He didn't like the feel of it. She'd had enough of him, end of story. She was done, period.

He wished he would've rolled the window down more.

His heart felt like it was pumping used, non-synthetic oil. He wondered if Filly was going to throw his stuff out the window like you hear about or, worse yet, pack *her* stuff and move out.

*Goddamn*, he thought. *Why the hell was my phone more important than Toots's rat?*

But he was still thinking of Chloe, too, out there somewhere alone and afraid, wondering what happened, what to do. One part of his brain, Toots, flicking her tongue; another part, Chloe, afraid. Sonny wasn't sure what to do: run inside to beg Filly not to pack, or run outside to try to find Chloe. Run to the pet store for a live rat or rabbit, or find Chloe and tell her everything was going to be all right.

He looked up and whispered, "Ma. Ma. Tell me what to do."

Suddenly he pictured his mother across the table at Nelly's, French-dipping her beef sandwich. He remembered the day he took her to the shelter, how most of the cats swarmed around them, as if knowing there was a better world out there and these two strangers were their gods. They couldn't decide which one to adopt. Then another customer walked in, and a kitten ran out the door, and the manager ran after it, and then they all ran after it, and the kitten hid under Sonny's pickup, smack dab where they couldn't reach it, and that's when his mother knew which cat they would take home. "Divine intervention, son," she said. "Heaven speaking."

He had forgotten all about that until right now. It was Ma up there making him remember. She had heard him whisper and was telling him what to do. She missed Chloe.

She was in that better world, and she missed her sweet kitten.

Suddenly Sonny knew what to do.

He got out of the truck, kneeled, and, sure enough, there she was! Just like that first time at the shelter. Ma had told him from heaven!

He didn't have to crawl on the ground to scoop her up this time because as soon as she saw him, she ran right over, right into his arms, purring, forgetting all about his leaving her in the basement. "I'm glad to see you, baby," he purred back, as they nuzzled faces.

He held her right up against his chest, and his heart wasn't pumping oil anymore, and he looked up at the sky, all blue and bright, full of the scent of Carl's fresh-cut grass and the memory of baloney and Ma's dish-soap hands, and he knew, just *knew*, that if he fed Chloe to Toots, everything would be all right.

# The Time I Accidentally Urinated on Idi Amin

We were in Mustique, an Eastern Caribbean "hideaway" island, and our taxi driver had just given us a drive-by of Mick Jagger's estate, Princess Margaret's winter mansion, and the vacation homes of two or three movie stars whose names didn't ring a bell, probably because I have not seen a movie since *The Exorcist*, which scared me so much that for a month I would not get up in the middle of the night to go to the bathroom, certain that Satan was waiting for me behind the shower curtain. It was not easy holding it in all night, but it wasn't the impossibility it would be now, my prostate currently being the size and consistency of a matzo ball. Not just any matzo ball, but one made by my cousin Linda, roughly the dimensions of the first atomic bomb. If President Truman had dropped one of Linda's matzo balls on Hiroshima, the Japanese would have surrendered in five minutes, and we would not have had to destroy Nagasaki three days later. I will get back to my prostate in a minute, which, I promise, has to do with Idi Amin.

I saw *The Exorcist* in a theater in an African-American neighborhood. Chicago is a city where ethnic enclaves are clearly marked by expensive, taxpayer-funded signs that arc over main streets. So it wasn't like I wandered into the neighborhood accidentally, got caught after the sun went down, and decided, what the heck, may as well see a movie about Satan. No, I went to that theater deliberately, because I happened to be dating Marceline, a Black beauty from a wealthy Chicago Gold Coast family, and wanting to show her I was open-minded and adventurous and would therefore work well in her father's business empire, I picked a theater on the South Side.

Traditionally, film is a two-dimensional, nonparticipatory medium that limits its audience to sitting passively in a darkened theater while entering a troubled world of pretend characters, secure in the knowledge that when the lights come back on, the real, safe world will comfortingly reemerge. That pretty much describes your typical White-audience film experience.

But watching a horror film with a Black audience is a different experience altogether, in which, Zen-like, the viewers *become* the movie, apparently believing not only that the events are actually happening to them personally and in real time, but also that, corollarily, they can control the outcome. It's not a bad philosophy, actually. I've always thought it more sensible than the zombic passivity we associate with Caucasian moviegoing—not unlike the difference between a staid Presbyterian church service and a rip-roaring Baptist get-down. Don't just sit there stupidly, tempting the devil into thinking you're there for the taking. *Make some noise! Let that muthafucka know you ain't going down without a brawl!*

So, for example, in the scene where Father Damien haltingly approaches the upstairs bedroom in which Satan, in the body of Linda Blair, lies bound to the bedposts, my South Side audience, screeching *"Don't go in there! Don't open that door!! You crazy, man?! Don't open that door!!!,"* jumped up, waved their arms at the screen, shrieked for their mothers, and fainted in the aisles—and getting up to buy popcorn was reminiscent of crossing the Gettysburg battlefield after Pickett's Charge. Except for the color, of course.

So you see that in that particular milieu, film was no longer a two-dimensional medium but one of at least eleven dimensions, including the Bizarro World, *The Twilight Zone*, the hotel in *The Shining*, *Nightmare on Elm Street* parts 1-4, and marriage. I will get back to that demented universe in a moment, and I still promise it involves Idi Amin. In the meantime, if Marceline happens to be reading this, I forgive you, and if you'll lift the restraining order, I'd still consider a position with Daddy's firm.

Our first day on Mustique, Debra, the woman I did marry and whose father was financially useless, was feeling giddy, thrilled to get away from her grueling Chicago routine of dog-earing catalog pages and having to repeatedly type her...my...Visa number into her computer. Her mood changed the moment we walked off the plane, and the redolent tropical air burled up her elated nose. I had not even checked into our guesthouse when she was hovering over her first poolside piña colada.

I returned from reception and handed her our room key. "Nice digs," I said. "What the hell is that?"

She followed my glance to a big, slobbering hog reclining two chaises over.

"A pig."

"He probably should put on some sunblock."

"Isn't this the quaintest place? Pigs running free!" She pointed her orange slice at some shrubs. "Have you ever seen such red hibiscuses? Such yellow bougainvillea? And a girl brings around a plate of fresh mango, and"—she inhaled—"doesn't it just smell like heaven?"

While she was going off on her Pollyanna riff, I couldn't take my eyes off the hog. I always try to see the bad side of everything, and the porker gave me the shivers. I knew something about voodoo, how the god Baron Samedi dresses up like a swine and visits people about to encounter grave misfortune. Debbie mistook those malevolent porcine snorts for quaintness. But this is the woman who sees affection in the smiles of plumbers about to charge us nine thousand dollars for recycled toilet seat bumpers. Of course, that would be my fault.

"They have diseases, don't they?" I asked.

"No more than we do."

"He wasn't in the pool, was he?"

"What if he was?"

"I was looking forward to a dip, is all."

"So take a dip. What do you want from me?"

"It hardly seems kosher."

"You know what?" she said testily. "Why don't you take a vacation in North Korea?"

Which, I suppose, did unintentionally reveal her true feelings about communism. Still, I figured it was time to find something cheery to talk about. Waving the daily activities sheet, I said, "Check this out. They're showing *The Exorcist* in the great house after dinner."

The waitress came over. I ordered a Diet Coke with lemon, and Deb ordered another piña colada. "Better go easy," I told her.

She scowled. "Why? Because it costs more than a nickel?"

So already I knew Baron Samedi was on the job. "Does this have anything to do with the fact that I tipped the taxi driver with Canadian money?"

"It has to do with the fact that you can't stand having a good time."

"I'm having a good time. They're showing *The Exorcist* in the great house. All week."

"For free, I suppose."

"What did I do wrong?"

"Diet Coke, that's what. Whoopee."

"With *lemon*."

"Can't you relax for once?"

"I don't need the calories, that's all."

"So now I'm fat."

"Did they make your drink extra strong or something?"

She sighed. "Here we are in paradise, and you want to stay around and watch a damn movie."

"With Black people. Trust me, it's special."

"Live a little. It won't kill you."

"You want me to drink liquor?"

"Yes, I do. I want you to sip rum and go criminally insane and never be able to write again and stagger into the surf and get eaten alive by eels. That's what you're worried about, isn't it? That and losing all your teeth while you still have some dental floss left?"

"You know the deal with my prostate. Alcohol goes right through me. One cocktail, and it's up and down the rest of the night."

"I know, I know. And booze gives you gas, and you're terrified you might fart in front of me."

I raised my finger. "I'll be right back."

"You can't live your life afraid!" she called after me. "There's a pig lounging at the pool! Enjoy the moment!"

I went back to reception, chatted for a few minutes

with the manager, and rejoined Debra in the sun.

"Scratch the movie. We're going dancing."

"Dancing?"

"At Basil's. World-famous nightclub."

"You're a horrible dancer. I wouldn't even call it dancing. It's like some weird quadriplegic thing. You hate music. Do you have any idea how sick it is to hate music?"

*Not as sick as putting ketchup on hot dogs*, I thought. But I kept my mouth shut. "True enough," I offered instead. "Okay, celebrity watching, then. They come to Basil's from all over the world. They tie up their yachts next door. Fly in on private jets."

"You hate celebrities."

"I thought you might like to get a little wild, that's all. First night in paradise? And then, who knows, afterward we come back to the room and—"

She got up and collected her towels. "You called me fat."

"Where are you going?"

"To the gift shop to max out your credit card."

So it was a pretty good bet it was going to be a long, lonely night.

◆

My wife and I pretty much have nothing in common. She loves nature; I hate nature. Dark meat; white meat. Pepsi; Coke. Raisinets; Goobers. She has one cocktail every evening and likes to dance. That in itself should have been the red flag. The happy-hour habit she inherited from her parents, who also had a drink every night and lived well into their eighties but were blithering idiots the last couple of decades. The dancing, I don't know. To the best of my knowledge her parents didn't dance, and if they had, they would have careened off into different counties.

So when, at the hotel pool, I had stupidly blurted, "Better go easy," it probably hit too close to home DNA-wise, and the instant it came out, I knew I was about to spend the next six nights in sexual solitary confinement. Here is a secret for all you newlyweds. Drinking may make you puke, and dancing may make you dizzy, but blurting will destroy you with the blinding finality of cousin Linda's matzo ball on Hiroshima. Don't do it.

Basil's is a thatched beachside restaurant and nightclub built on pylons, hovering over Caribbean surf. From a distance it resembles a giant tarantula, squatting over its prey and sucking out its juices to the beat of reggae music. *Thump-thump-thump. Thump-thump-thump.* On Friday-jump-up-night you can hear the steel drums across Mustique and maybe on nearby Bequia and probably in Eastern Europe.

Apparently still miffed, Deb refused to take my hand as we crossed the planked boardwalk, waves frothing beneath us. I had to trick her into coming, telling her that Mick Jagger himself was on island and likely to show up. She was still not convinced that I wouldn't have rather been in the great house watching *The Exorcist*—right again—but reluctantly agreed, provided I would ask her to dance repeatedly so she could turn me down repeatedly, and provided that if I ordered a caffeine-free diet soda she could stab me in the neck with her fork.

*"No problemo,"* I assured her. "Now let's go have a good time."

The waitress looked us over, wondering, I guess, if we were famous. She put us in the middle of the room, the only table without a view of the water. When my eyes adjusted to the dimness, I glanced around for celebrities, but saw none. I wasn't sure I would recognize any anyhow, so I sneaked a peek at Debbie as she panned the room. Well, it was early, and maybe someone famous would still arrive, maybe even someone I recognized. Larry, Moe, and Curly were all dead, but if Linda Blair happened to walk in, bingo.

I tugged my dewlap. "So, would you like to dance?"

"Oh, no thank you."

In an hour the place was mobbed, and my Eustachian tubes calcified, or ossified, or whatever they do when parked next to six bombastic steel drum musicians auditioning for a record contract with executives listening from Detroit— without the benefit of a telephone. I was not alive when they built the Panama Canal, but my tympanic membranes could imagine what the isthmus must have felt like when that huge, hardened-steel, saw-toothed gnawing wheel ground its way from one ocean to the other.

Unlike unionized American musicians, West Indian bands do not take breaks. Caucasians are spoiled and weak, but Blacks are robust and indefatigable. That is why eighteenth-century White men enslaved tribal Africans instead of union musicians. White slaves would immediately have called for collective bargaining, taken frequent coffee breaks, come down with carpal tunnel syndrome, insisted on cradle-to-grave health care and enormous pensions, and would have gone on strike anyhow, just for yuks. For a modern example: General Motors.

Deb was snapping her fingers, and her shoulders were dipping and gyrating. "Great music, don't you think?!" she shouted. "Good to dance to!"

"How about it?!" I shouted back, nodding at the dance floor.

"Oh, no thank you!"

I was pretty depressed knowing there wasn't going to be any nooky in my immediate future and that *The Exorcist* was probably half over. I glanced at my life partner licking her straw, and my ear canals felt like those rubber bands on toy propeller airplanes you wind up four hundred times just so they can fly two feet before crashing into your face. I thought that the only thing that could get me the hell out of there would be a fatal heart attack—either one of us, I didn't care—or, say, an international mass murderer waddling in and clearing the place out.

Well, guess what?

———◆———

It happened while I was outside smoking a cigar. I promised Debbie I wouldn't be gone long, so she needn't have worried about the band leaving before we had a chance to dance.

"Take your time!"

Fifteen minutes later, I tucked what was left of my cigar into its metal tube—waste not, want not—came back in and, not caring about other people, didn't notice right away that the crowd had become muted and brow-puckered. The band played as spiritedly as before, but now only one couple was on the dance floor, everyone else huddled at their tables and looking as if they had just seen a cannibal or something. It didn't register at the time because, my prostate having plumped, the only thing on my mind was the men's room.

"Wait!" Deb yelped, grabbing for my wrist.

"We'll do the next song!" I promised and headed in.

There were two urinals. One was being used by a large Black fellow shaped roughly like Mr. Peanut on cortisone but without the top hat. I was in the middle of attending to business, when I happened to glance in his direction, then glanced quickly away so he wouldn't think I was trying to cop a look at his you-know-what, did a double take, and realized that—*whoa!*—this was the brutal former Ugandan dictator, who enjoyed dining on his enemies' entrails. So I did a triple take, this time swiveling my pelvis and appurtenances thereof, and before I could reverse direction—you can't stop a battleship on a dime—peed on the man.

It wasn't a waterfall, mind you, and mostly it wound up on his shoes, the problem being, he was wearing sandals. Big sandals, probably size two hundred, extra wide. I wear a seven and a half, D. His toes glistened like tongues cut out of the mouths of people who didn't vote for him and tossed back over his shoulder into Victoria Falls for good luck.

To understand why, on the one hand, I stood terrified of being beaten to death by a madman with a possible taste for Jewish food, but, on the other, as I abashedly tucked myself back into my shorts, I felt a tiny thrill at having just whizzed on the man who had butchered thousands of his countrymen, you need to know something about me.

I was born poor and without much prospect of success. My family got evicted a lot, and when we did live in actual apartments, they tended to be above bars. For my first seventeen years I wore only hand-me-downs from my cousin Sherwin, whom I despised. Sherwin liked to beat dogs within an inch of their lives and pull the abdomens off lightning bugs and grew up to be a gangster. To give you a good idea of the kind of guidance I had as a child, my father used to say, "Why can't you be more like Sherwin?"

Sherwin took a great deal of pride in his father being a slumlord, and maybe that's what my father had in mind when he told me to be more like my cousin. To Dad, a first-generation American, owning a skid-row flophouse was the epitome of success, and I suppose in his own demented way he wanted to inculcate me with good capitalist values—even though he could never seem to get his own ass out of bed before noon. And so I was expected to wear my cousin's discarded pants, shirts, shoes, socks, and underwear with gratitude. Sherwin knew I hated him and always gave me his old clothes dirty, adding skid marks—some in appropriate places, some not—for laughs.

At the time of my urinal encounter with Idi Amin, cousin Sherwin was selling used cars on the East Coast and still trying to figure out how you carried a digit from one column to another when adding numbers. When we were kids this process mystified him, but now he had apparently figured out a way to make a pretty good living at being mystified— when he didn't get caught. The Virginia Department of Commerce did call him in a couple of times, but apparently in the Washington D.C. region, moral turpitude is not an impediment to staying in business.

So, having just peed on Idi Amin, along with abject terror, I felt a kind of pride. My first thought was of Sherwin slogging through dirty snow on his funky used-car lot to screw some poor schlemiel out of dealer prep charges and processing fees. I thought of his baggy jeans I had had to roll up seven or eight times and the stink of his underpants and the wads of newspaper I stuffed into his shoes to stop them from flapping. But now, thirty years later, here I was on a beautiful Caribbean island, in a world-famous nightclub, with a gorgeous wife *praying* for me to ask her to dance, standing next to a former tyrant-for-life and current international pariah. Would I have rather peed on Mick Jagger's foot? Yes. Princess Margaret's? Of course. But for a kid whose parents couldn't afford to buy him a tricycle until he was halfway through high school, whizzing on Idi Amin wasn't nothing. It was something.

So I offered him a cigar.

———◆———

My legs were wriggly, and I plopped myself next to Debra just before they gave out. Possibly sensing something, she took my hand. The musicians were still beating the shit out of their oil drums, and I couldn't help thinking that's what Idi Amin was going to do to my head as soon as he realized the cigar was already half-smoked.

"Did you see—"

"I urinated on him."

"Good God."

"It was the piña coladas. I tried to tell you."

"Why isn't he in prison?"

"Probably has something to do with the French."

"Maybe we'd better go."

I flagged down the check and forked over my credit card. But before the waitress came back with the receipt, out of the men's room waddled the mad cannibal, right over to our table—smoking my cigar stub. He asked Debbie to dance.

"Oh, no thank—"

"Yes, thank you," I piped, elbowing her to her feet. "She'll be glad to dance. She loves dancing. Have fun, you two."

"Well," she stammered, "maybe…just one. My feet sort of hurt."

I hooked Idi a thumbs-up. Off they went, and I looked around frantically for the waitress with my receipt.

You're wondering if Amin was a good dancer, and the answer is, I don't know. You can tell with a jitterbug or even the twist, but calypso dancing is as befuddling to me as honest arithmetic is to cousin Sherwin. Idi certainly was trying hard, gyrating like a, well, madman, my cigar garroted between his fingers as he flailed around the dance floor, which he and Deb had all to themselves, the old kleptocrat—Idi, not Debra—using every square inch to strut his stuff. His movements were spastic and exaggerated, but he was an eater of human flesh, not Baryshnikov, so you work with what you have. I sort of felt sorry for him, to tell you the truth, because apparently he'd had a lot of bottled-up emotion that he was finally able to let out in a nongenocidal way. The band fed off his volcanic energy and pounded their steel with foam-at-the-mouth frenzy.

Debbie, meanwhile, kept throwing me desperate glances. Suddenly dancing was no longer the litmus test of whether or not you were emotionally healthy. One part of me was getting a kick out of it, but then I thought if I rescued her maybe I'd have a shot later in bed.

The song ended, and, with obvious relief, she cantered to our table.

"We all paid?" she panted.

"Here she comes now with the receipt."

"Let's get out of here."

The waitress stuttered, "Seems to be a problem with the credit card. Maxed out, looks like."

I squiggled my eyebrows—in Debra's direction, if I'm not mistaken.

The band started playing again.

"Splendid!" Idi exclaimed, snatching her hand. "Then we have time for more dancing!" He turned to me. "You're right, she's a terrific dancer! What a pair!"

I wasn't sure what pair he meant, but I couldn't think about that now. I was too busy explaining the situation to the woman at the credit card company.

I don't think she believed me.

At ten-thirty the next morning the phone rang. I fumbled with it, but managed to get it to my ear. I answered, then handed it to Deb.

"Who is it?" she mumbled.

"Your new best friend."

She jolted up and gagged the mouthpiece. "Idi Amin is on this phone?!"

"I knew someday music would get you into trouble."

She tried to shove me the phone. "Well, hang up, for God's sake!"

But with last night's piña coladas still calling, bladder-wise, I refused the phone and went to the bathroom. When I came back, she had hung up, and she looked as if her face had been sucked on by the aforementioned giant tarantula.

"He wants to go dancing again tonight."

"Not with me, I assume."

"What are we going to do?"

"We?"

"You're the one who peed on him."

I didn't say anything about the cigar. "What did you tell him?"

"The only thing I could think of. That we're hanging around to see *The Exorcist*."

I brightened. "Really?"

"God, I hate you."

Contrary to appearances, though, things weren't going all that smoothly. I didn't tell her I had straightened out the credit card problem, so she wouldn't bolt off shopping again, and instead we sat at the pool all day, she reading Neiman Marcus catalogs, me blistering. Although I can't prove it without expensive lab testing, I swear she surreptitiously substituted my SPF 40 with Jell-O pudding. To further punish me, she ordered all the courses at dinner and ate almost nothing, which she knows drives me insane. At least I could console myself knowing that soon we'd be hearing the devil say dirty words to a priest. So it was back and forth like that, to see who could emotionally torture the other without actually admitting it—which had worked for twenty years, so why stop now?

Then, wouldn't you know it? At eight o'clock we're back in the room freshening up, all set to bound off to the great house, when she rubbed her temple and whimpered, "I've got such a headache. Why don't you go and see the movie by yourself? You don't mind, do you, hon?"

*Treachery, thy name is woman!* I should have seen it coming, I *should* have. *Twenty years!* But I had been so preoccupied with Satan and green vomit and Father Damien's dead mother groaning, "Why you do this to me, Dimmy?" that I had let myself get sucker-punched.

"It won't be the same without you there getting grossed out," I muttered.

"Dig three Tylenols out of my suitcase, will you?"

"I mean, you're going to have a headache anyway. Why not just have it there?"

"I'm going into the bedroom now. Please don't wake me when you get back."

And away she went with her pills, leaving me defeated and miserable.

Resigned to my fate, I started to go out, when I heard her mewl behind me. She was standing in the bedroom doorway, still holding her Tylenols.

"What?"

"It's…*him*," she whispered. "At the *window*."

"Him who?"

"*Him* him."

I took a peek over her shoulder. "I don't see anyone."

"He was *there*. Idi Amin. I'm not the psycho governess in *Turn of the Screw*."

"So in addition to being a mass murderer, he's also a Peeping Tom?"

"Get me the hell out of here!"

"I know. Let's go see a movie!"

And so it was that, on a starlit terrace, basted by tropical breeze, rum punch in one hand, conch fritter in the other, my beautiful wife close by, although admittedly not close enough, and Linda Blair screaming obscenities on a large-screen TV next to a coruscating pool, I reached vacation nirvana. On the horizon, a cruise ship's lights twinkled fetchingly. But I was not to be fetched.

I was content.

And then what homicidal madman do you think stopped by, standing eerily in the shadows of a pool floodlight, looking around for you-know-who?

"Holy crap," Debbie gulped, spotting him before he spotted her. "This isn't funny anymore."

He saw her, smiled, and waved.

"Don't panic," I said. "We've got plenty of witnesses."

"I'm not kidding. He's stalking me. Do something."

"Maybe he's just lonely, you know? I mean, everyone

runs away from him."

"Good idea. Let's go."

I pulled her back. "He'll think you're just being coy."

Idi found a seat two rows behind us.

I whispered, "Only one thing to do. Get close to me. Real close. Let him know how much you love *me*."

She slid her chair close to mine and leaned against me like she meant it. I put my arm around her as I had when we were dating, and she nuzzled her blond head against my neck and burbled, and I hugged her and kissed her eyelid and her nose.

"I hate you," she whispered. "You understand that, right?"

"Better get closer."

It must have worked, because just as Father Dimmy was walking upstairs to Linda Blair's bedroom, I snuck a glance over Debbie's shoulder and saw the former Ugandan dictator, no longer preoccupied with my wife, on his tiptoes, waving his fists and lunging at the TV, bellowing, *"Don't go in there! Don't open that door! Don't open that muthafuckin' door!"*

And then his eyes rolled up into the back of his head, and he hit the deck.

"You're in the clear," I told Deb.

"Good God. You think he's dead?"

"Trust me, he's fine. Check out this next scene. I promise, you won't want to go to the bathroom for a month. And with any luck, neither will I."

"What's that smirk on your face?"

"I was just thinking of my cousin Sherwin."

"What the hell for?"

"He's been married four times, and I've only been married once. Happily, too."

She nuzzled closer, right up against my sunburn. I winced.

"What's the matter?" she said, pulling away.

"Nothing." I hugged her tighter. "Not a thing in the whole wide world."

# Get Well Soon

Brutal emails back and forth, accusations, subpoenas, IRS threats, Sheriff Department threats, FBI threats, depositions, indirect hints of assassination from both sides. Their divorce had been ugly—even more than most. Not just bitter financially and legally, but verbally (e.g., *"I hope your safe deposit box falls on your fucking head."*). Their lawyers kept telling them to shut the eff up already (lawyers usually love stirring the pot, but in this case, when Irene and Roger each filed a complaint with the Attorney Review Board against the other's legal eagle, the opposing advocates agreed to spend the rest of their careers in the Wrigley Field bleachers, sharing popcorn).

Irene and Roger couldn't help it; radioactivity burst across their keyboards like Chernobyl meltdowns. Not just online, but hardcopy. Neither could successfully use the correspondence against each other in court because they were equally guilty. Not that they didn't try; every couple of months they'd appear before the same judge trying to convince him that their no-longer soulmate was a thief, cheater, clinical narcissist, pyramid schemer, HIV transmitter, reincarnation of Satan, embezzler, porn addict, paranoid-schizoid, atheist, anti-Semite, xenophobe, sex pervert, cross-dresser, racist, animal torturer, grifter; was bipolar, pathologically selfish, delusional, impotent, eggless, gluttonous, spermless, empathy-less, social-media crazed. Plus one or two others. The judge, a lookalike mixture of Judge Judy and Judge Joseph Wapner, never raised her voice to the combatants nor intervened because she thought the whole show was kind of hilarious, and also because she was usually plastered. Eventually, she entered rehab.

After a few years, the external acrimony dwindled. The last email Roger received from Irene read: *"I hope you get the help you need."* He was tempted, naturally, to write her back but knew damn well she wouldn't be satisfied unless she had the last word. By then he had read somewhere that the opposite of love isn't hate but indifference. Besides, all that lawyer money, not to mention the divorce itself, had left him pretty much broke.

As fifteen more years went by, they would occasionally hear rumors about each other and drop their own snippets of toxicity to former mutual friends. But otherwise, nothing. Roger and Irene had changed homes, email addresses, phone numbers. They had at last moved on.

Sort of.

When an old neighbor of theirs told him that Irene was in hospital ICU, possibly dying, Roger's first thought was, *Oh, shit*. His brow creased, his forehead dipped, his heart sank. But when his friend asked him what was wrong, Roger caught himself, pumped his fist, and honked, *"Yes!"*

In the hospital intensive care, Irene lay propped up, oxygen tube wrapped around her ears and dripping from her nostrils. From a chrome hanger, an IV bag dripped colorless fluid into her pencil-like arm. On her other arm, a strap was connected to a stand-mounted vital-signs monitor—her minimal breathing, blood pressure, and heart rate continually graphed in struggling green scratches.

She lay with her eyes closed, deep into thin, faraway dreams. Yesterday, to the nurse now standing next to her bedrail, she had whispered that she wasn't afraid of dying. She was worn out, tired of everything. Again today, the nurse tried to cheer her up, to at least let her know that people did care about her, that they loved her, that even "strangers" like the nurse herself couldn't bear to see her feeling hopeless. That she wasn't alone.

"Here, you got another get-well card," she beamed. "Want me to open it?"

No answer. No nod, no hand movement, not even an eye twitch.

"Okay, then," the nurse chirped, slicing open the card envelope with her surgical-gloved finger. "Let's see who else loves you."

No answer, no movement, no twitch—she was a puddle of candle wax—the vitals monitor just struggling along like her fading flame.

Leaning against the bed railing next to the IV, the nurse tugged out the card and described it merrily: "It's a beautiful, flowery design...yellow and pink tulips. Very cheerful. Let's see who it's from." She opened the card and was surprised to find no Hallmark-printed message, but instead, except for a handwritten one-liner, two blank pages. So, really, it was more of a greeting card than a get-well card. But instead of saying anything to that effect, the nurse simply read aloud the scrawled message: *"I hope you get the help you need."*

Concentrating on the card, she didn't notice that the patient's eyes not only twitched but opened. Just a crack, but definitely opened. Then a hard blink. Then devil-eyed fury.

"Isn't that *sweeet*?" the nurse cooed, still focused on the card. Realizing that the writer hadn't signed it, she quickly added, "Looks like a man's handwriting. A secret admirer?" Smiling, she turned to Irene.

The nurse's smile dropped. She jumped back, crashing into the IV, tripping over its stand, almost knocking it over. The patient's eyes were wide open, but not with joy.

"Wha...what?" the nurse stammered.

"Say...that...*again*," Irene hissed. Not a whisper this time.

Turning back to the card, the nurse again read aloud, this time with less enthusiasm: *"I hope..."* Frightened, she hesitated. But Irene's scowl forced her to go on: *"...you get the help you need."*

The vitals monitor jumped to life.

# We Must Take the Current
# When It Serves

After his divorce, in desperate need of a woman willing to tell him he isn't the worst human being on earth, Doug signs up on WaveMatch.com and soon meets Cricket, with whom he instantly falls in love and believes is the reason he was born. She works out at the gym every day, seven days a week, with a body to prove it, and if that's sexist, he doesn't care. How she manages to work out and still have those gorgeous fingernails, Doug has no idea, but at this point he's not asking too many questions.

So smitten is he that after two dates, though they have not yet been physically intimate, he offers to take her to Hawaii. In his post-divorce pathological fear of rejection, he supposes that taking Cricket on an exotic vacation *before* making love will prove his generosity and gentlemanly *bon vivant savior-faire*, *objects d'art*, *grand cheval*, and *chèvre noire*, and that his trilling command of the French language will guarantee his getting *shtupped*—which isn't French, but he doesn't care about that, either. Believing she'll be impressed by his romantic notion of metaphorically putting her on a classical, white-marble pedestal, he tells her it's his way of "making our first time poetic." How can she in good conscience accept such a romantic getaway if not with the tacit understanding that it will lead to sexual fortune?

It occurs to him only after he books the nonrefundable

trip that she probably sees right through the BS and, to take advantage of his needy extravagance and to teach him a well-deserved lesson in confidence-lacking, she fully intends to exploit his nerdy magnanimity without the slightest intention of letting him get anywhere near her love boat. He imagines her deliberately getting sunburned the first day so that nothing can touch her flesh. Or her pretending to eat a bad shrimp and having to vomit whenever he walks into the room. Or her claiming to have come down with tuberculosis, requiring Doug to check her into her own hotel room or, better yet, suite.

It's his own fault, of course. So he deserves the two weeks of anguish between the booking and bon voyage, certain of the humiliation sword the trip will run through his stupid guts.

During those two weeks, despite the several pre-Hawaii bouquets Doug brings her; despite his offering to pay for her new bikini; despite his letting her know that he'll be popping for limousines to the airport and back; and despite her apparent gratitude, her many and ebullient thank-yous and cheek smooches, during those couple of preflight weeks, Doug comes to despise Cricket very much.

Absolutely, totally, completely worst of all, though, is Doug's further imagining that he will be standing at the hotel desk, explaining to the receptionist why, TB-wise, he needs to book a separate room for Cricket, when he suddenly spots his ex-wife with her new boyfriend, she looking blond, bubbly, and, apparently, extremely sexually satisfied. The problem being, continues Doug's deranged hallucination, the blonde has been standing right behind him during his explanation of his present companion's communicable disease, hears every word he says. "Well, well," the ex will chime, "what a coincidence. Here we are in Maui, where I would have liked to come years ago, but you were always too terrified of flying over water, and look! Here you are now, with some bimbo with water on her lungs."

So here is Doug, terrorized by the specter of his ex, trying his best to be cheerful to Cricket, who he just *knows* is using him for a free vacation and is at this very moment figuring out how to avoid having sex with him for seven nights while still being able to use the beach, pool, restaurant, and nightclub facilities.

Doug's further head-trip vacation certainties:

He's lying on the beach next to his new soulmate (Cricket), whom he despises, she reading a *Globe* magazine with a scowling Meghan Markle on the cover flipping the bird to Queen Elizabeth. Doug stares out at an acrobatic windsurfer showing off on the sparkling waves. Doug thinking, *Wouldn't I really look cool if I could do that? Maybe if I could earn Crickie's admiration, I won't hate her so much.* "Maybe I should try that," he ventures aloud, testing the waters of machismo. Cricket, peeking out over her sunglasses, following his gaze, says, "Why don't you rent one of those yellow water tractors with the big wheels instead?" She gestures to a hotel *serve use* to come spritz her with Perrier. Apparently, Doug's manliness tide has waned.

In his imagination, he springs out of his chaise lounge, stubbing his toe and stumbling. "The next time you see me," he crows to his trophy date, righting himself, poking his chest, and rubbing his foot, "I'll be out...there!" He limps to the nearby activities shack, his lungs plump with Pacific Ocean air, his arteries adrenalin-flushed, his intestines churning with undercooked pork sausages.

The instructor's nickname is "Weed." That should be Doug's first red flag. Weed answers him three questions behind. That should be Doug's second and third. He asks the windsurf maven something, Doug's voice traveling to the planet Pluto, orbiting twice, eventually landing on Weed's frontal lobe. Seeing right away that Doug is tense, Weed offers him a relaxer, neatly tucked in a waistband baggie. Then the instructor breaks out in uncontrollable giggling, which he's able to stop only by hitting himself on his head with a conch shell. After which, he recites a poem: "If all of the flies/Were only one fly/What a splendid, great/Fly it would be."

Continuing with his mental projections, Doug gazes fifty feet over at Cricket, who peers over her *Globe* and flashes him a manicured thumbs-up. If he backs out now, his life as he knows it is over. His toe is throbbing, and his chest hurts from where he poked myself. Maybe just a passing whiff of Weed's baggie will help.

Doug mounts the board knees first, strains to raise the sail, his back to the beach, comforted by the reassuring tug of the beginner-board's safety tether. When, after several minutes, he looks back, he spots the rope stuck under the foot of Cricket's chaise. Weed is sitting on the edge of her lounger, flexing his pectorals at Doug's better half, whom he still can't stand. Cricket is now also giggling uncontrollably. Weed gets up to fetch his conch shell, tripping over the tether, releasing it from the chaise's grip. Neither Weed nor Cricket seem to notice.

The good news is that in the strong current, Doug's imagination drifts him to the coast of the Big Island, Hawai'i, before nightfall. The bad news is that its volcano, Mauna Loa, has just erupted, causing an earthquake and a ten-foot wall of salt water that bears down on him like that scene from *The Poseidon Adventure*, a movie he didn't like nearly as much as *Pee Wee's Big Adventure*.

The tidal wave having ripped his board from under him, Doug rides the gigantic breaker like Frankie Avalon lashed to an Exocet missile. He arrives back at his hotel beach much faster than he left. A crowd cheers and carries him on their shoulders to the lobby, where Cricket waits, apparently unimpressed. She taps her watch and foot. She's gone through the trouble of finding a quaint local restaurant with good seafood and a reputation for cheerful island service, which damn well expects its son of a bitching patrons to be on time. Her gaze is scalding—similar to the Duchess of Sussex's while shooting Liz the finger.

But when, responding to her silent demand for an explanation, Doug reveals his tongue, bloated and crusty with brine, something magical happens, something electric between them. Something as aromatic and enchanting as a Hawaiian lei.

Cricket leads him back to their room, sprays the top of his head with Solarcaine, nibbles his earlobe, orders room service, including tiki crab rolls and Mai Tai doubles. Outside, tree frogs chime. Moonlight shimmers on the now-placid sea. Ukulele music rises from the beach. Doug offers to take a shower, but Cricket won't hear of it. She wants to get to him while his tongue is still swollen and his head still slick.

Then the phone rings. It's the hotel cashier telling him that his payment was rejected by his credit card company, and they'll have to leave their room and the hotel immediately. "*Instantly*, as in *right now!*"

Which is just as well because Doug can't stand ukuleles.

So sometimes post-divorce paranoia works out for the best.

# Blood Brothers

If you look up the word *Lucifer* in the encyclopedia, you'll see a picture of my best friend's wife.

One night at eleven, Archie called me and weepily asked me to scoot over. "I'm in pain," he sobbed. "She left me again. The door's unlocked."

Because this was the eighth or ninth time Eva had ditched him, and Archie's pathetic pleas always made me feel better about myself, he knew he could count on me. This time, though, his "I'm in pain" would mean more than his usual emotional tar pit.

The term "scoot over" was a bit flippant. Archie lived an hour away. Still, it was only eleven at night, not, say, two in the morning, and my cat was fast asleep on my pillow—so, what the heck, may as well get dressed, scoot over, and give Arch the moral support that wasn't good enough over the freaking phone.

On the way, I wondered yet again why Archie couldn't see what was obvious to the rest of our poker buddies: how much better off he'd be without his rack-torturer of a life partner. Behind his back we had often discussed anteing up X amount each or maybe start a GoFundMe campaign to put a contract on the witch. We loved Archie. In twenty years he had won only three hands, and two of those we let him win so he wouldn't get discouraged. One thing I knew for sure: there was no way in hell that on his behalf I would ever call Eva again and beg her to come home. What kind of woman would leave her man at a time like this?

I rang his doorbell anyhow—just in case during the last hour he had managed to track her down, offer to put all their joint assets solely in her name, and pay for as many male prostitutes as she needed to feel intellectually fulfilled.

I heard a distant, hamster-like "It's open." In I creaked. Except for a flickering nightlight, the hallway was dark, but a lamp was on in the living room, which I followed like a moth about to be fried alive.

Archie, defeated and depleted, sat slouched on his sofa, naked from the waist down, knees spread eagle, casserole bowl directly under his testicles, phone tucked between sofa cushions. On the coffee table, an ER array spread out at his shins: tube of K-Y lubricant; boxes of Kleenex and rubber gloves; bottle of hydrogen peroxide; snake-like catheter coiled on plastic bag, ready to strike.

Of course I knew he'd just had his prostate removed, so this time when he said he was in pain, he might have meant not just his wife, but his schlong.

"I need help," he moaned. Reflexively I glanced at his wiener, but quickly looked away.

"What happened now?"

"She said she can't spend the rest of her life without normal sex."

"You want a seltzer?" I asked, heading for the fridge.

"I need a favor," he mewled.

I knew what was coming. He was going to ask me to call her and beg her to come back...again. But to my surprise, instead of reaching for his phone, he chin-pointed to the eighteen-inch-long catheter.

"Need help putting it in," he muttered.

Okay, maybe by "help" he meant that I should sing a Jimmy Buffett song while he was routing the thingy up his thingy. Maybe find a rerun of *Two and a Half Men* we had all found especially funny during one of our card-game snack breaks? Recite some of my favorite Shakespeare passages? "Our revels now are ended..." (*The Tempest*, IV, 1)? I could manage any of these, as long as I didn't have to sit within direct eyesight of his dong.

"I can't do it myself," he whimpered. "Too painful."

"She left you to put in your own pee tube?" I snarled, eyebrows stretched.

"I took it out okay, but I can't...I can't do it by myself... Please, man. It hurts."

I started to sing "Margaritaville."

"I cleaned and greased it," he whined. "That's the best I can do." Again he nodded at the snake. "It's ready to go."

Now we both whined. My carotid artery bulged. "How about if I'm your navigator?"

"I need you to put it in."

"Get it started?"

"The whole thing...all the way."

My retinas flashed. I felt woozy. I paced. Maybe this was just a bad dream. Maybe I was asleep in my own house next to my sweet cat. Maybe she was licking my eyelids. I paced some more.

I refused to look at Archie's crotch. Sure, we had been best friends since grammar school, but...*slip something up his willy?* OK, maybe I could bring myself to sort-of sit next to him. Maybe if we just cried together, he'd get his strength back and slip the effing thing into his own schmecker.

His eyes narrowed at the coffee table. "Please," he pleaded. "I have to pee."

I'm usually not religious, but, as they say, there are no atheists in foxholes.

"Look, Arch," I stammered. "Don't get me wrong: You're a decent guy and all—"

"The doctor said if I piss into my own body..."

"Oh, man."

"I'll die of—"

"Stop!"

"...toxic shock..."

Bile surged up my esophagus. God willing, I'd die of toxic shock first.

"...in unbearable pain," he pressed.

I bent over to vomit.

Archie took that for a yes. "I love you, brother."

What choice did I have? If I abandoned my stupidly love-sick, wife-needy, childhood best friend now, if he did indeed die in penile agony, my poker group would always hold me responsible for its sudden financial decline. So I stepped back and forced myself to look at Archie's naked lap.

"Hurry," he said. "I really, really, have to pee." He glanced down at his limp plonker. "Hold it with the tissue," he instructed, "and slip it in a little at a time, steady as she goes. I'll scream if you go too fast. Love you, bro."

I thought of Marlow steamboating down the Congo River into Kurtz's heart of darkness. I pictured Eva's head shrunk, her lips and eyelids sewn shut. Epiphany-like, I finally faced the karmic consequence of having always assured Archie that a straight beats a flush.

I scurried around shutting all the window blinds, hoping that when I returned to the couch I might find Archie dead. I turned the three-way lamp bulb down to its lowest setting, just in case anyone was peeking in from the skylight. I went to the kitchen to fetch several napkins; mere facial tissues would not do. Luckily, Eva had swiped a bunch from their neighborhood coffee shop—leaving them for Archie, I supposed, as her divorce settlement.

I came back to the sofa, tugged out a fresh pair of surgical gloves, and at arm's length daintily grasped his putz with three folded napkins, the way you might snatch a frog from your basement window well, ready to drop the lumpy little MF and bolt upstairs at its slightest wiggle or tongue-flick.

Then something even more terrifying occurred to me: *What if, wrapped in my grip, Archie got a hard-on?*

*Holy crappola.* What if...*I* got a hard-on?

So, napkins flying, I dropped the frog and spun around, searching for the stairs. Unfortunately, it was a ranch house.

"Help," Archie tooted, the life draining out of him.

In a minute I returned with more napkins and, holding my breath, again gingerly took hold of his weasel. (If the situation were reversed, would he do the same for me? Or would he consider my agony payback for all those times I had bluffed him at cards—revenge for his having to write end-of-game personal checks, his having to take out credit-card cash advances at twenty-eight percent? Maybe Archie wasn't really my pal after all, but a cunning, mortal enemy—Prince Harry's Hotspur whose catheter dirk I was about to insert, only to be sliced to ribbons by a multi-million-dollar personal-injury lawsuit sabre.)

"Please," he moaned. "I have to piss."

"Okay, tell me where to put it," I said, fearing future depositions.

Even though there was only a single opening staring me in the face, he pointed. "Right there. Go slowwww."

I inserted the tip of the lubed serpent into his one-eyed lair, forcing myself not to look away.

*"Ow!"*

I yanked it out. Blood spurted onto my chin. I jumped up, ran to the kitchen, scrubbed my face with Comet and Brillo, showered it with scalding water from his sink sprayer. Did I just contract one of Eva's STDs? Would my cheeks erupt into giant canker sores every time I thought of her? At twenty-two dollars per tiny tube, would I have to rub Abreva cream on my head from the neck up?

"Hurry, bro!"

I returned with a napkin tucked into the bridge of my glasses, kicking myself for not having thought of that sooner.

This time as I inserted the catheter, struggling not to pass out between my buddy's thighs, from the corner of my eye I could see him wincing, holding his breath, internally screaming, sweating like a Yosemite waterfall. (*Welcome to the club.*) It was a delicate balance between not wanting to rush so much that I actually killed him and having to explain same to the police, versus needing to get this thing over with as quickly as possible so I could get home and drink a bottle of bleach.

At last, he held up his hand and exhaled, letting me know the job was done. I released the napkins and jolted back, out of spurting range. He hauled himself up and limped to the bathroom, and I heard him tinkle into the bowl. Until that moment I never thought I could despise Eva to any greater degree, but now I wanted to track her down and rub my chin over her entire chubby body, so that every one of her limbs, joints, eyeballs, and digits would erupt into excruciating lesions.

On the other hand, as I was driving home, I did sort of see her point regarding Archie not being able to have normal sex anymore—if, indeed, any sex between those two had ever been normal. I also saw *his* dilemma: How would he explain his lack of erection potential on Match.com? What circumspect wording would he ask me, his English-major best friend, to come up with? How would I struggle to prove to him, and to myself, that I had actually earned my Ph.D. by knowing how to write engaging, persuasive, impotent-male, dating rhetoric? Alluring poetic passages? Romantic imagery? Compelling compound adjectives, captivating modifiers that beguilingly dangled (sorry), subliminal sexual tropes, seductive symbolism, Latinate torsos with Anglo-Saxon appendages? That I (like most of my English Department colleagues) could obfuscate meaning with long, complex sentences stitched with discursive subordinate clauses, phrase slathered upon phrase, comma after comma, digression after digression, turning on themselves in eddying pools, only to eventually emerge into grammatical Valhalla—the syntactical equivalent of vernal rapids rushing over a waterfall before settling into a placid Alpine lake?

I didn't even try. What I did instead was, the first thing in the morning, while still in bed, I called Eva.

"Oh, you," she said, pretending to be surprised. She yawned. "How may I help you?"

"Archie's crushed." I, too, pretended this was a first-time plea. "Devastated."

"I know what *crushed* means."

"I have another friend who had his prostate removed and now screws like an Olympic swimmer." The moment it left my mouth, I realized this analogy made no sense, but, remember, I'm a Ph.D., not a real doctor.

"What friend?" she asked accusatorially.

"Marty Mandelbaum."

"You're a liar," she said, not unreasonably.

"You can find him on social media," I lied some more. "He talks about it right on Facebook and Twitter."

I could hear her slap her head.

I pressed: "Maybe Arch will be emotionally better able to withstand the loss if you dump him after he fully recovers. Losing you, I mean."

"He's really a wreck?" She stifled a giggle.

"Suicidal," I assured her. "Can't live without you."

After a pause, she said, "I'll think about it, how's that?"

"He's a mess."

"I said I'll think about it. Don't push me."

"I've never known a couple so made for each other."

"Go fuck yourself."

"No, I mean it in a nice way. Our poker buddies talk about it all the time. Usually when we're watching those porn videos Archie brings to the games."

"He brings *our* movies?!"

"Maybe I shouldn't have mentioned that."

"I'm going to kill him. *Fuck*."

"If you can get back there today, he won't need to call that nurse."

"Nurse? What nurse?"

"He needs help putting in his catheter."

"What're you, crippled?"

"I have three classes and an English Department staff meeting."

"So...what? He needs a fucking nurse for one day?"

"I'm just going by what he said, Eva. I can't get inside his...um...head."

Silence.

"Eva?"

"I can't take this kind of pressure," she moaned... probably thinking, *I should have married my first cousin Adolf, instead.*

"I have to get ready for school. I know you'll do the kind thing."

"I never liked you, you know."

"Really?"

"You don't know the definition of loyalty," she pointed out.

"Can hardly spell it."

"I feel sorry for your students."

"Hanging up now...got to catch a train."

"Go fuck yourself."

After she disconnected me, I called Arch to let him know she was on her way.

"You're my best friend," he reminded me. "Love you, man."

"Tube still in?"

"Ten-four. A-OK."

We both knew Eva wouldn't be ditching him again for another six months or so. I just hoped it wouldn't be midwinter. I despise driving in snow.

"I'll check back in a couple days," I assured him

anyhow.

"Maybe better not."

I understood. No sense upsetting their marital equilibrium.

"Poker's not the same without Archie," I offered.

"So."

"'This sceptered isle...this happy breed of men,'" I agreed, reciting Shakespeare, the literary genius who didn't return home to his wife for twenty-three years.

At least yours truly, *moi*, was home now, away from squirting catheters, toxic peenies and wee-wee, post-op lovelorn derangement, and one-eyed frogs. At least I was no longer driving the highway in the middle of the night, struggling to stay awake while suddenly realizing I had forgotten to remove my rubber gloves. At least it was now logistically impossible for me to faint between my best friend's loins. I was in my own bed, exhausted, but relieved, safe and sound, snug as a bug, face next to my dozing cat.

Her name is Lynda, named after my wife. In an hour or so, just as I fall back asleep, she'll paw-pat my cheek to let me know it's time to get up. I won't be too tired. I missed her while I was helping Archie. I thought of her while I was driving alone in the middle of the night. I worry about her while I'm gone all day teaching.

Archie and I have a deal: If I should die before Lynda—my cat; too late for my wife—he'll adopt her and try hard to make her happy. As for Eva, well...she might wind up loving Lynda as much as I do and so not be in such a hurry to ditch Archie again. If I'm wrong, maybe Arch won't be in such a hurry to beg his wife to come back; he'll have the cat to sleep on his pillow.

This is what blood brothers do.

# El Max

I knew the bus driver was going to be trouble. He evidently had no first name, but his last name was Lopez, and he was small and angular, and his eyes were round and black like a rat's. He never looked at you, but stared out the windshield, even though the bus was still parked and it was the middle of the night. He didn't respond when you said *holá*, just tapped his gnarly fingers on the steering wheel, gazed out at the dim lot, and occasionally picked gook out of his eyes. He refused to budge.

We had landed after midnight, but some of the group were coming in on a separate plane, and there was no telling when they'd get to Havana. But our Lopez refused to take the first part of the group to our hotel and return for the others. We had been traveling for almost twenty-four hours. After delays in Chicago, Toronto, and Montreal, we had finally taken off in a blinding ice storm, terrorized by the paroxysms of a 1950s Aeroflot Soviet jetliner with chewing gum for hors d'oeuvres and rivets. We were too exhausted even to cheer when we finally touched down, and now the son of a bitch wanted us to sit on the bus and wait for the other plane. He wouldn't budge.

We found out his name was Lopez when our HavanaTur guide, a handsome, affable young man in his early twenties, whose name was Roberto Baez, but who asked us to call him Bob, kept yelling at him in Spanish to take us to the hotel. Most of us did not speak Spanish, but we got the gist of it, and every once in a while Bob would sprinkle his exhortations with the name *Lopez*, so that's how we knew. One of us who did speak a little Spanish said Bob called the driver a "dog's anus," but Lopez only replied by staring at his reflection in the windshield and scratching his butt.

After each vain appeal, Bob turned to us with a forced smile and, in pretty good English, said, "We assure you, your friends are almost here, and we will be on our way extremely shortly. We know it has been an extremely long day, and extremely shortly you will be asleep on your extremely soft pillow in your hotel. We welcome you extremely much to our extremely beautiful city, which you cannot see now, but you will surely see in the daytime."

Then he turned again to the driver and—for our benefit—pretended to engage in good-natured banter, but was really calling him combinations of names that included animals and orifices.

Lopez still wouldn't budge.

So right away I knew he was going to be trouble.

I'm cranky when I'm tired—also when I'm hungry, thirsty, have missed any episodes of *The Goldbergs*, or am visiting any country that doesn't have Starbucks or macaroni and cheese. Long about one-thirty, after another of Bob's futile go-rounds with Lopez, I'd had enough. I had been a courteous American for an hour and a half—way longer than average. Being a man of action, I got up to offer Lopez a bribe, when the long arm of the law, my wife, pulled me back by my elbow skin.

"Sit," she said.

When I looked down, my glance was met by the same malevolent gaze as Christ's detractors in Mel Gibson's *Passion*. I didn't actually see the movie, but I saw enough excerpts on TV to guess the main idea. When they showed Jesus with deep, bloody lacerations all over his face and body, I thought: *cat owner*. Oh, great, so in addition to killing the son of God, Jews were also responsible for not declawing their pets. That's what I thought. Sue me.

Five hours in an ice storm with Force 5 hurricane winds on a Soviet airplane with a beaded curtain for a toilet door and krill for meal service cannot compare with the terror-inducing of my wife's gaze, usually reserved for when I say something mean but truthful about her nephew, the thirty-year-old Nintendo wiz. I sat back down.

"You're not going to spend two weeks in a Havana jail," she hissed.

"How come?"

"It might distract me."

Our companion plane arrived from Canada at four-thirty in the morning, and by the time that group was interrogated and frisked, it was dawn over Cuba, but we were at last on our way.

On the plus side, our hotel had what appeared to be a real cafeteria. The problem being, in Cuba you can't eat without involving pig parts. Not a pork lover, I had to remind myself that Hemingway would not only have eaten the oinkers, he would have shot them. In that order.

At eleven-thirty, a knock woke us up. "It is I, Bob."

For a moment, I forgot who Bob was. Havana doesn't have peepholes or other basic security devices, probably because they don't have lawyers to sue someone for knocking on your door. Shirtless, I cracked the door and peeked at our tour guide's grinning kisser. "Bob," he repeated. "Might I come in?"

"My wife's still sleeping."

"I'm awake," Penny said behind me. She dashed into the bathroom with her clothes, afraid she might miss an excursion that involved purchasing carved coconut heads. "Don't let them leave without us."

Bob glanced up and down the hallway, then stepped in. "It's an extremely beautiful hotel, don't you think? They are holding breakfast until noon today, in honor of your extremely late arrival. Excellent pork." The front of his guayabera shirt bulged weirdly, as if his own breakfast had consisted of a cinder block.

"What can I do for you?" I asked.

"Lopez is a scoundrel. A worm's earhole. Complete turtle excretion...if I understand the term correctly."

"You're doing fine."

"My brother Alberto, a police *capitano*, would like to arrest him for being such a goat's ass." He raised an eyebrow. "He would take care of him extremely firmly, I assure you. No further visitors would be so inconvenienced."

I motioned to the chair. He pulled it out and sat, the bulge under his shirt rising to his chest.

"Unfortunately, my brother's hands are tied. Do I use the phrase correctly?" He lowered his voice. "Lopez is a good communist. Head of his CDR—Committee for the Defense of the Revolution." He lowered his voice even more, and his forehead furled. "He once broke bread with El Maximo. I myself am not political. I stay out of it. But Lopez is a pig's nostril. I am here to give you advice. Be careful what you and your friends say on the bus. The villain reports everything."

"I don't have any friends."

"Ah, I see. Extremely wise. Your wife, then."

Penny popped out of the bathroom. "His wife what?"

201

"Don't talk in front of Lopez."

"And, good heavens, never offer him a bribe!"

She glanced at me and whistled soundlessly.

Bob grimaced, the cinder block digging into his spleen.

"I think Bob brought us a box lunch. Pork, I'll bet."

"Oh," our guide said, pretending he had just remembered the hidden package. "Oh, yes, this." He motioned to the bulge. "Do you mind?" He slipped the bundle out of his guayabera. He plopped a filthy, fat manila envelope onto his lap and took a breath. "Your visa says you are a writer."

"A bad one," I assured him.

He patted the grease-spotted envelope. "I am wondering if you would read my novel. Not here, of course. Take it home and read it when you are relaxed."

"You want me to smuggle your manuscript out of Cuba?"

"I thought perhaps, and only if you like it, you might show it to a publisher—"

"We'll get into trouble."

Bob flicked a finger. "My brother would not allow that. Do not worry." His glance fell on my Star of David necklace. "We have a secret weapon." He whispered, "We, too, are of Hebrew persuasion."

Penny's toes did a little conga. "You? Jewish?"

"And Alberto, naturally." He chortled. "Fidel thought he was, too." He paused and looked around. "Not that we wanted him. But it came in extremely handy. My brother was teaching him Yiddish. Alberto didn't speak a word of it. He made it all up. You should have heard the Bearded One trying to talk like a Jew. Extremely amusing."

"Of course we'll take your novel," Penny piped. "And my husband is a *very good* writer." Always there when I need her.

"Wonderful! Wonderful!" He handed her the package. "You can tell no one in Cuba it is mine, naturally," he whispered. "I left my name off it entirely."

I took it from Penny and handed it back. "Sorry. Out of the question. Anyhow, I'm disliked in the trade."

She took it back and buried it at the bottom of my suitcase. "It's in good hands."

"Written entirely in English," Bob puffed. He slowly pantomimed scribbling. "In my good handwriting for ease of reading."

*"Longhand?"* Penny exclaimed.

"I will be glad to divide any money with you fifty-fifty, if I'm phrasing that correctly?" He got up and offered me his hand.

Penny took it. "Not necessary, we assure you. We're glad to help an oppressed artist."

"You will have a glorious ten days in Cuba, with me as your guide."

"I have no doubt."

"Well, *I* have a doubt," I said, reaching for the manuscript. But before I could shove it back into Bob's shirt, he was out the door.

I turned to Penny. "I thought you said my being in jail would be a distraction."

"This is different. He's probably a literary genius. A Cuban J.D. Salinger. Think of his determination and hardship, writing it out longhand. He's *Jewish.*"

"Apparently so was Fidel, but I wouldn't have trusted him with my pork chop."

"All right, if they make a fuss—which I highly doubt—*I'll* go to jail. How's that?"

"It doesn't work that way. Do the names Julius and Ethel Rosenberg ring a bell?"

"You're on vacation. Relax." She kissed my chin. "Who knows, maybe he'll dedicate it to you. That would be something, wouldn't it? Anyhow, they shoot you here, they don't electrocute you."

"It must be nice being married to a love-sick imbecile."

"It comes in extremely handy. Now get dressed and let's go for breakfast. Then I want to buy something shiny." She suddenly looked worried. "Commies sell shiny things, don't they?"

After lunch the bus was waiting. Bob had held the front seats for Penny and me. The other people in the group drilled us a look. One woman in particular, a manicurist from Detroit with six-inch fingernails painted to depict important events in the life of Black leaders—one pinky being Marcus Garvey's parade down Lenox Avenue, and a thumb Martin Luther King's "I Have A Dream" speech on the Washington mall—cut me a snarl, possibly sensing race-related shenanigans. I knew that unless I got on her good side, I would never leave Cuba with both eyes. Nevertheless, I sat. May as well enjoy the scenery while you still have depth perception.

"Today we are going to Veradero Beach," Bob reminded us, as Lopez swung the bus onto the Malecón. "We will have lunch and enjoy the sun." He sliced me a wink.

"Cubans themselves are not permitted on the beach." He glanced at Lopez accusatorially. "Only tourists."

I didn't wink back.

Twenty minutes later, I told Penny I had to go to the bathroom.

"So go. What do you want from me?"

"I have to pass that woman."

"Protect your eyes."

"What if she goes for the family jewels?"

"One hand on your face, one on your crotch. This ain't brain surgery."

"It'll look like I'm afraid of her."

"You are afraid of her."

"People will think I'm weak and eat off my plate."

"Think pork."

"Point taken."

"Besides," she whispered, "we've got Roberto's brother."

I smiled at Bob and, yes, winked. I got up and walked gingerly to the back, whistling "Candy Man" by Sammy Davis Jr. Other than her staring at my hand covering my crotch, there were no incidents.

Until, that is, I tried to leave the bathroom. The door stuck. I mean, S-T-U-C-K. I wiggled the sliding latch and jammed it back hard. *Nada.* I pulled it back and got my knee up and pushed my other leg against the commode and heaved, but the door didn't budge. It occurred to me that the Detroit woman was leaning on it from the other side. Perhaps she had recruited the other members of our group, many of whom had wanted to sit in the front seat. Perhaps some of them were familiar with my writing. Meanwhile, the bus was barreling down the coastal road, picking up speed, jouncing me like an asymmetrical Cuban-lottery ball, and the windowless three-by-three cubical, which was directly over the diesel engine, was getting ten degrees hotter a minute. And guess what? I'm claustrophobic.

Sometimes I get panic attacks when my sheets are tucked in too tight, even when I'm not in bed. If you've ever had a claustrophobia attack, you know they are terrifying, degrading, and make you regret all those times you promised to write something nice about a hotel or restaurant just to get a free room or food, knowing full well you were going to stiff them, review-wise. You're sure you're going to pass out and poop in your pants, and that strangers will rifle through your wallet and find a picture of your parakeet. You're also sure that no one else on the bus will have to go to the bathroom all the way to Veradero, and that your wife will fall asleep, which she likes to do, and that you'll pass out with your head in the potty, and that it will get so hot in there that by the time anyone notices you're missing, your skull will have shrunk to the size and density of a parakeet's.

It was time to pound.

With the engine roaring like an F-16 or my lawn mower after Penny's nephew borrowed it and forgot to put in oil, I wasn't sure if anyone could hear me. I took no chances. I pounded and yelled, yelled and pounded, my panic attack in full shock and awe. The louder I screamed and whacked the door, the more spiritedly Lopez revved the engine. The bus was going faster and faster, the bathroom getting hotter and hotter, my breaths harder and harder, my temples percussing like ten-thousand-pound bunker-busters.

The son of a bitch must have known I had Bob's novel.

"Help! I'm stuck!"

Bob yelled: "Pull the latch back!"

Penny shouted, "Take deep breaths and slow down your alpha waves, like Dr. Luce taught you."

"It's hot! I can't breathe!"

"Close your eyes and imagine yourself lying in a lovely meadow next to a country lake!"

"Tell Lopez to stop the bus! I'm going to pass out from the fumes!"

"I'll be right back!" Roberto hollered.

"Hurry!"

The bus went faster.

"You still there, honey?!" Penny shouted.

"Kill Lopez!"

"Roberto's talking to him! Close your eyes and pretend you're listening to Handel's *Water Music*."

"Kill the commie motherfucker!"

Finally, finally, finally, Bob ran back. "He won't stop! He said the nation depends on him to arrive on time! It is a matter of prestige! But don't worry, we will get you out!" He shoved something into the door jam. "I have a pen. If only it will go—"

But, writing instruments being useless when you really need them, it was too fat to reach the lock tongue.

"Do you have a tire iron?!" I shouted.

No answer. Penny might have been interpreting.

"A tire iron!" Roberto confirmed. "To fix flat tires! Of course!"

"*Pry* me the hell out of here!"

"It's with the spare tire! Under the bus! We would have to stop!"

Lopez went faster.

"I love you, honey!"

I felt woozy. The rumble of the diesel receded, approached, receded again. Penny's voice sounded tinny and far away—even more than usual. My vision blurred. I could feel my carotid artery in my toes. My tongue was the size and consistency of a Vienna salami, my flesh cold and lifeless. I lost sense of time. The walls began to swirl. My knees gave way. I would have collapsed, if only there had been room. I remembered being born.

Then, as if in a dream, I saw Martin Luther King slip through the door crack.

A moment later, the latch slammed back, the door jolted open, and the manicurist from Detroit filled the doorway. "You all right now, sweet baby!" she trumpeted, fanning me with her nails. Fresh air whooshed over my bloodless mug. "Charmaine set you free!"

She hefted me to my feet and hauled me down the aisle, pushing Bob and Penny aside, shouting, "Get outta the way, we marchin' to freedom!" She deposited me in my front-row seat, warning Penny, "Take care of him. Men with good nails don't grow on trees." Then she turned to Lopez and bared her teeth, but he was too busy picking gook out of his eye to notice.

The morning we were set to leave Cuba, I noticed my Star of David pendant missing. It was a stamped, fourteen-karat gold-plated cheapy, but my Aunt Rose had bought it for me in Israel, so I liked it. I lose things a lot when traveling, and this time it was my necklace. Still, after breakfast, I offhandedly asked Roberto if anyone had turned it in. He said no and, even though I assured him it was junk jewelry, he seemed extremely concerned and checked with the concierge. Shaking his head solemnly, he took me aside and whispered, "Do you think you lost it on the bus?"

"It's possible, I guess."

He pursed his lips. "I see."

"You do?"

"Lopez must have found it and kept it, that thieving sheep rectum. Well, we'll see about that." He lowered his voice even more. "You still have my...merchandise?"

I nodded.

"I await your verdict with pines and noodles. You can reach me through my brother."

When, a few weeks later, I finished reading Bob's manuscript, I handed it to my wife. Penny is always trying to sign over our home and other assets to foreign people who say they love America. Our Polish cleaning lady, for example, is an indefatigable young woman who hunts down dirt like Purvis hunted down Dillinger. Believe me, I like her, too. But I still don't see why I should marry her to make her a citizen. I also like our gardener, Manuel, even though he formed an offshore corporation to launder the money we pay him. Or Viktor, our Croatian house painter, whose rehab treatments Penny offered to subsidize, forcing us to cash in the savings bonds from my bar mitzvah, and who's only on step two.

So I knew she really, really wanted to like Bob's novel. She had been watching me from the corner of her eye as I leafed through the manuscript, stone-faced. Finally, it was hers.

A couple of days later, she handed it back. "It's horrible."

"What? Not worth rotting in a tropical prison for?"

"As near as I can figure, it's *Fiddler on the Roof*—without a fiddler or a roof."

"Or a shred of talent. In itself not enough to keep it off the *Times*' best-seller list."

Her eyes lit up. "You're not saying there's actually hope for—"

I hefted the manuscript. "Cat litter."

She deflated. "What are you going to tell Bob?"

*"Me?"*

"Technically, he gave it to you, not me. Let him down easy. Promise?"

I had her. She had lurched unwittingly into my trap. What she didn't know was that, at that very moment, hunkered in my desk drawer was a letter I had plucked from the mailbox yesterday, while she had been out shopping for something nice for herself.

*My Dear Señor*

*We are knowing about your stoling star and we opened a file on your theft. We will not rest, we will never rest, until we solve this badly crime. Our nation depends on us. It is a matter of prestige.*

*Yours truly,*

*Cpt. Alberto Paul Baez (Captain)*

*District Centro*

*La Habana, Cuba*

*Postscript: We have now a suspect into custody, your bus driver.*

"Okay," I agreed, promising Penny I'd let Bob down gently. Then, trying to appear depressed, I shuffled to my office, where I typed:

*Dear Roberto,*

*My wife and I read* Castanets on the Bus, *and we agree that it* [I dug deeply for the right phrase that did not include the words "total dreck"] *elicits great promise. I will keep you informed. Meanwhile, please tell your brother to keep the pressure on regarding my precious stoling star. Tell him I am extremely happy he has a suspect and that I will do everything I can to make you a famous author. I promise.*

Sincerely *(I really mean it!),*

*Your Honest Friend and Future Literary and Movie Agent*

*P.S. If enough pressure is applied, sooner or later the suspect will confess.*

I lobbed Roberto's masterpiece onto my desk, next to my framed eight-by-ten of Charmaine hugging the Reverend Al Sharpton, and admired my nails. Every month or so I'd write Bob another letter to keep his and, especially, his brother's hopes up. He wants to be a writer? *Fine.* Why should he suffer any less extremely than the rest of us?

Besides, the thought of Capitano Baez pistol-whipping Lopez clack-clacked off the rooftop of my brain like happy little concave shells.

# Strapped

"You're not worried?" Donna wanted to know. But her husband was too busy knotting his tie. "Sean?"

"'Sup?"

"What they'll find?"

He squinted at her in the mirror. "We've been through this, honey. You're overthinking it. I promise, it's nothing. Aches and pains are just a part of getting older."

"But it's every day."

"And your stressing over it makes it worse." He undid his tie and started over. He continued to talk to the mirror: "As soon as they give you the all-clear, you'll instantly start feeling better. You'll see."

"But something is wrong. We have to listen to our bodies."

"The mind and stomach are related."

"But what started it?"

"Damn it!" he snarled. The front of his tie was still too short. Again he whipped apart the knot. This time he spun around to face her, his face almost as red as the tie. "Donna," he growled.

"Okay, I'm sorry. I just thought—"

"Listen to me. It's nothing. Are you listening?"

She nodded.

"Nothing. You'll see. We've been through this. You don't need me to come with you for reassurance because there's nothing to reassure you about. If you wouldn't be so afraid, your stomach wouldn't hurt. Plain and simple. Be tougher than that voice in your head. Quit letting it make you miserable."

She sat on the edge of the bed. "You're right," she sighed. "You can't be my wingman for every little thing."

"I am your wingman...just more long term, that's all." He started to kneel in front of her, thought better of it, sat on the bench facing her instead. "Think of this as an opportunity, a chance to build your courage, to not give in to that mind voice."

"You're right. It's just that—"

"Besides, when the test comes back negative, how're you going to feel knowing I postponed my client's audit? In their warped brains, the IRS considers all cancelations admissions of guilt. The poor guy's having a nervous breakdown as it is."

"Of course...you're right."

"You have to be tough. Remember, someday I might not be here at all. What happens then? So this is sort of a gift, right?"

She started to tear up but didn't want to wipe her eyes in front of him. He got up, sat next to her on the bed, held her hand. "You'll see. You'll thank yourself for being strong. So the next time, that little devil in there"—he nodded at her skull—"won't waste his energy because he'll know you're tougher than shit."

He got up, tossed aside both ends of his tie, helped her to her feet, kissed her cheek. He glanced at his watch. "Got to get out of here before my guy has a heart attack." He turned back to the mirror, inspected his shirt, flicked away any trace of makeup that might have made its way from her face to his fabric.

"I love you," she said.

"I love you, too," he said to the mirror. "You'll see, I promise." He glanced again at his watch. "Shit." He gave up on the tie. "I'll do it in the car. Hopefully won't run someone over on the way."

"I'm sorry," she said.

"Never mind." He grabbed his suit jacket, flung it over his shoulder, and beelined for the stairs.

"I love you," she called after him.

He blew her a smooch. "You'll see," he called back.

"I'll see," she whispered to herself. She sat on the edge of the bed for a few minutes, breathing deeply, forcing herself to relax.

She heard the garage door open.

She wondered if it was the test results she was so frantic about, or just the idea of being strapped into that MRI tunnel. When she had made the appointment, the scheduler asked her if she was claustrophobic. The question caught her by surprise. She said no, but the moment she hung up, she panicked. Googling the heck out of it did nothing to calm her.

As usual, though, Sean just now helped again—a little, at least. She fluffed up her pillow and lay down fetally.

The garage door closed.

She tried to meditate, the way she often did to help herself sleep. She imagined two purring kittens curled up in her arms. Every time her thoughts drifted from the purrs to the MRI tube, she would drag her brain back to the fur babies, concentrate on their soft vibrations, snuggling foreheads, and pressing little paw pads...imagining them comforting her heartbeats.

She kept side-glancing the alarm clock, though. She had another hour before check-in, but not wanting to risk falling asleep and missing her appointment (she'd never, with a shred of credibility, be able to explain that to Sean), after fifteen minutes, she got up, went to her bathroom medicine closet, and plucked out her Lonapafil (Dr. Simon said okay, just go light).

She had already decided not to tell Sean, either about the sedative or the taxi—that she wasn't going to drive herself, not even the few miles to the hospital. She wouldn't tell him that in this case, meditation wouldn't be enough.

Driving wouldn't work. She'd have had to time the Lonapafil just right: not so soon that it impaired her reflexes, but not so late that it wouldn't kick in when they slid her into the MRI. So taking a taxi would be the way to go.

Even at that, she had decided on not one—the dose she sometimes took to help her sleep—but, this time, two pills: one as soon as the cab showed up, and the second tablet as soon as she got to the hospital. Assuming no inordinate delay, her timing would be close enough.

She hoped.

She called the taxi company, got dressed, removed her wedding ring (per instructions), tucked her jewelry box at the bottom of their dirty-clothes hamper, stayed out of the kitchen so she wouldn't be tempted to eat (per instructions), and from their bedroom kept one eye on her Kindle, the other on the driveway.

At ten-fifteen, the cab pulled up, and she popped the first Lonapafil. Because she knew it would take at least a half-hour to start making her drowsy, she wasn't worried about falling asleep on the way and not being able to pay the driver. Assuming he didn't get lost trying to find the hospital.

The driver, not being talkative, left her to her thoughts. Had Sean lost respect for her—for her wanting him to come with? He was right, of course: women talked a good game about independence, courage, power, equality—until the bullets started flying. So, no, her husband wasn't abandoning her in her so-called hour of need; on the contrary, he was teaching her how to be strong. Strong for herself and for all women.

Still, remembering what he had said about maybe not being here for her someday, she couldn't help but tear up.

He was loving that way, wasn't he? How many times he had sat her down to show her how to pay their bills? Just in case. He didn't want to die knowing she'd be perplexed by the bookkeeping. He printed out how much went where and when; to whom he wrote checks, charged credit cards, approved automatic payments; the websites and URLs of the utility companies; the amounts and due dates of insurance premiums, the names and contact info of their agents, brokers, advisers—every *t* crossed, *i* dotted. That was Sean. He did it for her. He did it because he loved her. True, for now he ran the checkbook, but that was only because that was his profession. It made sense. But he'd never be able to die peacefully knowing that, afterwards, she could not handle her finances.

So, sure: other husbands might have all-too-gladly offered to be with their wives for this kind of common, non-invasive medical exam. Why not make their women even more emotionally dependent on them under the guise of "caring"?

He loved Donna very much.

So what was the problem, really? Not nutritional, apparently. Since her pains had started, she had tried all kinds of diets: gluten-free; lactose-free; wheat- and oat-free. Physiological? Not likely. Dr. Simon had prescribed half-a-dozen different medicines—for heartburn, acid reflux, ulcers, irritable bowel syndrome: Previcid; Prilosec; omeprazole; esomeprazole; pantoprazole; famotidine. The problem being, she didn't have diarrhea, constipation, heartburn, acid reflux, vomiting, black stool, gray stool, loose stool, stool that smelled like petunias, marble-shaped stool, ribbon-shaped stool, or stuffed nose.

So no wonder the meds hadn't helped. None of them. The almost constant pain was still there.

"Could it be stress?" the doctor had asked a few times. "I doubt it," Donna had chuckled—also a few times. "What do I have to be stressed about?"

Sean loved her, didn't he?

She kept a log. When during the day did the pain get worse? After eating or on an empty stomach? After which foods? Morning or bedtime? Peanut butter? Chocolate? Sugar? Hot intake: coffee, tea, soup? Carbonation? Diet drinks? Acidic juices? Cheese? Potato chips? Corn chips? Red meat? Chicken? Fish? Roughage? Salt? Pepper?

But there seemed to be no *aha!* Nothing to connect the dots. She Googled the heck out of it: mayoclinic. org; *Web*MD; medlineplus.gov; digestivehealth.com; clevelandclinic.org; healthline.uk.co.; johnhopkins.org; rushmed.us. Nothing. For months now, nothing to explain it.

But if it was wearing her out, that was nothing compared to the toll it must have been taking on Sean. For the most part, he had kept his frustration corked nice and tight. Not that he wasn't as bewildered—maybe even as worried—as Donna. Maybe even more so, his silence a language of its own. Aside from asking her details about meds and doctor visits to determine whether they were covered by insurance, he pretty much kept his concern to himself. But she could tell. He didn't have to come out and say it: he was plenty worried.

Sean loved her very much.

The taxi driver asked if he should wait for her. "No, better not. I'll call when I'm done." When he assured her the waiting charge would be only twenty-five cents a minute, she silently calculated. Assuming it might take a couple of hours, she'd still be better off calling for a fresh lift. On the other hand, she'd then have to wait—who knew how long—for the fresh cab to arrive. Given how big the hospital campus was, how many different buildings and entrances, it would be a minor miracle if another driver would even know where to come get her—or, for that matter, what directions she'd give them.

"No," she decided, handing him a ten and a five, telling him to keep the change, "I'll just call when I'm done."

The driver shrugged and, considering the decent tip, got out, opened her door, and wished her good luck. Once out, she told him to hold on a sec, and forked him another two bucks.

As soon as she stepped into the hospital, she popped her second Lonapafil.

The lobby was the size and ceiling height of a medieval cathedral, including towering windows, except these were colorless instead of saintly stained glass. And rather than soul-terrifying paintings of horned devils ripping out sinners' intestines, the lobby featured colorful abstract canvases, meant, apparently, to cheer folks about to visit their dying relatives.

The buildouts were all twenty-first century: two rows of glass-enclosed check-in counters; chrome-legged, tufted-leather divans; two Calder-like mobiles dangling from the high ceiling, reflecting sunlight onto the walls and white-marble floor (as opposed to the hanging bodies of thirteenth-century apostates). At the far end of this welcoming purgatory, escalators either rose or fell, depending. At the top of the up escalator, an abstract Lady Liberty sculpture peered down at the hopefuls.

From here, there was no way to see what waited at the bottom of the down escalator.

Donna asked for directions to the MRI department. "Imaging," said the woman receptionist, pointing. "Left to the elevators just after the sign that says *Imaging*."

Another reason Donna really did wish Sean were there: she had never been great with directions. And, sure enough, she walked past not only the *Imaging* sign but the ground-floor elevators, coffee shop, gift shop, garage, and restrooms before deciding that she had gone too far. Even at that, she paused for a half-minute, facing an emergency-exit door, figuring she had made another mistake.

Which, now that she thought about it, was another reason that Sean was right. If she couldn't even find the *Imaging* sign, how would she ever be able to navigate the rest of her life if he were to die first? If she depended on him for every little thing?

Backtracking, she eventually found the sign, the elevators, the third-floor Imaging Department, silently congratulating herself for still being on time.

Sean was always on time.

The Imaging receptionist looked her up on her computer, had her fill out and sign two forms, confirmed aloud that Donna wasn't wearing jewelry nor had metal inside her body. She pushed a button under her desk, motioning Donna to an inner door. "Have a seat inside. A nurse will be right with you."

Donna unflipped her Kindle, but she didn't feel like reading. In a few minutes the nurse came in from an opposite door, introduced herself—"Julie"—and led Donna to a changing room.

"Is there any way I can see the machine before I actually go in?"

"You bet," Julie said. "Patients ask us that all the time. Do you have claustrophobia?"

"Just a little anxious. Am I the only one?"

"Oh, you mean like *today*?" Julie chuckled. "Sure. First get changed, then I'll show you around the party room." She handed Donna a sealed bag of gown and socks, told her to undress down to her underwear, tie the robe in the back, and to lock her clothes in one of the changing room lockers. "Make sure you're not wearing any metal. Just call my name when you're ready."

Donna's Lonapafil timing was good. By the time she changed, she was feeling a little less jumpy, but not yet sleepy enough for Julie's tour not to sink in. The nurse led her through a double door marked *No Visitors Allowed*. She showed her the yawning MRI tunnel, described the procedure, explained about the earphones and microphone, about holding her breath when the recorded voice said so, about when the chilly intravenous fluid would kick in.

"Whole thing less than an hour. In the meantime, if you feel uneasy at all, my assistant and I will be right on the other side of this window here. You'll see, finished before you know it. No big deal."

Donna eyeballed the monster contraption. "Will I be strapped down? I think that might make me nervous."

"Not *strapped* in, no. But I'll be putting a pad across your abdomen, and hold it in place with a couple of Velcros. Your arms will be tucked under those—but just loosely. Not really strapped down. But if you have to pick your nose, I suggest you do it beforehand."

Donna smiled. The Lonapafil was beginning to work its magic.

"Speaking of which," Julie said, "If you have to use the ladies' room, better to do it now. Thing is, if we do stop before the end, we'll just have to start over."

That last part sounded kind of far away.

"Ready?"

"Ready."

"Don't have to pee?"

Donna shook her head.

Julie took Donna's glasses and locker key. "They'll be with me the whole time," she said, slipping them into her smock pocket. "Okay, now, let's have some fun. Before you know it, you'll be back out, dancing."

Per instructions, Donna stretched onto the gurney, tugging down her flimsy robe while Julie adjusted the pillow. "Feel right?" she asked.

But Donna was already starting to daydream. "I took Lonapafil," she mumbled.

"Good girl," said the nurse, as she fitted the earphones over Donna's noggin. "Feel okay?"

Donna readjusted the right muff slightly and nodded.

"Remember, I'm always right there," Julie said, raising her voice next to the left headphone and nodding at the control room window, "and if you talk to me, I can hear. You don't have to shout. Just talk normal. Ready to rumble?"

When Donna didn't answer, Julie lifted the muff. "Ready to rumble?" When Donna still didn't answer, the nurse said, "I take that for a yes." She gently replaced the muff, shot Donna a thumbs-up, and headed for the control booth. "Remember," she said on her way out, raising her voice, "you're never alone."

On the ceiling above the gurney was a backlit, light-fixture tapestry, a colorful rectangular garden scene meant to help relax the patients. Donna stared at it for a minute, imagining herself in a field of sunflowers, her eyes soon pleasantly drooping. When the gurney began to slide her into the tube, the movement at first startled her, but her fists quickly untightened, her breathing resumed, her heartbeat again in rhythmic iamb. Her eyelids relaxed again in sync with the machine's low buzzing and slow slide.

Fully inside the tube, her eyes closed, her thoughts drifted to a lakeside beach where kittens and puppies frolicked, gently lapping waves pooling their paw prints. She believed she was floating on a pink inflatable, not far from shore, the water rocking her as tenderly as an infant's cradle. From the distance came her mother's sweet voice: "Can you hear me, Donna?"

"Oh, yes," she cooed.

"You okay?"

"Okay."

"I'm right here," Julie said.

"I love you, too."

"We love you, too," Julie giggled. "When the voice asks you to hold your breath, it'll only be for a couple of seconds. In the meantime, just relax and breathe normally. Okay?"

"Okay."

Every few minutes, her earphones prompted Donna: when to take in a breath, when to hold it, when to let it go. Occasionally, Julie would come on board: "Still awake?"

"Still awake," Donna assured her languidly.

"We're right here."

When, one time, Donna didn't respond, Julie again broke in: "You still awake?"

"Still awake."

"You're doing great."

Donna was still dreamily on her float, her heels dangling in the placid lake. Once in a while she'd scoop up a palmful of water and moisten her face, chest, and arms. Whenever she felt the shadow of a cloud, she'd creak open one eye and see a haloed nimbus curling between her and the sun, making sure she wouldn't get too hot. If, from the beach, children's playful shouts sounded too far away, with one-handed fingertips she would serenely paddle back towards shore.

All was calm.

The world was right.

Life was right.

Sean loved her very much.

Until the lifeguard's blaring megaphone screamed from the sand, trembling the water, jolting her float, scattering the clouds, terrifying the puppies and kittens, panicking Donna.

"I came home early and saw that your car is still in the garage!" the lifeguard blasted.

Donna's eyes shot open. It was Sean's voice screeching from the megaphone.

"Don't tell me you took a cab! You've *got* to be kidding!"

Her heart bashed her ribs.

"Donna, honey, baby...even at the current high gas prices, back and forth would only amount to two-fifths of a gallon, or about a buck and a quarter. Even if you factor in wear and tear...tires, battery, grease, and oil...we're still only talking less than two bucks! But what did the cab cost you... *us*?! Seventeen smackers each way! Seventeen! Each way!"

She jerked up her arms to yank off the earphones— only to remember that, no, her wrists were held down under the straps.

"Donna, can you hear me?!" bellowed Sean's voice in her earphones. "Remember what I told you? It's not how much you make, it's how much you don't spend! You said you understood. What happened?!"

The megaphone stopped, and the gurney started sliding out of the tube, feet first. Ceiling lights came on. The wildflowers light fixture slithered into view. Donna held her breath, clenched her jaw. Though she hadn't eaten in twelve hours, vomit seared her throat.

"Hey, honey," Sean said.

She blinked hard. He was there, standing next to the machine. Alone. No nurse. No assistant. Just Sean, in suit and red tie, clutching his briefcase in one hand, his calculator in the other.

"I'm here to bring you home," he told her.

She squinted into the control room. No one behind the glass, either. Julie gone. Everyone gone.

Except Sean.

He didn't unstrap her, didn't help her up. He just stood there with briefcase and calculator, his tie perfectly knotted.

Unstrapping her would be encouraging her weakness. She knew he wouldn't help her off the gurney for her own good, even if the Velcro was too tight.

Sean loved her very much.

# His Military-
# Industrial Complex

The check-in line at José Marti International was for tourists what every other line in Cuba was for Cubans: long and languid and as listless as a python after eating an agouti on a sweltering afternoon. The Stanfords had barely moved for almost two hours—sitting on their suitcases, reading, playing blackjack, muttering obscenities, occasionally standing to regain circulation and nudge their bags with their feet, playing "Name That Tune" on zippers and "Hang the Butcher," with the Butcher sporting a beard, smoking a cigar, and wearing guerilla fatigues from the 1950s. But, like the COVID-19 shipping and supply chain backlog, in all that time they had gotten absolutely nowhere. One crummy check-in agent for a couple of hundred sunburned, bunion-throbbing, pissed-off Yanquis. Eventually the python began to bulge here and there, then break apart like on that New Hampshire Revolutionary flag—"Live Free or Die."

When Earl couldn't stand it anymore, he moseyed outside and found a nine-year-old kid—Raphael—selling stale coconut fragments, and gave him ten dollars to come inside and stand in line for him and Wendy.

In Cuba you can bribe anyone to do anything for a U.S. dollar. One night Wendy and Earl went to the Museum of the Revolution, only to find it closed for "remodeling"—a term that is to Cuban economic reality what "international" is to a Cuban airport. One buck, and the security guard not only let them in and turned on the lights, he invited them to help themselves to whatever mementos they might like, such as *Granma*, the boat on which Castro and a hundred of his men sailed from Mexico to launch their revolution. "Go on," he said, waving, "just take it."

If you got sick on hotel food, and they diagnosed you with needing an entire upper-body transplant, and there were three thousand desperately ill Cubans on the upper-body waiting list, a dollar would do the trick, and you'd be flying home with a spanking new thorax.

So in offering Raphael a sawbuck, Earl was not only giving him at least a thousand times more than necessary, he was also single-handedly reviving the Cuban gross domestic product. Unfortunately, his wife didn't see it that way.

"What's the matter with you?" she hissed.

He explained about the Cuban economy.

"He's not standing in line for you. It's demeaning."

"Not as demeaning as constantly losing at 'Hang the Butcher.' What the hell kind of a word is *sphygmomanometer*? You made that up."

"Not you. Demeaning for *him*, you nitwit."

"Now there's a word I can wrap my brain around."

"Send him back out there."

"He's selling chunks of old coconuts for a nickel. He'll be dead before he makes ten bucks."

"Then let him keep it."

"It's not slavery," Earl pointed out. "He wants to work for it, and if you send him away, he'll think it's his fault. Anyhow, what's so demeaning about standing in line?" He glanced around at their fellow travelers. "I'll bet they wish they thought of it first."

Wendy magnetized his molecules with her MRI glare—usually reserved for when Donald Trump said something idiotic.

"Hey," Earl reminded her with an accusatory nod, "we all work for someone."

"Not standing in line for spoiled Americans," she said.

A fat Canadian with a ponytail in front of them shook his head—in disgust, if Earl wasn't mistaken. "Right on, sister," the Canuck muttered. Instead of a respectable, bourgeois suitcase with gimpy wheels, he nudged a backpack across the floor, the kind usually seen on the bony shoulders of pimply college undergraduates, not middle-aged men shaped like Shamu the whale. Earl knew he was an escapee from the Great White North because his passport was tucked into a strap on his backpack, as if he wanted to make damn-well sure everyone knew he wasn't a Yank. You can pick out a Canadian passport from across a room because its cover features a gold-embossed portrait of Queen Elizabeth eating a bacon sandwich. You can tell it's bacon by the curlicue tail sticking out of the bread.

Earl happened to like Canadians. Before he was married, he and his best friend, Steve, spent a week at a fly-in fishing camp in southern Ontario, on a system of lakes that, had Livingston been fishing there, Stanley would not have found him in a bazillion years. The landscape was so unremittingly wet and featureless and bland, even Canadians considered it boring. It was like a beer sign had fallen off the wall into the sink, and the bartender accidentally left the cold faucet running overnight, and a storm came and blew the roof off the bar, and the bartender, who had fallen asleep drunk in the storeroom, drowned.

The lakes were so easy to get lost on that Earl and Steve were supposed to wear bright orange ponchos so the seaplane that had dropped them off would be able to find them in a week, and if they heard the plane, but didn't see it, they were supposed to make a fire and, if necessary, burn all their clothing to attract attention. The problem being, they and all their belongings were so thoroughly soaked to the bone—if their belongings had had bones—that they could have doused themselves with kerosene from their sleeping-bag warmers, had they not run out of kerosene four days earlier, and had their sleeping bags not fallen out of their capsized canoe, along with their food, tent, clothes, and themselves, and they still would not have caught fire.

So they wound up fishing naked, which they found liberating and glorious and spiritual, until Earl's accident with the lure. Then they had to call for an air ambulance, which cost three thousand dollars Canadian—sixty-five dollars U.S.—but which at least supplied them with dry hospital gowns. They flew them to Winnipeg, where a surgeon removed the lure and related minnow, and, after a massive dose of antibiotics, Earl and Steve saw an American movie with Canadian subtitles and went to a "massage" parlor where they could be with actual women, as opposed to walleye pikes dressed up like women. Earl's "massage therapist" was a nifty brunette named Margo, who at the time reminded him of a young Jill St. John, but in retrospect more resembled Herbert Hoover. In any event, there he was lying on his back, "massage" towel draped over groin, and Margo dribbling warm "massage" oil into his navel while they engaged in preparatory idle chitchat. Then she asked him if he would like her to remove the towel, and he said sure, and, when she saw what was underneath, she screamed and asked what the hell was that. He told her it was a fish-hook accident, but she probably didn't believe him because she blew a whistle, and in ran a seven-foot-tall Canadian

229

with a hockey stick who threatened to slap-shot Earl stupid if he didn't scram and take his weird-looking groin and his friend with him. Or it may have been the other way around.

So you might wonder why Earl liked Canadians. Here's why. A couple of years later the Blackhawks made it to the Stanley Cup playoffs versus the Maple Leafs, and who should turn out to be Toronto's star defenseman but Matt Powell, Margo's seven-foot bouncer. Earl had just met Wendy, and he wanted to impress her on their first date, so he asked her if she wanted to go to a playoff game, only to find that tickets were pretty much impossible to get. So in desperation, he found out what bar the players hung out at, and he took a chance and cornered Powell, and after very little prodding the defenseman remembered that Earl was the fish-hook guy whose arm he had threatened to tear off and beat him with, and Earl bought him a Labatt beer, and they became new best friends. Matt got his new BFF two front-row seats, and Wendy thought Earl was some kind of CEO or something, and he asked Powell not to mention the Margo/lure incident in front of her, and he never did. So they fell in love—Earl and Wendy, not Earl and the hockey player—and he thought she was a Republican, so he married her.

And she was a Republican, too, until Donald Trump got elected, at which time she became a communist and started blaming Earl personally for everything that came out of the Donald's mouth and tweets. Somehow or other it was Earl's fault that Hillary didn't get elected, that the levees failed in New Orleans, that there was a volcanic eruption on Montserrat, and that Karl Rove was the moral equivalent of smog. Earl was not allowed to watch Fox News while Wendy was in the room nor turn off any TV while set to that station, in case she should be the first to turn it on again. She was suddenly gung-ho for Hugo Chavez, reparations for everyone except Earl, and changing the University of

Illinois mascot's name from Chief Illiniwek to Chief Rotten Imperialist Pig. She now believed that *The Wall Street Journal* was an example of ideological state apparatus; that maybe Thomas Jefferson wasn't such a great guy after all, considering he liked brown booty; that Fidel Castro was Jesus reincarnated, except possibly for the cigar and Jeep; and if Trump had his way, Havana would be a Walmart and the rest of Cuba a parking lot, as though the previous fifty years had been a figment of the earth's imagination.

Earl reminding Wendy that she had married him under possibly false pretenses fell on "audibly disadvantaged" ears, she replying that if he wanted a divorce, fine and dandy, and if the "Repubrobates" nominated one more conservative lunkhead to the Supreme Court, she had her divorce lawyer, Adolph Hitler Mendelbaum, ready to file, so Earl better pray for the justices' good health.

So, yes, Earl did like Canadians, but the muttering former hippie in front of them at José Marti "International" was a tad suspicious-seeming. For one thing, Earl had seldom seen a fat Canadian—they worked off their bacon by cleaning fish, he guessed—and, for another thing, all the hippies he had ever known pretty much grew out of it in their twenties, when they traded in their roach clips for Audis and condos. The last time he had seen a ponytail on a man the age of this so-called Canadian was when they found that Green Beret alive in the Cambodian jungle, having survived there for thirty years and never knowing the war was over or that Nixon had resigned and that America had matured to the point where they would teach creationism again in public schools, and all he could eat was capybara poop until long and intense psychotherapy, during which he was gradually introduced to current movie prices and *The View*.

So right off the bat Earl didn't like this corpulent, time-warped freakazoid, although based on what you already know about Wendy, you probably thought she would have answered his clearly provocative, anti-American crack, "Right on, sister," with a raised-fist, Black-power salute, like those guys in the 1968 summer Olympics whose names no one even remembers, and that she would have given him a hippie handshake and trucked-on-down with him to the airport lounge, where they would have shared carrot juice and a toke, and they would have exchanged notes on how to blow up oil tankers.

You might think so, but you would be as wrong as a naked fisherman trying desperately to reel in a twelve-hook, Godzilla-brand lure that happened to be snagged on a sunken Canadian log. You cannot get more wrong.

Because here was an interesting thing about Wendy. On the one hand, she would make a mad dash to Michael Moore's latest movie with the enthusiasm of one dog's nose up another dog's poo-poo, and return home spewing all manner of wokeness to her emotionally needy, Donald-voting husband, who desperately craved a bit of nooky before bedtime. On the other hand, you can't make a sow's ear out of a silk purse, and Earl knew, just *knew*, that when it came down to it, if some foreign, Jefferson Airplane-loving weed-sucker dared to say peep against her country, she would de-spleen him with the efficiency of mongoose on snake.

And sure enough, recognizing that murderous, patriotic gleam in her eye, Earl both feared for the unsuspecting, pony-tailed lard bucket and, at the same time, braced himself for some yuks.

But, oddly, Wendy pinged the guy only an indifferent glance and said nothing. Instead, she turned to Raphael, folded his hand around Earl's ten dollars, so he knew he could keep it, then pointed to the door and smiled maternally. "It's yours, honey. Go."

The kid looked at Earl, confused. "Got...no...change," he stuttered—probably a phrase he had learned phonetically.

Wendy shook her head. "It's okay, keep it."

Again, Raphael, frowning, glanced at Earl.

*"No problemo,"* Earl said, loud and slow and showing his palms. "Keepo itto."

The Canadian clacked his tongue, flicked his ponytail, and rolled his pork-loving eyeballs.

Okey-dokey. Now he was really in for it. True, Wendy had been perfectly willing to deal the Canuck a beginner's good hand. It had been his lucky day. He had pulled a pair of aces. But with that clacking he had pressed that luck, split his pair, and was about to get his head handed to him. He was about to be blonded.

Earl held his breath. This was it. *Cobra, prepare to die.*

Wendy turned to him. "Fork over a twenty."

"Twenty what?"

Her eyes bulged. Earl whipped out his wallet and found a double sawbuck. She snapped it nice and loud—to irritate their Canadian enemy, Earl assumed. She handed the money to Raphael. "For you," she said. "You don't have to do anything. We have lots."

"We do?" her husband whispered, making a sound like a sneezing hamster.

She motioned for his wallet again.

"Um, don't you think this is the kind of thing we should discuss as a couple?"

She thrust out her palm and wriggled her fingers malevolently, this time Earl hoping rather than assuming, for the benefit of their northern friend.

He handed her his wallet. She went right for the hidden pocket, where Earl kept his bail money. She handed Raphael two crisp hundreds. "For you to do whatever you want, sweet boy. Don't forget the rest of your family."

The Canadian said nothing. Evidently humiliated, demoralized, and defeated, he had returned to his crossword puzzle.

Wendy took out two more hundreds from their leather lair, creased them lengthwise, and tucked them into the lad's pocket. "We're rich," she told him. "Wealthy *Americanos*. Very spoiled." She turned to her husband. "Aren't we, dear?"

Earl cleared his throat. She handed him back his wallet with three dollars in it.

Did they show that Canadian, or what?! *These colors don't run!*

She patted Raphael's head. "Have a nice day."

The boy turned to Earl, who could see what was left of the kid's lunch on his back teeth. Coconut.

"Yeah, have a nice day," he said. "Try real hard."

Wendy tilted her head at hubby.

He held up his hand. "Okay, I'm not saying another word."

"And you're going to keep me company in line and not get any more bright ideas?"

"You bet, and no way."

"Deal the cards, bright boy."

He did, and she drew twenty-one, and Earl busted. They sat on two suitcases and used the third as a table, and every now and then they'd inch along and continue playing, and after another hour he dealt her a ten and a six and was waiting for her to indicate stay or hit, and when she didn't he glanced up and saw her looking around the hall, her mouth twisted weirdly, her eyebrows gnarled. Earl followed her gaze and saw it too. He was the last one to see it, but that was the story of his life.

Raphael had put out the word, had rounded up a horde of his young *compañeros*, who were stampeding the waiting line with offers to stand in for passengers at a U.S. dollar each. In a few minutes Wendy and Earl were pretty much the only non-Cubans still in line—the Canadian having been one of the first to fork over his buck, no doubt so he could rout up a pork sandwich.

It all worked out, though.

Earl taught the urchins how to play blackjack, and when they lost their money, he explained about what they call in English the "learning curve" and made them repeat the phrase several times until you could hardly detect an accent, and after he won back his bail money, Earl let them play on credit, and when they continued to lose he was willing to let them work off their debt by walking on his and Wendy's backs, which were killing them from having waited so long in line. At first she didn't like the idea, but when he pointed out that they were teaching the kids the evils of gambling, ancillary to the evils of capitalism, she, too, saw it as a life-lesson master stroke and flipped over on her tummy.

# Tools

When Neal turned forty he decided to teach his wife how to use tools. Marilyn always said she never would live anywhere except in their present house, followed by the cemetery, so he figured she'd better learn some basic handyman...handyperson...skills, so if Neal died first she wouldn't get screwed over by contractors who prey on maintenance-clueless widows. Their house was built on an Indian burial ground, and ticked-off warrior ghosts rose up and broke at least one thing every weekend.

Lesson One would be to simply get her comfortable with the nomenclature. So one October Sunday afternoon after a World Series game, Neal moseyed to the basement and lined up some basic tools on his workbench in a neat row—he thought if it vaguely resembled a jewelry display case he might hook her subconscious—and then he called her downstairs.

"What for?" she shouted. She was always a little afraid of descending into that dank, dark, demonic space, believing it had something to do with why Neal's favorite TV program was *Jerry Springer*.

"I want to explain some things before"—he stopped himself—"dinner," he decided.

"Why can't you explain up here?"

So he hauled the tools to the kitchen.

"What the hell are those and get them off my counter."

"It's time you learned how to make a couple of simple repairs. You don't want to have to call a plumber to fix a toilet seat."

"What's wrong with our toilet seat?"

"Nothing."

"Then why would I want to fix it? If you broke it, *you* fix it."

"You're not getting my point."

"You're the one who keeps lifting it up."

"It's not broken."

"Then what did you bring all this junk up for? Get it off of there."

"I'll die easier knowing you won't waste my hard-earned money, that's all."

"*Your* money?"

He knew that would get her.

"Okay, pal, let's see what you got."

He held up a screwdriver. "What's this?"

"How would I know? You're the intellectual."

"Fundamentally, of course, it's a screwdriver. But what kind?"

"Blue."

"Phillips. See how the point is shaped?"

"Like a putz." She one-eyed him.

"And this other kind. See how it runs straight across?"

"Phil is gay?"

"Phil who?"

"The guy who invented the penis screwdriver."

"What are you talking about?"

"Well, the guy who invented this one obviously wanted people to know he wasn't gay, or he wouldn't have made a point of calling it *straight*."

"This has nothing to do with sex."

"Then why did you wear your tool belt to bed the other night? And why are they called *screw*drivers?"

He sighed. "Okay, let's leave these for later."

"Can you hurry a little? I'd like to get back to the food."

He held up the wire cutters. "Do you know what these are for?"

"Your toenails?"

"Wire. They're called *dikes*."

She snipped him another look.

"Here, hold them."

"Not on your life."

"Not *that* kind of dyke. "It's short for *diagonal*."

"So why couldn't you call them *Al*s? I'll tell you why. *Real* men wouldn't be caught dead gripping an Al, but you want *me* to hold a dyke. Why aren't I surprised?"

"Okay, okay, never mind."

"Maybe you want to take videos of me and the dyke?"

"We'll do this one, then."

"Which is?"

"Stripper."

"You're sick."

"*Wire* stripper, for God's sake."

"What's that one, a *lap dancer*?"

"Resistance meter."

238

"To see how far you can get with the stripper?"

"It's a coincidence, and you're getting off topic."

"To see if you can *nail* her to the wall before she tightens your *nut*?"

"Stop."

"Of course, you might have to get her *hammered* so you can *drill* her and put some good *lumber* on her before you *washer*. Oh, yes, it's definitely a coincidence they're called handy*men*."

"Why are you being such a…I mean, why are you being so difficult?"

"Because I'm trying to make dinner, and you've got all your implements of male oppression on my cooking island." Then something occurred to her. She opened a drawer. "Here, look. Can you name all these utensils?" She held up a big spoon. "Go on."

"Big spoon."

"Ladle, you ninny. Try this one."

"Cow syringe."

"Turkey baster, you twit."

He shrugged. "What's the difference? If you die first, which I highly doubt, I'll just eat out."

"And if you die first, I'll just live with a dripping faucet. It'll remind me of you."

"What did I do wrong?"

"You think I'm stupid, that's what."

"Well, we're all stupid about some things. Turkey thingamajig, for instance."

"I know what you're really worried about," she said. "It's not the money, is it? You're terrified that instead of paying the plumber, I'll offer him sex. Admit it."

"The plumber? Barry?"

"What's wrong with Barry?"

"He's fat and he has no front teeth. Plus, he's a drunk and chews tobacco, and, oh, I almost forgot: he's a moron."

"That's it, isn't it? You don't want me screwing a fat, toothless, drunken, tobacco-chewing moron after you're dead. Trying to control me from the grave. You can't stand to think of me as a *lead pipe* cinch? The thought of Barry *Roto-Rooting* me drives you crazy? *Packing* my threads? Afraid his *tool* is too big for my tool*box*? My *monkeying* around with his *wrench*?"

On the bright side, she did seem to know more about tools than Neal had thought.

"I'm making *dinner*."

"Okay," he said, gathering up his stuff. Then, not wanting to entirely admit defeat: "We can go over this some other time."

"Eight minutes. Wash your hands."

He shuffled back to the basement but couldn't find the energy to put away his... um... equipment. He dragged himself back upstairs to the bathroom to get cleaned up. He wasn't exactly famished. Gazing into the mirror, he imagined Barry's fat, toothless, drunken, nicotined, moronic head, his pulsating nose, his idiotic 1950s buzz cut. Neal pictured his blubbery torso and tried but failed to imagine him naked.

He shuddered. *Barry...the plumber*? Really? Why not Manny the gutter-cleaning guy? *At least Manny's bilingual... sort of.*

Then he reminded myself that, no, Barry would never make a service call for flesh instead of money. Barry was a good union man, plain and simple. The rate was the rate.

He turned down the dimmer switch, squinted at the mirror, and tried to see Barry the way an affection-starved widow might see him. Maybe in the really, really, *really* dim light, their plumber might even shed a hundred pounds, might appear to have at least a few teeth and a pink, rather than brown, tongue. Maybe being a physically and mentally hopeless case, he would arouse a sympathetic widow's maternal instincts, the compulsion to clean him up, make him presentable to civilized society. Perhaps where Neal saw bib overalls, Marilyn would see a rent-a-tux.

He dimmed the light even more.

But hard as he tried, dark as it was (completely now), no matter how he racked his brain, he just couldn't see Barry with his wife, tux or no. Even if an asteroid ten times bigger than the one that wiped out the dinosaurs and ninety percent of all other life on earth were to fall directly onto Illinois, and by some biblical miracle Barry and Marilyn were the only survivors—perhaps he was giving her an estimate for a new water softener at the moment of impact, and the fortuitous mingling of salt-pellet and cheap beer fumes with chewing-tobacco electro-magnetic waves created instant immunity to sulfuric asteroid fallout—and they spent the next decade futilely roaming the earth for intelligent life, Neal still could not imagine them checking into the same now-reasonably priced room at LaRamano Resort on St. Barts, even if the room overlooked the beach.

So, with a relieved sigh, he brightened the light, finished washing, and headed down to dinner.

Then near the bottom of the stairs, he stopped. Where the hell *did* Marilyn learn all those tool terms? As far as Neal ever knew, she couldn't tell the difference between PVC pipe and, say, a cocker spaniel, and now suddenly she was a maven on Roto-Rooting? He tried hard to recall the last time Barry was around fixing something and where Neal was at the time. Last summer they'd had him over to replace their leaking outside spigot, but there was no reason he would have been inside the house. *Or was there?* Neal remembered running out for a Quiznos because in addition to liking their chicken carbonara sandwich, he enjoyed feeding the parking-lot seagulls. So while he was out being a decent human being to birds, was his plumber Roto-Rooting his wife? Yet still have the temerity to ask for his credit card number?

He went back to the bathroom, turned around, and, peering over his shoulder at the mirror, pictured Barry's gigantic, undulating butt.

"It's still hot," Marilyn said when he finally sat down at the table.

"What?" he demanded. "What's hot?"

"Dinner. What do you think?"

"Oh, dinner. Oh."

"Oh what? What's the matter with you? Where've you been?"

"No place."

"So eat your dinner. It won't stay hot forever."

And he did, too. He skipped the butter and the excess salt, but polished off the fish and string beans and wild rice. He decided he would eat healthy from then on. No fat, nothing to rot his teeth. Definitely no cheap beer. He would make a point of exercising regularly and not driving too fast or changing lanes on the expressway without checking over his shoulder and always making sure his tires were properly inflated, and he sure as heck wouldn't swim too far out on Lake Michigan without a life vest or ever again climb down into the gorilla enclosure at Brookfield Zoo.

Yes, he silently vowed then and there to do whatever necessary to assure himself a long, happy life.

He looked up from his plate across the table.

"Good?" she asked.

"Healthy." He looked back at his plate, considered, then gazed up at her as if for the first time. *Could it be?*

"What?" she said.

"You served me a healthy meal. I just realized something. You *always* serve me healthy meals." He peered into her soul.

"You're creeping me out."

"You *want* me to live a long time."

She batted her eyelashes. "Who, stupid little me?" She came over, nuzzled her face into the crook of his neck, and tapped his chest. "Wouldn't want to clog these good old PVCs, would we?" She smooched his chin. "You just can't replace workmanship like this anymore—for any hourly rate." She started clearing off the table. "Now get off that skinny butt and help me clean up around here. You can start by passing me those"—she pointed to the silverware—"whatchamacallits."

# The Power of MasterCard

$M$y wife is smarter, better read, better educated, and more cunning than I am. She has a degree in some kind of literature from Northwestern University, whereas I have only a safe-driving certificate from the State of Illinois. She enjoys watching PBS and Discovery; I dig MeTV and the Sci-Fi Channel. She reads Dostoyevsky on the beach; I tear into Walter Scott's Personality Parade with the gusto of a Chihuahua scarfing down a Goobers. I was lucky she married me. Just ask her. If I hadn't met her, I would be drinking out of a paper bag and peeing into my shoe.

And it's not only in the intelligence department that we have nothing in common. For example, traveling. She loves visiting exotic locales; I love visiting my couch. Or temperature. Between taking expensive vacations, she likes the house as hot as Venezuela, whereas I prefer it to have the geothermal properties of Antarctica during that 1950s movie *The Thing*, in which an interplanetary fiend lives in a chunk of glacier until a scientist diddles with the thermostat, causing the ice to melt and releasing the monster, who starts to kill everyone and take over the earth until he gets to Dallas, where the size of the women's hair terrifies him into returning to outer space. More on thermostats in a moment, which I promise has to do with traveling.

Connie and I have been married for so many years, I don't remember who was still alive among the original cast of *Saturday Night Live* when we tied the knot. I do recall that

I'd wait all week with coiled anticipation for *Fantasy Island*, just to hear that lisping French midget shout, "De plane, boss! De plane!" Or he might have been a dwarf. I never could get those two straight—but I have the same problem with mostaccioli and rigatoni. Whichever it is, it's the pasta Connie's family always serves during surprise birthday parties while wearing *I'M WITH HIM* T-shirts.

Although marrying me was certainly a come-down for her and agonizingly tedious on a daily basis, she has kept the intellectual side of her brain active by finding new and better ways to torture me without making herself look bad. For instance, I'll be sitting quietly in front of the TV, minding my own business, threatening not a soul, watching great comedies from the 1960s, my cat curled up on my lap, when Connie appears out of nowhere like an avenging angel and, without a word, turns the room thermostat up ten degrees and then immediately leaves the house.

Because Babs is curled comfortably, and Connie knows how much I love my kitty, she can be confident that I will now suffer infected sinuses, cracked and bleeding lips, eyelids that creak along my eyeballs like haunted-house doors, shriveled tongue, desiccated bowels, and peeling brain pan before I'll get up to turn the temperature back down. If, when I see her next, I have the temerity to ask her what the heck she did that for, she'll merely claim she was trying to make our philodendra more comfortable. Young couples, take note: In any argument in which your spouse has to choose between your welfare and the welfare of a house plant, it's always better to be the plant.

Or the time my best friend, Arnie, left me a phone message that our old high-school groupie, Bambi, was in town for the day and was *dying* to meet Arnie and me for dinner, and that she was very wealthy now, having married and outlived the Oman of Ublabla, and, in appreciation for our having shown her how to play strip poker, wanted to buy us brand new Lexus SUVs with built-in GPS systems and lifetime supplies of SiriusXM and gas, which cost her nothing, since she now owned Ublabla. And—this is the "new and better ways" part—when Connie came home, listened to and erased the message, and "forgot" to write it down because she was preoccupied thinking about starving children in Darfur, and when I pointed out that having specifically asked her if there were any messages for me before she cleared the call memory, she could just as easily have said "yes" as "no, not a one, no messages today, not a single one, sorry." And, when it came right down to it, in terms of number of syllables, actually a lot easier. So it was clear that I was more concerned about my own pathologically selfish gratification than about pitiful African children.

Or the time she gave my Pee Wee Herman doll to Goodwill without my permission. Or when she took my cherished car in for an oil change, not to All-View Auto Repair, where owner, Tim, has been working on it for years and treats it like his own offspring, but to her cousin Bruno, who needed a few bucks to sort out that parole glitch and who held an Aryan Nation White Power rally on the hood of guess what? "I was just trying to be nice," she snapped, "and, *no*, I have no idea how a swastika got carved into your back seat. It's just leather. It doesn't have *feelings*. In all this time you've never gotten to know *me*."

Many men, especially those who do not admire their wives as much as I, would have at that point, say, killed her. But really, how can you not bow down trembling before majesty like that?

Don't get me wrong. I'm not entirely guiltless. For a while I retaliated by secretly wiping the cat's water bowl with Connie's face towel. And once, when she had the stomach flu and ran out of Imodium AD and was writhing around the toilet bowl and groaning for me to please, please, please, *please* rush over to Walgreens for her, I stopped on the way home for a take-home sack of White Castle cheeseburgers, which I know she usually craves, but, getting a good whiff, seemed not to thrill her on that particular occasion.

Shrinks call this "passive-aggressive behavior"—a feeble and ultimately ineffective way to one-up your wife without making marks—which would be the "aggressive" part of "passive-aggressive." And, let's face it, my fraternity-prankish stunts are pathetically crude sight-gags compared to her torture brilliance.

Which brings me to traveling.

Our vacationing trouble began on our Jamaican honeymoon, when I was still too polite to ask her why her suitcase weighed roughly the same as Luciano Pavarotti— the difference being that I didn't drag the actual opera star around O'Hare Airport, from ticket counter to snack bar to coffee shop to bookstore to men's room to cocktail lounge to security check-in to gate and back to cocktail lounge. Nor, in Montego Bay, did I schlep the real tenor from gate to car rental to cocktail lounge to gift store to parking lot, into car trunk, repeating the trunk part when the car broke down and we had to wait six hours for the car rental outfit to send three ganja-sucking, shirtless Rastas who wanted to know if my wife ever partook of "de tru weed," to which she said, "What the hell, when in Rome…"

The point being, I didn't even get a good aria out of the deal, although I did get a collapsed spinal disk and fourteen choruses of "I Shot the Sheriff," so all these years later I still can't stop humming the goddamn thing. By the time we got to our hotel room—Connie and I, not Connie and the Rastas—and I hauled her suitcase onto the bed, and she unpacked her iron, folding ironing board, ghetto-blaster with built-in cassette player, battery-operated TV, hair-curler steaming contraption, electric toothbrush, power nail buffer, kerosene lantern, and Black & Decker variable-speed electric drill with carbide-tipped bit set, I was in too much pain to ask the obvious—so, sorry, I can't tell you why she had packed a drill. She was not then the experienced traveler she is now, so maybe she was afraid we would get caught in a hurricane and have to personally rebuild our hotel. Or maybe she thought if I broke a tooth on a coconut and needed a root canal, rather than cut her holiday short she would just take care of the matter in our room. I just don't know. It's not like I've ever mentioned it after all this time because the truth is, we really don't talk to each other much. (See "oil change," above.)

Anyhow, the ganja must have made her not only horny but irritable, because when I suggested that my back pain was too severe to let me perform my husbandly duty, and that maybe propping myself up and watching the midget (dwarf?) shout "De plane, boss! De plane!" might cheer me up, she spun around Tasmanian Devil-like and accused me of being a "Euro-centric, uptight colonial oppressor," and what was the point of a honeymoon in the Caribbean if I didn't want to get stoned and have nonstop sex on the beach? I honestly don't know how the beach got into it at this point because our room didn't overlook anything remotely resembling sand—I was just starting out then—but rather was on the first floor next to the service driveway and garbage bins, on which having nonstop sex would have been uncomfortable and possibly dangerous.

And so it was that vacationing immediately became a "bone" of contention between two in-love but mutually spiteful people, in as implausible a marriage as vacationing/ bone is an implausible metaphor. But we work with what we have, and as you see, my safe-driving-certificate spite wasn't in the same league as her Northwestern University spite.

So the following winter when she wanted to cruise up the Amazon (anthropology of Arawaks), and I lobbied instead for the Electronic Games Convention in Las Vegas (Wayne Newton), we wound up booking Brazil, where I contracted an intestinal parasite the size of her mother's rigatoni (whatever), after which I spent a quality week at Mayo Clinic in Rochester, Minnesota, eating barium-and-jelly sandwiches and having PVC pipe shoved up my tuchas, while she trudged off to LaSamana resort in St. Martin—her logic being that since I apparently loved frigid temperatures (see "household thermostat," above), Minnesota in January would probably be a great place to cling to life, should I have an adverse reaction to the anesthetic, while, because she appreciated warmth, it was only appropriate that she should spend my ICU time in the Caribbean.

The year after that, she wanted to take a cruise around the Mediterranean (history and art), but I was more inclined to Oktoberfest in Milwaukee (beer and bratwurst). Our marital compromise got us booked to the Aegean, where I spent the next two weeks being seasick and throwing up into my suitcase, so I had to buy a whole new wardrobe at our next port of call, which happened to be Kabul, and for the next three days I lay on the Lido Deck wearing a burka and drinking Pepto Bismol through a mosquito screen.

Then it was African photo safari (vanishing species) vs. Wisconsin Dells (Minnetonka moccasins); Eastern Australia (Great Barrier Reef) vs. Dubuque, Iowa (paddle-wheel boat with slot machines); China (Terra Cotta soldiers) vs. Lake County State Fair (corn dogs); Netherlands (tulip festival) vs. Branson, Missouri (Dolly Parton)—the upshot of which was that "we" decided to save the American destinations for when we'd be too old to lift ourselves out of our bathtub.

Can you spot the pattern here? Connie, convinced that life is short, likes to experience all things exotic, while I, convinced that sometimes life isn't short enough, enjoy hanging around my creature comforts. I simply don't like any country whose restaurants don't serve tuna melts, where you can't watch *Wheel of Fortune* in English, and where there is a suspicious lack of stray dogs and cats.

Besides, I detest flying. I once got run over by one of those stupid airport carts that carry octogenarians from one gate to another, and now every time I hear that *eee-eee-eee* I freak out and cower behind the check-in counter, which weirds out the check-in ladies, although one of the check-in guys did give me his home phone number. And why the hell do octogenarians fly anyhow? Aren't they supposed to be driving around in motor coaches with dachshunds as comfort animals?

And yet, year after year, Connie managed to drag me from one corner of the earth to another under the implied threat of taking away everything I own in an ugly divorce, wherein she would reveal in public records that I polish my cat's toenails.

But then, two years ago, there was a miracle.

One night at dinner, Connie passed me the pepper shaker and said, "Let's go to Montserrat. I've got the trip all planned out. It'll be fun. The third week in January when it's the worst weather in Chicago and the best trade winds in the Eastern Caribbean. We'll send our friends postcards to torment them."

"That's Super Bowl week. The only thing they show on Montserrat TV is Queen Elizabeth's coronation...which they think is happening now."

"You can watch the Super Bowl anytime. Tape it for when we get back."

I passed her the salt. "But then I'll already know the score."

"So what're you saying, football is more important than me?"

"The guys expect me, that's all. We missed last year, remember?"

"And nobody died."

"They're going to order in hotdogs and Italian beef." I neglected to mention that Bambi was going to stop by for a little poker.

"And while they're clogging their stupid arteries, you'll be eating fresh grouper with mango chutney. Where it's *warm*."

"But don't you remember, you promised me last year if I—"

"We're going to be dead soon, and we won't have *lived*."

"We're in our forties, and we've been on every continent and every ocean."

"Like you know exactly when we're going to die. Punxsutawney Phil."

Which was another of her brilliant tactics because now it wasn't about the Super Bowl anymore but about my being a fat rodent.

But there was no point probing, because she having already made up her mind was as immutable as the Great Pyramid of Cheops, and my appealing to her sense of fairness would have been the equivalent of the Egyptian contractor going to Ramses when the project was three-quarters finished and saying, "Problem, boss. The Hebrew Slave Union is calling a strike."

And so it was that, for the umpteenth winter in a row, my wife made me face the gloomy prospect of lying under a mosquito net in the middle of nowhere, watching mandibled moths the size of drone bombers gather on the ceiling waiting for me to go to the bathroom, while my buddies were going to be dealing Bambi deuces from the bottom of the deck and gloriously stuffing their faces with Vienna all-beefs.

I did not want to go. I plunged into a depressive abyss. I couldn't sleep. I lost weight (Connie actually put on a few pounds). I began to fantasize about my old girlfriends—both of them. It's true, my mother had warned me about getting married before I'd had a chance to take a girl out more than twice, after which they always dumped me on the grounds that I was a mama's boy. But I had pointed out to Mommsy that I was almost thirty and therefore perfectly capable of making a marital decision on my own, and, besides, of all three women, Connie was the one who most reminded me of her. But now, in retrospect, those previous two girlfriends were looking pretty attractive, like Ginger and Mary Ann on *Gilligan's Island*, although in reality they more resembled Thurston Howell III and, for that matter, Gilligan.

But the more I suggested alternatives—for example, having children—the more Connie dug in, her trump card being that she had studied West Indian literature in college while I was wasting my brain making a living. So what's the point of earning a degree at a great university like Northwestern if you don't derive the full value of your tuition by actually seeing the very places you read about? When I pointed out that having wasted my brain working for a living had allowed *me* to pay her tuition before we were married, and so technically and probably legally it was *my* money from which we would not be deriving full value by not lolling around gift shops that featured rubber alligators, she merely counter-pointed that if having helped further her higher education was making me so intellectually insecure, maybe I should have married a bonobo chimpanzee or a real estate agent.

"But okay," she said, turning up the thermostat twenty-five degrees, "I can live with that."

So as I faced the prospect that if I somehow managed to avoid joining her in Montserrat—unlikely—I'd have to spend the remainder of my married life stuffing ice down my pants, I knew I was beaten. It was like when an overweight Mohammad Ali climbed with false bravado into the ring in pursuit of a fourth title, and everyone felt sad for him and angry because they didn't want to be reminded that their own aging selves were figuratively climbing into that ring with him, and they wished time could have stopped with the Rope-a-Dope in Zaire. I was tired, and I didn't want to climb over anymore. I didn't want to go to Montserrat. I wanted to watch the Super Bowl with my pals and Bambi. So I overdosed on vanilla lattes and drove around the neighborhood through dark, forlorn, lonely streets.

During which I thought—yes, I finally thought it—maybe, just maybe, after all those years of maneuvering and counter-maneuvering and in-out-sideways maneuvering—bobbing, weaving, ducking, jabbing, feinting, blocking, hooking, collapsing in the corner, jumping up when the next round started—the marriage referee had finally counted me out.

I just didn't want to answer the bell anymore.

When, late one night, I crawled into bed, Connie was already asleep—dreaming of conch fritters, I suppose. I kissed her on the forehead—maybe my last—and she snorted, "love you" and rolled over. She could afford to love me; our plane tickets had arrived that morning. I lay awake for a while, peering spiritlessly into the darkness, contemplating bachelorhood. I'm not religious, but I watched enough of those late-night TV preachers to have more or less figured out that if you start mumbling to some Mexican guy named Jesus, who lives in your attic, and you call in more money than you can afford to the number on the bottom of the screen, then the *amigo* will sneak down into your bedroom in the middle of the night and kneel next to your wife's nightstand and threaten her with a switchblade in her sleep, which is effective because, like hypnosis, it involves her subconscious, which has historically proven to be more rational than her conscious, and—this is the best part—if you had sent in enough money, your wife's subconscious will do what he says, so it doesn't matter if he's legal or not.

"Who are you talking to?" she grunted from her half-sleep.

"No one."

"Well, quit it," she muttered. "Get to sleep. We need to be rested for the trip." Then she rolled over again, snorted, and returned to her fritters.

To tell you the truth, I wasn't expecting much, attic-wise. From what I gathered, the best results came from calling in your credit card number to the twenty-four-hour hotline, rather than depending on the U.S. Postal Service, which, frankly, didn't care whether I went to Montserrat or not and doesn't even know how to spell it. But here I was, totally desperate, soon to be eyeball-to-eyeball with giant moths, my toes about to be nibbled on by lizards, my stomach deprived of any food not containing sand, my teeth brushed with water that, every time you turned on the tap, would squirt out with a lamprey eel.

So I sneaked out of bed, crept across the bedroom and

stealthily turned on the TV. With the volume muted, I found my favorite late-night ministry, the Heavenly Certificates of Deposit Evangelical, founded by Reverend Leon Griswold, whose wife, when she caught him compromising with one of the women who passed out hymn books, compromised his skull with a combination Old-New Testament Bible, putting him in a coma for three years, after which he woke up a blithering idiot and a great spiritual leader and went on to collect millions with his rousing sermon, "Leap Out Onto the Highway of Truth!" before he got run over by a church minibus.

So I memorized the 900 number and gently plucked my wallet from my pants—always a tricky enterprise when Connie was in the house—and, leaving the bedroom TV on so I could see where I was going, tiptoed downstairs to the kitchen and made the call. The woman on the other end said my donation was a decent first effort but not enough to earn a free copy of Reverend G's latest DVD, "Drain That Account for the Lord!" and I told her it was a marital emergency, and she assured me that Jesus was listening. I don't know about him, but my rummaging around my pants certainly woke Connie, because no sooner did I hang up the phone than I turned around and there, standing pretty as you please in the kitchen doorway, was the fist-pumping, lips-curled, eyeballs-ablaze-with-searing-yellow-red-flame-licking, jaw-rippling, nostrils-flaring, teeth-clenching love of my life.

"It was nothing," I said sheepishly, holding up my credit card. "I just wanted to make sure we have enough cash balance to cover rubber alligators."

"You lousy dirty rotten selfish bastard," she growled satanically. So right away I suspected Jesus was probably a heavier sleeper than the 900-number lady thought.

In truth, I was frightened. The prospect of my wife being possessed by Beelzebub—flattering though it was on a certain level—was especially terrifying because it was now too late to request separate beds at the Montserrat Plantation Inn.

Reckoning this irrational fear was the result of my guilty conscience, and further reckoning that I had been caught red-handed, I 'fessed up. "It was only fifty bucks," I whimpered, referring to my donation. "We'll spend more than that on carved coconut heads."

"Bastard," she repeated. "Crummy, selfish, stinking bastard."

Perhaps she was overdoing it. I looked around, but no one else was there. "Me?"

"It's always just about *you*."

I peeked over her shoulder. Nope, I was the only stinking bastard in the place.

Her head twitched, and for a moment I really did think it was going to spin around on her neck. Her eyes quivered malevolently, she sucked her teeth, snort-sprayed something slick and ominous, hissed, swiveled, strode to the guest bedroom, and locked the door.

It took me a minute to collect my thoughts, such as they are, and then I went back upstairs to see if maybe I had left the toilet seat up again. The instant I entered the room, I spotted the problem.

A "Breaking News" alert was strobing in the corner of the screen, probably having roused Connie's subconscious from its QVC-limited-time-offer sleep. It was no longer the preacher on the screen but a newscaster I didn't recognize. The volume was already back on. He piped, "We again interrupt our regular programming to bring you this breaking story. We are getting word of a major volcanic eruption on the tiny island of Montserrat in the Eastern Caribbean. We do not yet have specific details or know the full extent of the catastrophe, but a reliable source is quoted as saying that 'a monumental eruption has occurred, a horrible natural disaster.' Facts are sketchy, but apparently there have been many fatalities, among which may be European and American tourists. The U.S. State Department has put the region on travel alert, pending evaluation of the eruption's current damage and future danger. Stay tuned to this station for details as they arrive in the newsroom. We now return to our regularly scheduled program…"

I muted the set again, pumped my fist at the ceiling, and whispered, *"Amigo!"*

And then a commercial burst on the screen with the headline, *The Power of MasterCard.*

———◆———

She was pretty ticked off at me at first. She sulked for a couple of weeks, as the pyroclastic ash billowed over the Caribbean, and the pundits were all giving odds on whether it would lower the temperature of America's eastern seaboard. We were lucky, I guess, not to be living on the coast. Good old Illinois, nestled right in the country's womb, cozy and safe next to mother's heartbeat. But as the volcanic cloud rose to the stratosphere, Connie's frostiness began to thaw, and before long we were watching the news cuddled together on the couch.

I'll tell you what I think really happened. In spite of that Northwestern University education, her fancy degree, all those books and intellectual mumbo-jumbo, in her soul she was really scared crapless. Seeing how much clout I had with the guy in the attic must have given her a lot to ponder. That I and my Latino hit man were perfectly willing to destroy an entire island, including European and American tourists, to avoid missing the Super Bowl, gave her a new kind of…"respect," shall we say? And even if she had been skeptical at first—what Northwestern University intellectual wouldn't be?—when that fifty-dollar charge showed up on our credit card bill, she figured she'd better start to ratchet down her exotic-holiday wish list. That's what I think.

One night about a week after the disaster, I came home early from my monthly poker game (I was going to tell Connie that I had busted out, but the truth was, I was a little shaky about that traveling poisonous cloud and thought if she and I were going to get ashed to death, we may as well be together—call me a hopeless romantic). But I couldn't find her anywhere, not in her office, not in the media room, not even in the kitchen scarfing shoestring potatoes. Her car was in the garage, all right, but when I went back in the house and called her, there was no answer. Finally, I drifted upstairs to the master bedroom but stopped cold when I saw that our walk-in closet door, usually closed, was now weirdly half-open. Something didn't seem right. Believing she might be in peril, I garnered my courage, braced myself, and started to slowly enter the closet.

But the door opened only a few more inches before bumping against something solid. I peeked in and saw that someone had pulled down the trap-door stairs to the attic. I looked up and saw Connie's legs near the top step, her upper half in the attic, sweeping a flashlight beam across cobwebs. I didn't want to announce myself and risk scaring her and having her fall off the ladder, so I quietly backed away and crept downstairs, where, in a little while, once she was down from the trap door, I would pretend to first come home.

"Hey, how's it going?" I would say.

"What're you doing home so early?" she would ask.

"Busted out. Sometimes you win, sometimes you lose. What've you been up to?"

"Nothing. Nothing at all."

And I wouldn't say a word about that wisp of pink insulation in her hair. In a little while, when we would be canoodling on the couch, I would simply reach over to give her ear a nibble, nudge the insulation away with my nose, and surreptitiously tuck it between the sofa cushions for later disposal.

# Fertilizing Raoul

I was pretty sure that my wife was having an affair with our landscaper (well, grass mower), Raoul. Never mind that she is a thin, pearl-white blonde, and he is a dark, corpulent Argentinean. I could think of no other possible explanation as to why, when she had come up with the idea of remodeling our yard to resemble a Caribbean garden (we live near Chicago), the South American, fingertip in dimple, trilled, "Yes, it can be done, *señorita*, though requiring research."

*Research*, I believed, was the code word they used when they wanted to rendezvous later at the Sybaris motel. I was convinced they weren't going to be happy until they collected the last of my IRA and life insurance, after I had impaled myself on a frangipani bush.

But that would be somewhere down the road—or, more accurately, down the driveway. Until then, that tree-frog-croaking shrub was only a red squiggle on Raoul's sketch prints, which he unrolled with a flourish over our dining room table, accidentally knocking my checkbook to the floor. Momentarily losing sight of his retirement plan, he panicked, threw himself onto the table and thrashed around like a bonito until Lilly mercifully retrieved the checkbook and comfortingly guided *el gauch's* fingers around its reassuring vinyl.

"It'd probably be good if we just let him hold on to it," she suggested, Raoul pressing my routing number to his bosom.

Raoul's English was very good. With his free hand, he went on to point out the "symmetry," "aesthetic logic," "visual balance," and "chromatic value" of all those other colored squiggly circles. I believed those were all code terms which he and my wife would later repeat with sidesplitting laughter over frozen margaritas while sharing a hot tub in the Anthony and Cleopatra suite.

"The yellow allamanda will contrast nicely with the red flamboyant and subtly bring out the pinks of the poui, hibiscus, and oleander," the Argentinean purred, running his stubby finger over the plans, secretly completing a connect-the-dot picture of Benjamin Franklin.

Two things occurred to me. First, some of these flowers do not grow on miniature bushes but on gigantic trees. Second, oleander is one of the most poisonous plants in the known universe.

Not wanting Raoul to think me unappreciative of his botanical genius, instead of choking him, I tactfully cleared my throat and raised my anemic finger. "Question?" I said.

"Café au lait grande with two carmelita cookies," he replied over his shoulder. *"Gracias."* He grazed Lilly a smile. "And whatever the *señorita* would like," he said, full-tongued, as if gargling on a fresh papaya. He called her *señorita* instead of *señora* because, I gathered, that made her moist.

I cleared my throat again. "Well, another question," I said, interrupting their little wet fest: "Since it remains below zero here about eleven and a half months a year, won't all these tropical plants sort of, um...." I faltered, not wanting Raoul to re-apoplex.

*"Señor?"* he snorted, reminding me that he wasn't charging us for this preliminary consultation. "I am waiting."

"Sort of, um, well...*die*?"

Lilly glared at me. Raoul glared at my wife. I glared at my checkbook, desperately clutched to the landscaper's *botones*.

"It is apparent the *señor* does not have faith in Raoul," he huffed, one-handedly rolling up his prints.

"Wait!" Lilly exclaimed. "The *señor* trusts Raoul completely!" She spun to me. "Tell him, you horticulture *idioto*."

"Very well," the shrubbery maestro conceded, letting her take back the plans. "I will explain." Arms spread over his prints like Columbus over nautical charts, on his way to slaughter the Arawaks, Raoul tutored me: "Each autumn we will move the *magnifico* plants inside and fertilize them with Dominican vervet-monkey poopies. These monkeys eat only natural sugarcane, and their little *excrementos* are quite delectable to the soil. You will have the most *espléndido* garden. One of a kind! Tourists will stop in front of your home to take pictures! We will be enormously famous!"

I poked my chin. "Excuse us *uno momento*," I told him, as I nudged Lilly into the kitchen. Out of the landscaper's earshot, I whispered, "Based on a novel I once read by the Nobel-winning West-Indian novelist V.S. Naipaul, I vaguely recall the flamboyant tree being taller than a two-story house."

"So?"

"*Way* big," I explained in non-academic terms.

She drew an impatient breath.

"For bringing inside?" I said.

"Well, sure, we'll have to make some room. Raoul and I have talked about it at length."

Over Julio Iglesias and love oil, no doubt.

"We'll just have to use some of your office," she

explained. "Now let's go back before he starts feeling unappreciated."

"Flamboyant trees in my office?"

"It faces east, so they'll get the morning sun. Very important, especially for the oleander bush."

"The *poisonous* oleander?"

"I'm doing it for your own good," she assured me. "The truth is, you get pretty gloomy around the holidays. A little monkey *excrementos* might do you good."

We returned to the landscaper, whose lower lip was quavering.

"I have an idea," I ventured. "Why don't we explore the idea of a greenhouse."

"A greenhouse!" Lilly beamed.

"Greenhouse!" the South American exclaimed, snapping his fingers and hopping a quick flamenco. "The *señor* has made an interesting suggestion." He shot me a stern frown. "It will not be inexpensive, of course."

"I know!" Lilly added. "Raoul can design a greenhouse to look just like an authentic West Indian cottage, complete with a veranda!" She took the remaining blank checks out of the leatherette, handed them to Raoul, and tossed me the empty case.

*"Magnifico!"*

*"Magnifico!"*

*"Magnifico!"*

I didn't have a hat to throw on the floor, so we all danced around my Visa Card.

"We can put some plants in the *señor's* office in the meantime to cheer him up," Wifey pointed out.

"Oleander," the landscaper agreed. *"Magnifico!"*

263

*"Magnifico!"*

That night, while *mi esposa* was fast asleep, no doubt dreaming about Zorro's sword, I was lying awake, wondering how in the future I'd ever be able to work in my little home office without inhaling.

First thing in the morning, before she woke up, I Googled it.

# St. Maarten

He went back to find the cat.

He checked into the hotel, on the beach in downtown Philipsburg, where he and his bride had spent their honeymoon and three anniversaries. The beach was more the color of nutmeg than sugar, and the high-tide line was oil-splotched and garnished with dead fish. But it was right in the middle of things and had a fine view of the harbor and the hills enclosing Great Bay. When they got married, their quaint, eighteen-room hotel was new and clean, and their room had a balcony with the kind of view you never forget. The hotel lobby was open on one side to Front Street, to the beach on the other, and its palm tree canopy between the Jacuzzi and sand was like a portal to heaven.

But it was different now. Philipsburg had grown up too fast. Front Street was now chaotic with tourists and souvenir shops, and the beach was crowded and littered. Their hotel was still there but shadowed now by condo midrises, and the receding tide left not just fish but the detritus of cruise ship buffets. The hotel still featured a lobby bar, but their bartender, Neville, was long gone, the Jacuzzi was covered with warped plywood, the mahogany bar top scuffed and dull, and the ceiling fan was missing a blade. The narrow stairway to the rooms smelled like rancid mop, and their honeymoon room, though only a dozen years old, was world weary and forlorn. The television volume knob was missing, the sink and toilet rust-streaked, the shower caulk-peeling, and the mattress sagged. The floor tiles were cracked and chipped. The sliding balcony door no longer wanted to move. It was heavy and stubborn and moaned as if in great pain.

But the view was still something you don't forget.

Standing on his balcony now, hands on the same railing he and his wife had touched together, he gazed up and down the boardwalk for the cat. It was not yet dark, so he wasn't expecting much, but you never know.

He came prepared. Regulation-wise, bringing a pet into the U.S. was no small task. He had filled out the forms, paid the fees, and, for a hefty premium, arranged for a St. Maarten veterinarian to check them out right away and, he assumed, give them the all clear. He brought with him a fleece-floored cat carrier and stainless-steel food and water dishes, six cans of premium cat food with gravy, a pouch of salmon- and chicken-flavored treats, and a large zip-lock baggie plumped with cat chow. He had even packed a feather-on-a-stick and a squeaky mouse.

On the way from the airport he had the taxi driver stop at Bryson's Hardware on Cannegieter Street, where he bought a shallow plastic tub to serve as a temporary litter box. They didn't sell litter, but as much sand as he needed would be just outside the hotel. The biggest problem was his return ticket. Because he didn't know when, or if, he'd find the cat, he couldn't know when he'd be going home. His airline miles wouldn't work, so he paid cash and, as with the local veterinarian, a premium for a flexible date.

As far as he could tell, he was ready.

All he needed was the cat.

She had first come to them on their third anniversary. They were scraping along the boardwalk from a restaurant at the edge of town, sipping Drambuie out of paper cups. A half-moon shone on the bay, masts motionless, ripples lapping languidly. They also carried leftover rolls soaked in marinara sauce, in case they were greeted by one of the stray dogs that roamed the beach. Usually the mutts came during the day, but sometimes they would appear after dinner. These were often new moms whose pups were hidden and snug under a nighttime porch.

No dogs came that night. But from under a lamplit bench, the cat came prancing over, head-butted and rubbed their ankles. They had never seen a cat here before, let alone one so friendly. She was tawny with a striped tail, and her nasal bridge was arched, making her resemble a miniature sheep. She followed them back to the bench and sat between them as they fed her marinara morsels. Fifteen minutes later, the cat climbed onto his lap, curled up, and fell asleep.

He was in love with two girls now.

The cat was young, maybe a year old. She was thin but not emaciated, and her fur wasn't matted, so, even though she wore no collar, they assumed she belonged to someone. West Indians don't think of their dogs and cats the way Americans do. Even their so-called pets they seldom take inside, letting them wander, apparently not much caring if they return. If once in a while the animal happens to accompany a tourist back to the States or Canada to start a new life as a real member of the family...oh, well.

But they, too, were young, he and his wife. They couldn't imagine that pets were so easily forgotten. It didn't occur to them that whoever owned this *puddy tat* wouldn't have been waiting up for her. She wasn't feral; she wasn't underfed, and she (obviously) liked people. So they figured that her owner was, if not overprotective, at least not abusive. That's the reason they didn't name her. They just called her "our baby."

In half an hour he lifted her from his lap and placed her on the warm spot where he had been sitting. But she didn't go back to sleep. Instead, she followed them back to their hotel. They sat for a few minutes on the steps from the beach, scratching their new baby's tush. They brushed away sand from the steps and left the rest of their bread morsels there and whispered good night.

In the morning, she was waiting for them.

Neville said he had seen her before but had no idea to whom she belonged. "She's yours now," he beamed. But being inexperienced, they took that figuratively: she was theirs only as long as they were on vacation.

And she was, too—until the night before they left. That night, and the next morning, she didn't show up. They strolled the length of the boardwalk; they sat on that same bench under the lamplight; they sat on those same steps to the beach. But she didn't show up.

In a way, it was a blessing. It saved them from any afterthought about leaving her there (even later, when they'd learn they could have taken her home). The decision had been the cat's, not theirs.

Now, back on St. Maarten these seven years later, fully prepared to bring her back home, feeling guilty for not having done it sooner, and not even knowing if he'd see her again, he decided to give her a name. If his mission failed, at least he'd know she had a name.

Naturally, he called her Diane.

She'd be about eight. If all went well, she'd have ten years of easy life, never having to head-butt tourists, never having to beg for food, always having a full bowl of Fancy Feast. The very best. No chance of worms. No fleas. None of the outside dangers: cars, predators, hurricanes, drunken tourists. No more fly-polluted drinking water. No more fish bones to scrounge. No more competing with gulls for scraps. With him, she'd be able to drink from the faucet. Bottled water, for all he cared. Spring Mountain. Perrier.

But the first day and night, despite his pocket stuffed with cat treats—nothing. He was reluctant to ask strangers if they had spotted her or ask Front Street shopkeepers if they knew to whom she belonged because in the unlikely event her owners did care, he didn't want to tip them off. So he nosed around *in oculto*, walking up the beach and down Back Street, winding through alleyways, peering beneath porches, scraping through shrubs. Then up and down Hendrikstraat and Zout Steeg and Voges Straat, circling cottages and yards, trying to seem lost so as not to arouse suspicion. In their newlywed days, the worst crime in Philipsburg had been someone stealing someone else's goat. Times had changed. Now there were burglaries and assaults and even an occasional murder. St. Maarten had grown up too fast.

So he tried to seem innocent.

The second day, the same. No Diane. The locals were starting to wonder. A woman was sweeping her porch the same time as yesterday. She stopped, dirked him a one-eye, and didn't sweep again until he moved on. He felt her gaze following him until he turned onto Vlaun Straat.

That night he wandered to Debrot Street near the library and spotted a pair of low, yellow eyes staring at him from between a pharmacy and a bank. He knelt on one knee and slowly raised his keychain flashlight beam. But it wasn't Diane. It was a black-and-white that dashed away.

The third afternoon was the same, except he was wearing out his welcome. The St. Maarten gossip whip cracked fast and hard. Word got around fast. On Korte Steeg a barber strode out with his scissors. "You lost?" he wanted to know. "You look lost." He didn't mean it to be helpful.

The average lifespan of outside cats is only four years.

It was time to give up.

On the last night before leaving, he went out to the boardwalk again to the bench they and their baby had sat on, where they had watched the tide's shallow breathing, listened to one another's hearts. The moon was rising now, casting a cruise ship's shadow. He wondered if its passengers were really happy or just yearning to be somewhere else. He wondered if any of them were standing at the railing, watching him.

He was now so preoccupied with the bay, he didn't see her. She startled him when she rubbed against his ankle. His heart raced. It was Diane, all right. She had come back. She knew him. She came back.

He scooped her up, scratched her, head to toe, kissed her ears, kissed her neck. He hugged her, talking baby talk, telling her how much he missed her. She remembered him— he was sure of it.

Not wanting to take a chance on her not following him back, he cradled her to the hotel, telling her how much he loved her, how safe she would be from now on. "No more scrounging for a meal," he whispered. She didn't resist. She purred. And when he asked for a kiss, she looked up and touched her nose to his.

"We're going home. You'll be safe."

It took only a couple of minutes for him to set

up the litter box, water bowl, and food dish, while Diane explored the room. She didn't seem to be thirsty, but when he whooshed open a can, she trotted over, licked the juicy food tentatively, then gobbled. She wasn't starving, but she was hungry. He was relieved; it seemed to confirm that she was homeless. Some restaurant owners put food out at night for the strays, but it's first come, first served, and if they were late, they were out of luck.

After eating, she returned to exploring the room. He showed her the litter box and scratched the sand—whose smell she was all too familiar with—to suggest what it was for. He opened a couple of dresser drawers for her to check out. He put a towel in one, in case that's where she wanted to sleep. He whispered to her reassuringly, telling her about the cushy life that waited. "You're going to have not one but two litter boxes, kiddo, and towers up the wazoo. And all the cat treats your little heart desires."

In an hour, he filled her dish with dry food, washed up, left the bathroom light on and its door ajar, and crawled into bed. He didn't expect her to jump up there with him, so he was pleasantly surprised. On top of the blanket, she curled up next to his leg. They were both very tired.

He didn't think he had fallen asleep until the scratching woke him up. For a second he didn't remember where he was, and he was scared. The sliver of light from the bathroom door reminded him. Diane wasn't next to him. He reached for his glasses on the nightstand and glanced at the clock. Two-thirty. He got out of bed and opened the bathroom door all the way, spilling in light. *Scratch, scratch.* Squinting, he spotted her pawing the front door. She padded over, weaved between his feet, meowed. He knelt and massaged her, ear to tail. But her mewl was more a whimper than a greeting. She wanted something. She returned to the door again. *Scratch, scratch, scratch.*

He picked her up and carried her back to the bowls. When she ran to the door again, he hauled the litter box to her. But she ignored that, too. He offered her a cat treat. When she ate it, he thought all was well again. But before he could get under the covers, she was again scratching and mewling.

She wanted out.

He carried the desk chair to the door, sat on the edge, and tried to reassure her. "I know it's not what you're used to, but you'll see, it'll be great. You'll have all kinds of toys: feathers and balls to chase and catnip mousies and scratching pads, and"—he twirled his finger—"spinning things and stuff to bat around and stuffed buddies to cuddle. You'll have stairs to climb and towers to sit on and tissue paper to maul and blankets to hide under, and I won't even care if you claw the furniture to smithereens."

She stopped listening and went back to pawing the door.

"You'll be inside where it's safe and cozy, see? A life of luxury. You're a lucky girl."

But that pep talk didn't work, either. She stood against the door on her hind legs, and her mewls were louder and more insistent.

"You can't go out," he tried to explain. "Don't you get it? It's not safe out there. You'll be happier inside, I promise."

She pawed toward the doorknob.

"It's for your own good."

She turned and hissed.

He pulled back.

She flattened her ears and whiskers. Her tail curled under her. She puffed out her fur, and her eyes narrowed and blackened.

"Okay.... Okay."

She flashed her teeth and hissed again.

He sat on the bed, out of claw reach. They stared at each other. Her gaze shifted fiercely from him to the door.

He wanted to hiss, too, wanted to remind her how much trouble he had gone through to save her, yell at her for being ungrateful.

But what would be the point? If he did bring her back with him, she'd just want to go outside anyway. She'd claw at the window, mewl all night. She wouldn't sit on his lap. She wouldn't sleep with him.

They'd both be miserable.

So instead of raising his voice, he got up and opened the door.

———◆———

On the plane ride home, the seat next to him that he had bought for the cat carrier remained empty. He hadn't asked for his money back; he welcomed not having to talk to a stranger. He watched the island disappear behind him while he daydreamed that Diane would return to the hotel that night and scratch at his door again, this time wanting to be let in.

# Bachelorhood

Bachelorhood was not treating Eric well. For one thing, he was now forced to buy his own shampoo, an experience that went badly. It never occurred to him that, little though there is, he didn't have normal hair (he assumed that's not what Leila meant when she told him to get help), but when he perused the Walgreens hair care shelves, all he saw were shampoo bottles with labels that read, *For Frizzy Hair*, *For Short Hair*, *For Curly Hair*, *For Oily Hair*, *For Brittle Hair*, *For Shiny Hair*, *For Straight Hair*, *For Transgender Hair*, and so on. When all he really needed was to wash his freaking head. So he roamed the aisles asking strangers, including a young woman he swore looked over seventeen, if they thought his hair seemed normal, and now he's not allowed within a hundred yards of grammar schools or public libraries.

Also, he had no idea which cleaning products to use for particular household jobs so wound up washing his bathroom mirror with Brillo and softening his laundry with licorice Twizzlers. Grocery shopping was a total mess. He stood in front of cereal boxes for an hour, agonizing over whether to buy a regular or large box of Cheerios. He always got a shopping cart with a gimpy wheel, forgot his phone number when the cashier wanted to apply his membership discount, sneezed on the *National Enquirer*, and dropped his debit card into that gap at the end of the conveyor.

Once, he wanted to buy a couple of oranges but

had no idea which, among the many types the supermarket offered, he preferred. All he knew was, he liked oranges and wanted an orange. But they had pyramids of oranges of many different names, colors, sizes, and shapes. They even had an orange that was oblong. It was insane. A woman would come capering by and, apparently without a single brain glitch, rip off a plastic bag, open it with a deft slice of fingernail, reach into her orange pile of choice, squeeze one or two, toss them into her bag, and be gone, as if she had just completed an everyday task as simple as...oh, buying oranges.

Meanwhile, Eric would be standing there with tears in his eyes, not knowing which type of orange he had always enjoyed (mentally flagellating himself for not having asked Leila in their divorce pretrial conference), well aware that everyone in the grocery store was watching him, and that the store had issued an urgent announcement to the Willow County emergency alert system, and at that very moment a message was scrolling across the bottom of local television screens: *URGENT COMMUNITY alert! alert! small-penised, newly-divorced pantywaist crybaby is currently in the Argosy supermarket, incapable of deciding which type of orange to buy!!...lol!!!*

So, on the verge of a food-choice mental breakdown, Eric forewent the orange idea and turned to apples.

There could be only one type of apple, yes?

Although he was a proud, patriotic American and a staunch believer in the glories of capitalism and the free-enterprise system, bachelor food-shopping was one of those times when Eric wondered if the penuries of communism hadn't had their good side. Before the fall of the Soviet Union, if you were, say, Bulgarian and had a taste for an orange, you would line up before dawn in front of a food stand, and, if you were lucky and still had not starved to death by midnight of the next day, a burly, sourpussed Stalinist bouncer would let you approach the stand, where you would be allowed to buy one orange, and that orange would be small, round, rock hard, and almost never colored orange. If a Bulgarian had seen an oblong orange, she would have drowned herself in her toilet bowl—if she'd had a toilet bowl.

Eric's poker buddies convinced him that grocery stores were a good place to pick up women. They gave him some valuable pointers. So now the first thing he did to project his manly image was to put three items in his cart: 1) a six-pack of Budweiser (implied reference to large-hoofed stallions); 2) a copy of *Big & Buxom Biker Chicks* magazine (not normally available at your friendly neighborhood grocer, except that, as luck would have it, Eric's was managed by a big & buxom biker chick named Peg, who appeared to have two pygmy hippos stuffed down her leather bodice and wore a *Make America Great Again* cap and was often preoccupied slapping the crap out of the Guatemalan bag boy); 3) a twelve-pack of extra-course toilet paper with the logo of a Tyrannosaurus rex gnashing a caveman.

On the other hand—again, according to Eric's poker group—here was a partial list of items he should *never* put into his cart:

Bay scallops

Bread with more than two multi-grains

Mueslix cereal

Shallots (whatever they are)

Chef Boyardee miniature ravioli

Any magazine with George Clooney on the cover

Evian water

Cocktail parasols (*duh*)

Presliced carrots with unidentified cream sauce

Any salad dressing containing cilantro

Any gel for any purpose

Cocktail salamis

*Fun with Sudoku* magazine

Low-calorie anything

Because sliced turkey was not on his buddies' prohibited-food-and-beverage list, Eric felt a measure of confidence when he was overcome with a craving for a sandwich consisting of two-multi-grain bread and that particular meat.

Offhand, sliced-turkey shopping did not seem an invitation to degradation. But as it happened, the same burly, sourpussed Stalinist bouncer who worked that Bulgarian grocery stand and who had emigrated to America after the Iron Curtain fell now stood behind the meat counter demanding to know what the *goddamn hell* he wanted—reminding Eric that the reason they make butcher department counters so high is the same reason medieval Europeans made cathedral ceilings so towering: to remind you, as a human being, when you walk in and feel awed under the majesty and greatness of the sublime Almighty, the sublime Almighty, like your ex-wife, thinks you are a lowlife piece of dreck.

Eric stood there on the other side of this majestic, humility-infusing and terror-inspiring meat counter, reliving in his memory all those times he had engaged in sin—which, it must be said, took a while. So the butcher tyrant barked, "Something wrong with your hearing? You want meat or don't cha?"

"Sliced turkey," Eric peeped.

"What do you mean?"

"Sliced turkey?" he repeated, this time with a question mark.

"Well, that doesn't tell me much, does it?"

"No, ma'am."

"Smoked turkey? Honey-baked turkey? Fresh turkey? Turkey loaf? Turkey breast? White meat? Dark meat? Thin-sliced? Thick-sliced? Deli-cut? Skinless? Salt-free? Low sodium? Nitrate-free? On the bone? Off the bone? Huh, huh, *huh*?"

"Never mind," Eric stammered and began to slink away to the parking lot.

"Halt!"

He halted.

"Turn around!"

He obeyed.

"Say, you're from around here, ain't you?"

"Yes, ma'am."

"I've seen you here before, haven't I?"

"Yes, ma'am."

"Sure, I remember now. You were the asshole making your wife push the cart while you stood around checking prices when she wasn't looking."

"Yes, ma'am."

"The pond-scum douchebag who thought it was so easy buying groceries."

"Definitely me, ma'am."

"The guy who thought that pushing a cart and checking prices is being an equal partner."

"I recognize my mistake now, yes, ma'am."

She stroked her mustache. "Any sins you'd like to confess, now that you feel so insignificant and worthless before my sublimely magnificent meat counter?"

"Yes, ma'am."

"Start talking, my son."

So he told her he didn't know how long you're supposed to go between washing your sheets; what the term "low-rise" means relative to underpants; how to defrost your freezer without flooding Holland; whether to have the driveway patched in the fall or spring; how to remember your computer administrator password; if you're a sucker for buying movie-theater medium-size popcorn for fifty cents more; on which dishwasher shelf the cups go; which scouring pad you use to wash the bathroom mirror; how to get cat vomit off the counter...

He took a breath.

Continuing his confession: ...what kind of vacuum cleaner bags to buy (if any); how to find the dryer lint filter; how you work the outside spigots; how to reach your house painter in Croatia; how to call Jung Ho carryout on Monday to find out if they're closed on Mondays; why facial tissues stop popping up halfway down the box; how to record a new message on the answering device in your own voice so your friends don't think you delusionally believe you're still married; how to get the dust off your dust mop; how you program call waiting; how to turn off the garbage disposal; how to get cat vomit off the carpet...

Another deep breath, slow exhale.

The Stalinist tapped the counter with the edge of her butcher knife.

He marched on: ...when you're supposed to use tin foil versus Saran Wrap; what the *Quick Thaw* button means on the microwave touchpad; what, for that matter, any of those little numbers mean on the microwave touchpad; the difference between "super strong" and "super absorbent"; how often you're supposed to change razors; how to get the cap off the Extra-Strength Tylenol; if you're supposed to smother toaster fires or douse them with water; if you're expected to tip the ER nurses; how to get cat vomit off your pillow.

By the end of his confession, Eric was a quavering, glistening wad of snot kneeling before the precooked chicken cordon bleu, his face pressed pitiably against curved glass. When he finally did manage to right himself, stagger to the checkout line, make the near-fatal error of standing in the ten-items-or-less line with eleven items, drawing the wrath of an old hag who, under normal circumstances he could have taken out with a left hook, but now let her beat him stupid with a rolled up *Big & Buxom Biker Chicks* magazine, guess what?

He accidentally dropped his debit card into the gap at the end of the conveyor.

By the time he got to his car he had a maxi-force migraine headache that had him wondering why his mother hadn't flushed him down the toilet when she'd had the chance. And, oh yeah, a seagull who apparently had eaten beef stroganoff for lunch crapped on his head. And, oh sure, he was halfway home when he realized he had forgotten to transfer his groceries from the shopping cart to his trunk, and the seagulls were now burping up his sliced turkey. And that *still* wasn't the worst of it.

What could possibly be worse than predigested beef stroganoff dripping into your eyeball? How about this: You're driving along, head imploding, forehead starting to itch from some rapidly reproducing avian parasite, wondering what the hell your parents ever saw in each other; you round a bend, and what jolly couple do you see jouncing toward you along the road, hand in hand, happy as hamsters, the guy sporting a post-orgasmic smirk, and the woman looking suspiciously like your ex-wife, who, when she recognizes your car—which, of course, she would since you've had it for twenty-five years—lets go of her new love's grip, grins, and *waves to you*!

Be honest. Wouldn't you have mowed them down, too?

# Previous Appearances

- **"Killing Sparrows"** appeared in *The Gettysburg Review* (1999) and *Short Story America* (Vol. 1) and Quiddity Public Radio.

- **"Secret Cigars"** appeared in *Troika* (2000) and *A Rotten Person Travels the Caribbean* (Travelers' Tales, 2008).

- **"Lanterns of Fear"** appeared in *Best Travel Writing 2011* (Travelers' Tales).

- **"Nasdaq 16,000"** appeared (as "Nasdaq 5000") in *A Rotten Person Travels the Caribbean* (Travelers' Tales, 2008).

- **"Kap'n Cy"** appeared in *Wake Up and Smell the Shit* (Travelers' Tales, 2015).

- **"The Time I Accidentally Urinated on Idi Amin"** appeared in *Story Quarterly* (2008) and *Narrative Magazine* (as "Don't Open That Door").

- **"El Max"** appeared in *South Carolina Review* (2005) and *What Color Is Your Jockstrap?* (Travelers' Tales, 2006).

- **"His Military-Industrial Complex"** appeared in *Heartlands, A Magazine of Midwest Arts and Culture* (2006), and *Best Travel Writing 2007* (Travelers' Tales).

- **"The Power of MasterCard"** appeared in *Big Muddy* (2007-2008).

All other stories have been written exclusively for this ***Champagne and Sour Grapes*** collection.

# Acknowledgments

My sincere appreciation and love to RuthAnn Taylor, Marc Buslik, Babs Buslik, Rex Buslik, Ileen Falk, Kirsten Koza, James O'Reilly, Sean O'Reilly (RIP), Larry Habegger, Benjamin White, and Lisa Kastner.

# About Running Wild Press

Running Wild Press publishes stories that cross genres with great stories and writing. RIZE publishes great genre stories written by people of color and by authors who identify with other marginalized groups. Our team consists of:

Lisa Diane Kastner, Founder and Executive Editor
Joelle Mitchell, Licensing and Strategy Lead
Cody Sisco, Acquisition Editor, RIZE
Benjamin White, Acquisition Editor, Running Wild
Peter A. Wright, Acquisition Editor, Running Wild
Resa Alboher, Editor
Angela Andrews, Editor
Sandra Bush, Editor
Ashley Crantas, Editor
Rebecca Dimyan, Editor
Abigail Efird, Editor
Aimee Hardy, Editor
Henry L. Herz, Editor
Cecilia Kennedy, Editor
Barbara Lockwood, Editor
AE Williams, Editor
Scott Schultz, Editor
Rod Gilley, Editor
Kelly Ottiano, Editor
Carolyn Banks, Editor

Evangeline Estropia, Product Manager
Kimberly Ligutan, Product Manager
Pulp Art Studios, Cover Design
Standout Books, Interior Design
Polgarus Studios, Interior Design
Learn more about us and our stories at
www.runningwildpublishing.com

Loved this book and want more? Follow us at
www.runningwildpublishing.com, www.facebook/
runningwildpress, on Twitter @lisadkastner @
RunWildBooks

RUNNING WILD PRESS

www.ingramcontent.com/pod-product-compliance
Lightning Source LLC
Chambersburg PA
CBHW052019020726

47501CB00004B/1136

www.ingramcontent.com/pod-product-compliance
Lightning Source LLC
Chambersburg PA
CBHW052019020726
47501CB00004B/1136